AUTHOR	**CLASS**
LIPMAN, E.	F

TITLE   The dearly departed

THE DEARLY DEPARTED

Elinor Lipman, who grew up across the street from a nine-hole golf course, is the author of the novels *Isabel's Bed*, *The Way Men Act*, *Then She Found Me*, *The Ladies' Man* and *The Inn at Lake Devine*, as well as a collection of short stories, *Into Love and Out Again*. She has taught writing at Simmons, Hampshire, and Smith Colleges, and lives in western Massachusetts with her husband and son.

ELINOR LIPMAN

—

The Dearly Departed

A NOVEL

FOURTH ESTATE • London

This paperback edition first published in 2002
First published in Great Britain in 2001 by
Fourth Estate
A Division of HarperCollins*Publishers*
77–85 Fulham Palace Road
London W6 8JB
www.4thestate.com

Copyright © Elinor Lipman 2001

1 3 5 7 9 10 8 6 4 2

The right of Elinor Lipman to be identified as the author of
this work has been asserted by her in accordance with the
Copyright, Designs and Patents Act 1988

A catalogue record for this book is available from the
British Library

ISBN 1–84115–655–8

This book is a work of fiction. Names, characters, and incidents either are
a product of the author's imagination or are used fictitiously. Any resemblance to
actual events or locales or persons, living or dead, is entirely coincidental.

Printed in Great Britain by Biddles Ltd, Guildford & King's Lynn

This book is dedicated to my son,

BENJAMIN LIPMAN AUSTIN

THE DEARLY DEPARTED

CHAPTER I

Come Back to King George

Sunny met Fletcher for the first time at their parents' funeral, a huge graveside affair where bagpipes wailed and strangers wept. It was a humid, mosquito-plagued June day, and the grass was spongy from a midnight thunderstorm. They had stayed on the fringes of the crowd until both were rounded up and bossed into the prime mourners' seats by the funeral director. Sunny wore white—picture hat, dress, wet shoes—and an expression that layered anger over grief: *Who is he? How dare he? Are any of these gawkers friends?*

Unspoken but universally noticed was the physical attribute she and Fletcher shared—a halo of prematurely gray hair of a beautiful shade and an identical satiny, flyaway texture. No DNA test result, no hints in wills, could be more eloquent than this: the silver corona of signature hair above their thirty-one-year-old, identically furrowed brows.

The King George *Bulletin* had reported every possible angle, almost gleefully. MARGARET BATTEN, LOCAL ACTRESS, AND FRIEND FOUND UNCONSCIOUS, said the first banner headline. *BULLETIN* PAPER CARRIER CALLS

911, boasted the kicker. An arty photo—sunrise in King George—of scrawny, helmeted Tyler Lopez on his bike, a folded newspaper frozen in flight, appeared on page 1. "I knew something was wrong when I saw them laying on the floor—the woman and a man," he told the reporter. "The door was open. I thought they might still be alive, so I used the phone." Inescapable in the coverage was the suggestion of a double suicide or foul play. Yellow police tape surrounded the small house. Even after tests revealed carbon monoxide in their blood and a crack in the furnace's heat exchanger, *Bulletin* reporters carried on, invigorated by a double, coed death on their beat.

A reader named Vickileigh Vaughn wrote a letter to the editor. She wanted to clarify something on the record so all of King George would know: *Friend* in the headline was inaccurate and possibly libelous. Miles Finn and Margaret Batten were engaged to be married. Friends, yes, but so much more than that. An outdoor wedding had been discussed. If the odorless and invisible killer hadn't overcome them, Miles would have left, as was his custom, before midnight, after the Channel 9 news.

———

Sunny was notified by a message on her answering machine. "Sunny? It's Fletcher Finn, Miles's son. Could you pick up if you're there?" Labored breathing filled the pause. "I guess not. Okay. Listen, I don't know when I can get to a phone again, so I'll give you the news, which is somewhat disturbing." Another pause, too long for the machine, which clicked off. He called back. "Hi, it's Fletcher Finn again. Here's what I was going to say. I'll make it quick: I got a call from the police in Saint George, New Hampshire—no, sorry, *King* George. They found our parents unconscious. Nobody knows anything. I've got the name of the hospital and the other stuff the cop said. What's your fax number? Call me. I'll be up late."

Sunny phoned the King George police. The crime scene, she was told by a solicitous male voice, was roped off until the lab work came back. Sunny pictured the peeling gray bungalow secured with yellow tape, its sagging porch and overgrown lilacs cinched in the package.

"Are they going to die?" she asked.

"Sunny?" said the officer. "It's Joe Loach. From Mattatuck Avenue? We were in study hall together junior and senior—"

"I got a message from a Fletcher Finn, who said his father and my mother were found unconscious, but that's all I know. He didn't even say what hospital."

Loach coughed. "Sunny? They weren't taken to a hospital. It was too late for that."

He heard a cry and the sound of her palm slipping over the mouthpiece.

"It was the damn carbon monoxide. It builds up over time, and then it's too late. I'm so sorry. I hate to do this over the phone . . ."

When she couldn't answer, he said, "I saw your mother in *Driving Miss Daisy* at the VFW, and she was really something."

Sunny pictured her mother's grande-dame bow and the magisterial sweep of the arm that invited her leading man to join her in the spotlight. It had taken practice, with Sunny coaching, because Margaret's inclination was to blush and look amazed.

"You're where now? Connecticut?"

She said she was.

"Okay. One step at a time. Nothing says you can't make arrangements by telephone. Maybe your mother put her preferences in writing—people do that, something like, 'Instructions. To be opened in the event of my death.' I could walk anything over to the funeral parlor for you. In fact, remember Dickie Saint-Onge from our class? He took over the business. He's used to handling things long-distance."

"I'm coming up," said Sunny.

"She and her fiancé didn't suffer," said Joey Loach. "That much I can promise you."

"Fiancé?" she repeated. "How do you know that?"

"That seems to be everyone's understanding. Her cleaning lady wrote a letter to the editor to set the record straight. Plus, there was a ring on the appropriate finger."

Sunny cried softly, her hand over the receiver.

"Can I do anything?" he asked. "Can I call anyone?"

"I'd better get off," she said. "There must be some phone calls I should make. I'm sure that's what I'm supposed to do next."

"Just so you know, the house is okay now. They found the leak and fixed it, the town did, first thing. You don't have to be afraid of sleeping there. I'll make sure that everything is shipshape."

"I think my friend Regina used to baby-sit for your sister," she said. "Marilyn?"

"Marilee," said Joey. "She's still here. We're all still here. So's Regina. You okay?"

"I meant to say thank you," said Sunny, "but that's what came out instead."

"You're welcome," said Joey Loach.

———

Fletcher sounded more annoyed than mournful when he reached Sunny the next morning. "Under the circumstances," he said, "I would have thought you'd have returned my call."

"You didn't leave your number," said Sunny.

"I'm sure you can appreciate that I wasn't thinking about secretarial niceties last night," he snapped.

"Such as 'I'm so sorry about your mother'?"

"I didn't know her," he said. "And at the time of my call I believed she was still alive."

Sunny quietly slipped the receiver into its cradle. It rang seconds later.

"My father's dead because he was watching television with someone who had a defective furnace," blared the same voice from her earpiece. "He was as healthy as a horse. How do you think I feel? And on top of that, some backwater police chief delegates to me the task of calling the date's daughter."

Forcing herself to sound composed and rational, Sunny said, "Are you the only child, or is there a humane sibling I can do this with?"

He paused. "Unfortunately, I'm it."

"You don't have to torture yourself with the idea that this was some blind date that went awry—that he was in the wrong place at the wrong time—because he was there every night. She was his fi-ancée."

Fletcher said, "Unlikely. I never met her."

"She had his ring, and the date was set."

After a silence, he asked, "Were you invited to a wedding?"

"Of course I was," Sunny said.

———

Reached by phone, the funeral director said he preferred not to stage a wake in a theater, even if it had once been a house of Congregational worship. Sunny heard his flimsy argument, which was grounded in what she felt was personal convenience, and answered in a shaky voice, "I think it's what my mother would have wanted. I don't think I'm being unreasonable, and if it requires a little creativity and flexi-bility on our part, so be it."

No one in King George had ever asked Dickie Saint-Onge for creativity or flexibility, so he rose to the occasion, promising to accom-modate the loved one's undocumented dying wishes: a coffin in a hard-wood that was stained to resemble ebony, white satin interior, no variation on her hairdo, which should be styled by her regular hair-dresser and not by some mortician. Sunny herself would get permis-sion from the King George Community Players to have her mother buried in her *Mourning Becomes Electra* costume or the black dress she wore in *Six Characters in Search of an Author*. He would tell the town's only florist this: no daisies, no carnations, no mums. Say that the daughter wants flowers cut from the vines creeping up her mother's porch, in combination with the Russian sage by the mailbox. And if they aren't in full bloom, find wisteria on someone else's trellis around town. Everyone knew Margaret. Everyone loved her.

———

Fletcher announced that he'd be flying to King George on the morning of the funeral with an associate. Unfortunately, he couldn't get away one moment before that, due to the campaign. Was there an airport nearby?

"Forgive me for not owning a copy of your résumé, but what campaign are we talking about?"

"Right now, a congressional campaign."

"And you're too busy to get away?"

"That's not what I said. I'm coming up for the funeral."

"On the morning of. In other words, your father died and your boss won't give you a few days off?"

"Just the opposite: She very much wants to attend the funeral, but we can't get away until Saturday morning, because there's a state fair—"

"What state?" Sunny asked.

"New Jersey. Sixth Congressional District."

"What's her name?"

"Emily Ann Grandjean. She wants to be there," said Fletcher. "For both of us."

"How kind," said Sunny. "Too bad she can't spare you for a couple of days."

"Every second's scheduled. It's brutal. Our election's in September."

"So I imagine that you won't be staying very long after the funeral."

"To what end?"

"To go through your father's things and decide what you want to keep. Someone's got to do his packing."

"Packing?" Fletcher repeated, as if Sunny had said *sharecropping.* "You *pay* people to pack—moving companies pack. They can do a whole house in two days."

"If it's the cottage I'm thinking of on Boot Lake, it won't take you very long."

"Whatever," said Fletcher.

"I'm going up tomorrow. You can reach me at the King's Nite Motel," said Sunny.

"Fine."

"Do you know my name?" she asked.

"Sunny?"

"Batten," she said, and spelled it.

The night she returned to King George, the local news reported that a motorist, after running the town's only stop sign, had shot the chief of police. Sunny, watching on the motel television, first thought, Good—people in this town will have something to talk about besides my mother; and second, It's him, Marilee's brother, the cop. She crawled from the head of her bed to its foot for a closer inspection. Indeed, Chief Joseph J. Loach *was* Joey Loach, the kid who'd swaggered around the halls of King George Regional more than a dozen years before, the detention regular and goofball who could fold his eyelids up and inside out, now a hero wounded in the line of moving violations. Because his bullet-proof vest had saved him, Chief Loach was being presented a state-of-the-art model by the vest's proud manufacturer, bedside. "I guess it wasn't my time," Joey told the reporter.

Mentioned obliquely in the hushed wrap-up: The perpetrator was still at large.

CHAPTER 2

Meet You at the Lake

"Actress" in the obituary's headline, especially without the modifier "amateur," would have delighted Margaret Batten, who'd been stagestruck in middle age, recruited at the beauty parlor by the wife of the superintendent of schools. Might Margaret, she asked, consider a tiny but vital role in the King George Community Players' fall production of *The Bad Seed*? Duly flattered and only briefly deflated to learn that she had no lines, Margaret threw herself into her first production—understudying, baking for the bake sale, and embracing the subculture that was the King George Community Players. She was a woman alone, a divorcee looking for a social life in a town of 1,008 year-round residents.

Sunny was in high school when the acting bug burrowed under her mother's skin. They lived on the edge of the King George Links, a semi-private golf course, in a small house with rotting trellises, leased for a pittance under an odd historical footnote concerning a runaway slave and a host abolitionist, now moot and inapplicable. Still, it carried with it a legacy and the taint of a scholarship awarded on the basis of need. Historically, poor people lived in the gray bungalow, visible from the seventeenth fairway; their underprivileged children fished waylaid golf balls out of the course's water traps. Margaret had qualified as a lessee under the unwritten widow-with-child clause: Sunny's father was dead, or so the tale on the application went.

Margaret was not a habitual liar, but the little house had been vacant when she moved to King George. A real estate agent, sizing her up correctly as a single mother without means, said, "I know I'm shooting myself in the foot to let you in on this, but there's this little house that belongs to the town ..." Margaret asked to see it. The pine floors had been stripped of linoleum and left a tarry black; instead of doors, faded blue burlap hung from curtain rods between rooms, and the kitchen sink was a soapstone trough. But Margaret was a great believer in soap, water, ammonia, bleach, lemon oil, paint, shellac, wallpaper, and fresh flowers. She could see the small provincial print she'd choose for fabrics and the museum posters of lily pads and haystacks she'd frame for the walls. "How much?" she whispered.

"A dollar a day—and that includes utilities."

"And you think I could get it?"

The agent confided, "They don't check, so lay it on a little thick in the application. They like widows and orphans—the more the better."

"I only have Sunny."

The agent said, "I happen to know from personal experience that if they like you, they're not sticklers."

The truth would have been nowhere near good enough: Margaret had lost a husband in the most prosaic fashion, to nothing more tragic than an uncharacteristic slip—hers. She still couldn't believe she had sinned and that the perfectly decent John Batten, who updated kitchen cabinets with laminates, had not forgiven her. It hadn't even been a love affair but a temp job, a professional courtesy: The lawyers for whom she worked had loaned her and her shorthand skills to an out-of-town client running for Congress. He hadn't announced yet; he told the newspaper that he was visiting primarily on business and, yes, maybe to shake a few hands along the Saint Patrick's Day Parade route.

And when he did, as Margaret would observe, it was with such penetrating eye contact and warm, two-fisted handshakes that the woman in his grip felt more attractive and interesting than she knew herself to be.

Pretty in a round-faced, wholesome way; short, with a generous bust and small waist, Margaret was in her mid-twenties and looked eighteen. Safe, her employers thought. Not bait. Harmless as a secretarial loan to a reputed womanizer. At the end of Miles Finn's visit, after two days of depositions, he invited her to dinner, in a hotel dining room famous for its Caesar salads prepared at the table.

Thank you, but she couldn't, Margaret said.

"A previous engagement?"

"I'm married."

"I am too! This isn't a date. I'm so sorry that's what you thought. This is a thank-you for a job well done and a grueling two days of boring testimony. Dinner seems the least I could do. . . . Perhaps your husband would like to come along."

"He's on a job," she said.

"Out of town?"

"Camden," she said. "A school renovation. It's supposed to open the day after Labor Day."

She seemed torn, concerned about something other than the appearance of social impropriety. Her hands ran down the sides of her brown cotton A-line skirt.

"What if we made it for seven or eight?" he prompted. "That way you can go home and change into something for evening."

She nearly curtsied with relief, and said, "I do have something new I was saving for a special occasion."

"How old are you?" he asked. "I only ask because I'd like to toast my campaign."

"I'm twenty-six!"

"Twenty-six." He smiled.

===

He asked for a quiet table, away from other diners. Margaret arrived in what his wife would call a little black dress, poofy and crisscrossed with chiffon at the bosom, in very high heels that looked a size too big, and carrying a long, thin clutch purse with a rhinestone clasp; a heart-shaped barrette held her brown hair off her shiny forehead. She ate her Caesar salad and her veal rollatini with such earnestly exquisite shop-girl manners, refusing to speak until she had chewed and swallowed every morsel of food and washed it down with a ladylike sip from her water goblet, that he felt chivalrous, which, in turn, impelled him to in-vite her upstairs to have Kahlúa on his balcony. He wanted to flatter her; wanted this sweet-faced girl to feel that she had been an excellent dinner partner and that Miles Finn enjoyed her company. If he needed a secretarial pinch-hitter again—say, next month?—could she get away?

———

She shouldn't have spent the night, shouldn't have assumed that her heretofore nonpregnant state was her failing and not her husband's; should have checked her good black dress for the long, prematurely sil-ver hairs that John removed with tweezers and saved in an amber pill bottle. He filed for divorce, gallantly characterizing it as no-fault. Their two lawyers privately agreed upon a paltry monthly payment in lieu of a paternity test.

When no one had a good word for John Batten, the brute who di-vorced his sweet, pregnant wife, Margaret told her family, "It's not what it appears to be. Don't blame John. That's all I'll say," and took her wispy-haired baby girl to King George, a town in the shadow of the White Mountains. Candidate Finn had recommended it unwittingly as the site of idyllic boyhood summers and a future retirement. John Bat-ten moved his laminating business to a booming Phoenix and sent Margaret a wedding announcement ten months later. "She's a keeper," he wrote in one ecru corner.

———

Believing that the bungalow on the golf course would provide a month or two's shelter, Margaret typed in the space allowed that she had been briefly married to a wonderful man, who had died an accidental death in a helicopter crash. In parentheses, she wrote that her late husband flew critically ill people, or sometimes just their hearts and kidneys, from the scenes of accidents to hospitals, from country to city, where teams of specialists met him atop hospital helipads. He had died in the line of duty, whereupon *his* organs and corneas were harvested and transplanted into no fewer than five near-death breadwinners. The committee for the Abel Cotton House had considered the poorly punctuated appeals of too many teenage mothers who came to interviews in cutoff jeans. Times had changed. Runaway slaves had given way to war widows, who'd given way to church-sponsored refugees with extended families. English-speaking applicants were scarce; people who would fit in were scarcer. With a house in suburban Philadelphia as her last address, an associate's degree, a dented Pinto, a thin, sad gold band and diamond chip on her widowed left hand, and a little blond daughter, the soft-spoken Margaret Batten was the happy choice of every philanthropist on the committee.

⸻

The invitation to act with the Community Players brought changes for the better for Sunny: Her mother took her to the movies now that she had techniques to study, gestures to borrow, dresses to copy. Dusty blues and greens accented her eyelids, and her fingernails went pink. She began squirting hand cream into new rubber gloves by day and massaging her heels at night. Various upstanding professionals, including an optometrist and a pharmacist, took Margaret out for bites to eat after Thursday rehearsals.

Her fellow thespians uncovered a talent Margaret didn't know she had, the ability to memorize lines more quickly than anyone else—not just her own, but the whole cast's. "Photographic memory," she'd apologize, unable to swallow the prompts when her fellow actors missed their cues. She understudied both leading ladies and ingenues, and finally had her break when the woman playing Mrs. Winemiller in *Summer and Smoke* needed emergency disk surgery. Sunny ushered at her mother's opening night, and was both pleasantly surprised and disconcerted. Margaret became someone else onstage, gesticulating, enunciating, and projecting, in an accent that was all Blanche DuBois. Sunny thought she looked pretty at a distance with her face painted and her taffeta church outfit rustling, prettier than she looked in real life. The *Bulletin*'s freelance drama critic, who taught at King George Regional and had Sunny in driver's ed, reported that "newcomer Margaret Batten brings an understated ardor and energy to the role of the minister's wife." It was a gift to an unattached, shy, forty-three-year-old woman in a town where everyone read the same newspaper. Men in the KGCP teased her. The crème de la crème of King George society, she liked to say, was opening its circle to her. The bachelor Players called her at home, asking for "Maggie." Confidence changed the way she dressed, the way she drove—with a chiffon scarf tied around her neck, in Grace Kelly fashion—and the way she entertained. She rented a floor sander, polyurethaned the pine boards to a high gloss, and painted the front room in a color called Caviar. When the KGCP needed sites for their annual progressive dinner, Margaret energetically volunteered what she now was calling the Cotton homestead for the canapé course.

Confined to the stage, Margaret's mild airs and new self-esteem were bearable, even lovable. Sunny knew what play was running on which nights and how to stay out of the refracted limelight. She would baby-sit costars' kids; would paint scenery and post flyers on two dozen bulletin boards around town. But she refused to act—refused to answer even the desperate call for teenage daughters in *Fiddler on the Roof* and *Cheaper by the Dozen.* She studied, she caddied at the golf course that was her backyard, fished golf balls out of the brook that divided the eighth and ninth fairways and sold them back to the original owners at half price. Her mother allowed her to golf as long as she wore culottes and an ironed blouse and didn't look like one of the ragamuffins who had preceded them in the peeling gray house. Margaret frowned on her daughter's carrying other people's golf bags—like a bellhop, she said; like beggars who dived off Acapulco cliffs for coins. Sunny helped her own cause by describing the nice doctors and lawyers, owners of the big houses on Baldwin Avenue, who let her play through and admired her swing.

Too many male caddies were impatient and contemptuous of the ladies' league, but its members finally had an alternative. Sunny took them seriously. She knew the course, and dispensed tips that she'd picked up on loops with the assistant pro. When their husbands surprised them with new clubs for Christmas, the ladies offered their perfectly good woods and irons to Sunny.

It was a small town, but big enough for the theater fanatic and her mildly mortified daughter to coexist until Margaret played the president's wife in *Of Thee I Sing* and came away with an idea for a moonlighting job: impersonating first ladies at private parties, trade shows, or ribbon-cuttings. Since the cameo sideline began, she had dressed as Mmes. Carter, Reagan, and Bush; had added Sandra Day O'Connor and Queen Elizabeth as the occasion warranted. Her appearance at an event injected a guessing game into the dull photo opportunity—this faux-pearled and eagle-brooched character was which woman in Margaret Batten's repertoire?

"Please don't do it," Sunny would plead. "Please don't let them put your picture in the *Bulletin* again."

"But that's exactly why they hire me—so someone reading about the event will say, 'Oh my goodness. Look! A famous person came to the ground-breaking of the new branch. Isn't that Barbara, hon?' "

"It doesn't fool anyone. It's not being an actress. It's a sight gag. And then you leave and go to the supermarket, and my friends say, 'I saw your mother yesterday at Foodland in a gray wig.' Or, 'She was wearing a necklace of shellacked peanuts. Must have been Rosalyn's turn,' with this look that says, Is she *mental*?"

"It's theater," her mother would say, "an acting job that pays—which makes me a professional. It's your college fund. Besides, you of all people know I don't care what the neighbors think."

———

Sunny wrote to the long-absent John Batten every few months, and he wrote back. "Sincerely, John," he signed his dull, typed letters on the firm's letterhead. Neither correspondent invoked the terms *father* or *daughter;* Sunny did not accuse him of abandoning or failing her, because she understood without being told that there were complications that no one liked to discuss. Sunny studied her mother's wedding pictures and puzzled over the groom's dominant brown eyes and dark wavy hair, his short arms and thick neck. Artificial insemination, she guessed after reading a cover story on the subject in *Time*.

John's wife and office manager, Bonnie, added a banal postscript to every letter—"8 straight days of temps over 100!" or "driving to San Diego to see the pandas," which Sunny interpreted to mean: John and I have no secrets. I know whenever he writes to you. I protect him. Mostly, Sunny and John corresponded about golf, which he'd taken up in the Sun Belt. He hoped she was taking lessons, and Sunny told him no, but that she took illustrated books by Sam Snead and Ben Hogan out of the library and closely watched the best players at the club. He advised her which hand-me-down clubs, which compounds of steel and new alloys, she should keep and which she should put on consignment. He told her not to ignore her short game. She wrote back and said she was trying to spend an hour a day on the putting green. Was that, in his opinion, enough? "If you're sinking those three-foot whiteknucklers with some consistency, it is," he answered. He never asked about Margaret, and Sunny didn't ask about his wife. He didn't call or send gifts or ask for custodial visits. "I never really knew him," she'd explain to friends who asked about a father. Or, to close the subject: "He died before I was born."

═══

From Pennsylvania, Miles Finn continued to pay taxes on his New Hampshire property, an unheated Depression-era cottage with three dark rooms and outdoor plumbing. It was on a minor lake so ordinary and unscenic that one would wonder what inspired him to travel six hours to swim in black water and pee into a fetid hole. The crawl space housed an ancient canoe and an antique archery set; inside, there were moldy jigsaw puzzles, scratchy wool blankets, rusted cooking utensils, mildewed canvas chairs, mouse droppings, the occasional bat, and the empty gin and beer bottles frequently found in near-forsaken cabins.

Margaret aired out the place every spring, defrosted the shoebox-sized freezer as needed, kept clean linens on the bigger bed. If it was a quick trip to close a window before rain or to leave a welcome casserole, Sunny would wait in the car. The cottage, Margaret explained, belonged to friends from Philadelphia—"Finn," according to slapdash strokes of white paint on a slat—who'd been coming to King George forever.

"Do they have any kids?" Sunny asked hopefully.

"It's just one person," Margaret said. "An attorney. I worked for him before you were born."

It sounded right to Sunny that her mother would bring casseroles to an old, childless man who could afford nothing better than vacations at Boot Lake. Over the years, as Margaret headed off alone with her pail and sponges and a flush particular to this mission, Sunny adjusted her view of Mr. Finn. She sensed that the former boss had become a boyfriend—so typically charitable of her mother. Not that sex was involved, Sunny thought. Sex didn't fit Margaret. It had to be a crush, durable yes, but no more fertile or reciprocated than the ones Sunny herself had on teachers at King George Regional or on golfers on TV.

═══

Miles called it his retreat, and if any woman—first his wife, then subsequent girlfriends—voiced suspicions about his treks to Boot Lake, he would say, "If only you could see the camp. I don't even bathe when I'm there. No woman would set foot in this dump. Of course *I* love it, but that's a childhood thing. No one else will go near the place."

He made the romantic terms clear to Margaret, semi-annually. He was married, with everything to lose personally and professionally. He wasn't inviting love affairs or headlines.

He didn't volunteer personal details unless she inquired: Yes, there'd been a separation. Yes, in fact, a divorce. Yes, he was dating in Philadelphia, but only when necessary; only when he needed presentable companions for black-tie events. They had sex quickly on her fabric softener–scented sheets during her lunch hour, and didn't speak again until he called six months later with a jangle of quarters from a phone booth. "Guess who?" he'd say each time, and always she'd have a clever answer ready: An old boss? A charming dinner companion from Philly? Tomorrow's lunch date?

For a long time, she thought she had no right to mind. Twice-yearly dates didn't make her his girlfriend or his confidante. She wasn't above this flimsy attention—she who'd broken her marriage vows and several Commandments. But eventually she joined the Players, and was lauded in print for her understated ardor. Now when he called from the road, Margaret was not being coy when she hesitated before answering his "Guess who?"

"Is someone there with you?" he asked.

"Miles? Oh, sorry. I wasn't sure. How *are* you? *Where* are you?"

"I'm about twenty-five minutes from there, and you know how I am." He dropped his voice. "Ready, willing, and able."

She began to ask, as she sat on the edge of the bed, rolling her panty hose back up, if they could go out, if he could pick her up, if they couldn't have something approximating a date. "I know what you've always said: 'No calls, no letters between visits, no paper trail.' But we never get a chance to talk. We could drive to Vermont, to an inn, then stay the night. Sunny can stay with a friend. We're both divorced. There wouldn't be a scandal even if we were caught." She didn't say, "You lost the election sixteen years ago. You're a private citizen. No one knows who Miles Finn is anymore."

He always answered the same way: Communication didn't always have to be spoken, did it? Wasn't what they had special and unconventional? Did she prefer a restaurant dinner to a passionate lunch?

If he asked about Sunny, it was from the polite distance of a man who had no reason and no desire to meet his occasional paramour's child. On these trips—fish all morning, fuck Margaret at lunch without any wining or dining or conversation; nap, read, drink, sleep—he didn't want to think about anyone but himself. His son, Fletcher, was a teenager, the same age as the girl. These visits wouldn't last forever: Fletcher was asking questions, and Margaret was asking for proper dates. She'd even used the words "Maybe this isn't such a good idea anymore." Margaret, he gathered, had other men calling her among the locals. And soon a devoted, alternate-weekend father like himself, claiming to be tying flies and frying trout alone in New Hampshire, would have to invite his kid along.

CHAPTER 3

You Should Run

Fletcher knew that managing Emily Ann Grandjean's congressional campaign would mean fourteen months of spinning, baby-sitting, and chauffeuring, followed by a loss of the most humiliating kind—a landslide victory for an incumbent who didn't have to shake one hand.

And then there was Emily Ann herself. In an exploratory meeting, she demonstrated one of her most annoying tics: constant sips from a large bottle of brand-name water, then the ceremonial screwing of its cap back on once, twice, full-body twists as if volatile and poisonous gases would escape without her intervention.

They met in a conference room at Big John, Inc., the family business, founded by Emily Ann's grandfather after he took credit for discovering exercise in the form of a stationary bike. Subsequent generations invented a rowing machine with a flywheel and, most recently and profitably, a stroller for joggers. Emily Ann's three older brothers, whose tanned and photogenic faces anchored the annual report, went happily into the booming family business. But the baby sister made a fuss about striking out on her own—like those Kennedy cousins who went into journalism or the Osmond siblings who didn't sing. Emily Ann went to law school, dropped out, went back, and at her graduation heard Congressman Tommy d'Apuzzo—beloved, honest, monogamous; a man for whom a district's worth of highways and middle schools were named—urge the new lawyers to consider careers as public servants. "Where are the dreamers?" he cried, waving his arms. "Where are all the little boys and girls who wanted to grow up to be president? Are you all heading for Wall Street? To white-shoe law firms in New York skyscrapers? We need your energy and your idealism. Run against me! Challenge me! Provoke me! Defeat me!"

Only Emily Ann thought he meant it; only she thought a seat in the House of Representatives was attainable to a member of the Class of '96. When she returned from her graduation grand tour (London, Paris, Venice, and the Greek Isles) she took a bar-review course by day. By night she found a campaign to work for. Conspicuously wearing outfits of Republican red and Betsy Ross blue, she volunteered for an earnest young firebrand running for the city council. She stood in for him at a Republican kaffeeklatsch after practicing answers and sharing aphorisms with a voice-activated pocket recorder.

"You should run," said an elderly man by the dessert table as his wife dusted confectioner's sugar off one of his veiny cheeks.

"Maybe one day," said Emily Ann.

"Don't wait too long or I might not be able to vote for you," he said, chuckling.

"This evening," she reminded him nobly, "is about Greg Chandler-Brown and *his* race, and about the bond rating of a dying city."

"I didn't catch your name," he said.

"Emily Ann Grandjean."

"Mrs. or Miss?" he asked.

"I'm not married."

"Have a piece of fudge cake," he said. "You could use a little meat on your bones."

A year later, Mr. Grandjean was sliding a Big John catalog across the conference table to Fletcher, who had managed the last candidate to lose to d'Apuzzo, under budget and with dignity. "You look like you work out. Is there anything in here that appeals to you?"

Its glossy cover displayed the rowing machine that was the Rolls-Royce of Fletcher's health club. Through some trick of digital photography, it appeared to be gliding past pyramids on the Suez Canal. Fletcher didn't open the catalog; didn't even touch it.

"No obligation. Absolutely none," said Mr. Grandjean. "A thank-you for your time and attention today, no matter what you decide. And, please. It's nothing to us. This is what we do. We assemble parts and turn a few screws and—presto—we have a bike."

Fletcher turned the catalog facedown. Equally compelling was the back cover—a computerized stationary bike, titanium, featuring a built-in CD player and a Tour de France winner perched on its fertility-friendly seat.

"She can win the primary," continued Mr. Grandjean. "I don't think there's any question about that."

"When you run unopposed, you win," said Fletcher. "But I'm not interested in being the campaign manager for a sacrificial lamb."

Emily Ann snapped, "You've never heard of upsets? DEWEY DEFEATS TRUMAN?"

Fletcher folded his hands in front of him on the hammered-copper conference table. "Let me paint a picture for you: Yesterday, in the village center of a very staid Republican suburb, in a chic café named Repasts, I ate a sandwich called The d'Apuzzo. Not a sandwich meant to be an insult, like baloney or marshmallow fluff, but one named out of affection and respect and because it was what Representative d'Apuzzo ordered on his last whistle-stop there."

"What kind of sandwich?" asked Emily Ann.

"Tuna club. Traditional yet popular. No negative symbolism there."

"Your point being that a man who has sandwiches named in his honor is unbeatable?" she asked.

"When he's a Democrat and it's on a Republican menu? Yes."

"Rather unscientific," grumbled her father.

"Can I be blunt?" asked Fletcher.

Both Grandjeans sipped their water.

"Miss Grandjean would be a gnat on the campaign windshield of Tommy d'Apuzzo and nothing more. He wouldn't respond to her speeches, he wouldn't pay for ads, he wouldn't campaign, and he sure as hell wouldn't fly home from Washington to debate her. And the editorial writers? Forgive me—they'll dismiss her as a rich girl without experience or convictions, looking for a career after law school."

"That's so unfair. I have convictions! I'm deeply committed to education—"

"Who isn't?" he asked.

"And to cutting taxes and to term limits—"

"Every man or woman who's ever run against Tommy d'Apuzzo has supported term limits. It ain't going to get you elected."

"This is about exposure, about building myself a base—"

"I just don't think I'm your man," said Fletcher.

Emily Ann gathered her water bottle, her Filofax, her pen and cell phone and said, "Then let's not waste anyone's time. A can-do attitude is the very least I would expect in a consultant."

"I agree wholeheartedly," said Fletcher.

She walked to the door, the skinniest girl on the skinniest legs he'd ever seen. Mr. Grandjean motioned that Fletcher should stay behind. As the door closed, Mr. Grandjean's fond, fatherly smile collapsed. "I'm going to ask you one more time to take this job. I'm going to name a salary that is the going rate plus—"

"Based on . . . ?"

"A dark-horse congressional race."

"Un-uh. Not interested."

Mr. Grandjean screwed the cap back on his water bottle and looked thoughtful. "It's September. The election is fourteen months away."

"I know that."

"Exposure for her is exposure for you. You can lose, and six months later I'll tune in to MSNBC and see you opining about presidential politics with REPUBLICAN STRATEGIST superimposed across your tie."

"Here's my problem," Fletcher said. "Tommy d'Apuzzo chairs two committees. He loves his wife and doesn't fool around. His secretary is widowed, Native American, disabled, and loves him like a son. His kids went to New Jersey public schools, then to Seton Hall, Rutgers, and Fairleigh Dickenson. His father was a cobbler. His mother was a Freedom Rider. His dogs came from the pound. Everybody except your daughter knows it'll take plastic explosives to unseat Tommy d'Apuzzo."

Mr. Grandjean shrugged. "You must have a price."

Fletcher scribbled numbers on his legal pad and slid it across the table.

Mr. Grandjean shook his head even before the notepad came to a stop in front of him. "Can't do. It's money out of my own pocket—a price I have to justify to her brothers."

"Are they in or are they out?" Fletcher asked.

Mr. Grandjean shifted in his back-saver chair. "You know how kids are. They keep score—who got a new car and who got a used one; who got semesters abroad. On one hand, they resent this pissing into the wind; on the other, they're glad to have her . . . gainfully distracted."

"I'm getting the picture," said Fletcher.

Mr. Grandjean wrote a sentence on the top sheet of Fletcher's yellow pad, tore it off, folded it into the most elaborate and aerodynamic paper airplane Fletcher had ever seen, and sent it sailing across the table.

2,000 shares of Big John stock, it read.

Fletcher rose, and walked it around to the other side of the table. "For your signature."

"Aren't you going to ask me what they're worth?"

"I know what they're worth," he said.

———

First, he tried to drop the Ann and make her only Emily. The double name lacked authority, he said. It was too cute, too wholesome, too Miss America.

"Too bad," said Emily Ann. She was not pandering to the small percentage of the electorate who cared about the sociological implications of a conjoined name. She was proud of it. It was her two grandmothers' names. People were so superficial. Like that reporter for the *Times-Rec-*

ord who was obsessed with her weight and her percentage of body fat—as if *that* had anything to do with her capabilities; as if anyone would even mention it if Emily Ann had been a man. When eating-disorder speculation became the only thing about Emily Ann's candidacy that engaged the public, it was Fletcher's unhappy task to pour Diet Coke into Classic Coke cans when she drank in public, to insist that she stop pulling the doughy insides out of her bagels, and to answer questions about the candidate's preternatural thinness. She allowed herself to be photographed with her teeth around a clam fritter at a state fair, a sausage-and-pepper grinder at an Italian street festival, a knish at a B'nai B'rith brunch. But she didn't consummate any of those acts; didn't even sink her teeth into the first bite after the photographer's flash. If there had been a position paper on her weight, it would have said: *All the Grandjeans are fit and rangy. Long and lean. Their veins show under the epidermal layer of their inner arms. Their faces are pinched and skeletal. It runs in the family. It's not a disorder. Candidate Grandjean's metabolism is incredibly efficient. If she appears to pick at her food, it's because she eats six or seven small meals a day and never much at one sitting. She may look as if she's been constructed of Tinkertoys, but that's because she works out faithfully on a Big John SB2000. All rumors about anorexia, bulimia, and terminal illnesses are defamatory and false.*

Worse, and just as he had feared, Emily Ann warmed to Fletcher. The first time she reached over and took a sip from his coffee in the van's cup holder, he saw it as an overture, especially when he was faced with the two coral blots on the rim. "Hey," he said. "That's mine."

"So?"

"It's polite to ask first. Some people don't like sharing."

"Big deal—my lips on your cup. Do you get so annoyed when someone kisses you?"

He didn't look over and didn't answer.

"What a grouch."

He was tempted to say, It has cream in it, which I know you'd never let pass your lips unless you are before a convention of dairy farmers.

"Doesn't coffee have a diuretic effect on you?" she asked.

Pissing, she meant: urological. Personal. He wasn't going to discuss the properties of coffee with this annoying bag of bones. "I don't like lipstick on my cup because it tastes like perfume," he said. "If you want your own cup, you should say so at the appropriate juncture."

Emily Ann turned away and studied the scenery.

"Let's go over some questions, Em." When she didn't answer, he asked if she was sulking.

"No I am *not*. I'm meditating."

"Here. Be a baby. Drink my cold coffee. I wouldn't want you arriving at the meeting with a long face."

"You work for me," she said. "I'm the candidate and you're the hired help."

Emily Ann reached down to the giant turtle-green leather satchel at her feet for her water bottle.

"Are you really thirsty all day long, or is it just a prop?"

"Neither. Everyone needs eight glasses a day." She took her usual swig, like punctuation. "I won't always be running for Congress. The question of who's the boss and who's the employee won't be an issue after Tuesday, November ninth."

Fletcher turned on the radio.

"Because we'll be equals when this is over," she said. "Possibly even friends."

"Not advisable," said Fletcher. "Lines get blurred."

"Not that I need any more friends," she continued. "And not that I intend to lose. I was only thinking it would be an interesting experiment."

"What would?"

"The occasional informal meeting over a glass of wine, post-campaign: candidate and manager minus the occupational constraints."

Fletcher took a gulp of cold coffee from the clean half of the rim.

"I sense you're uncomfortable parsing feelings and emotions," Emily Ann said, trying again, her bottle nestled in the crook of her arm.

"Correct," said Fletcher.

CHAPTER 4

Harding

Every spring Nancy Mobilio, assistant headmaster of Harding Academy, found the school's varsity golf coach at the center of the same tedious rumor: that he was having sexual relations with the school's newest female hire. For compelling personal reasons—she was married to him—Mrs. Mobilio chose to ignore the latest groundless gossip, namely that Sunny Batten, who'd been recruited as j.v. golf coach, equipment-room overseer, and part-time health teacher, was this year's crush.

Mrs. Mobilio was best known on campus for looking old enough to be her husband's mother, a genetic swindle that fueled the legend of her husband's roving eye. She was, in fact, only three years and eight months older than Mr. Mobilio, a difference barely worth noting, she felt; still, she dyed her once-dark hair and eyebrows an unbecoming gold and swam laps so religiously that her suits never dried. Truth or fiction, the rumors were humiliating. Real life and campus life blurred at boarding schools: Dorms were your home, colleagues were your neighbors, students were your baby-sitters. Alleged girlfriends emeritae were everywhere, rookies no longer, displaced by newer and fresher blood, untouchable job-wise thanks to rumors of romance.

So it was with well-disguised delight that Nancy Mobilio listened to a committee of three ninth-graders complain that Miss Batten couldn't teach health to save her life.

"You should hear her," said Ogden, who already wore the haughty look and out-of-season striped wool scarf of a future society hooligan.

"She calls us names," said Hugh.

"Such as?"

" 'You little shits,' " Rufus provided. "That was today. Yesterday I think it was . . ."

" 'Jerk! You jerks,' " yelled Hugh.

"Tell her that other thing," said Rufus.

Ogden unwound his scarf and cleared his throat. "The stuff we're learning? In health? My father saw my notes over March break and he thought it was porno."

"I beg your pardon?"

"It was the handouts she gave us on female anatomy. It listed the words and then the definitions."

" 'Clitoris: Female organ of pleasure!' " Ogden shouted gleefully.

"That's quite enough," said Mrs. Mobilio.

"My father called her up to ask what the hell she was teaching us, and she said it was science," Rufus continued.

"Do you know if your father called the headmaster as well?"

"I think he changed his mind because Miss Batten gave me an eighty in health and it was my highest grade."

"I see," said Mrs. Mobilio.

"Is she gonna get fired?" asked Hugh.

"We don't fire teachers because our students complain about them. What kind of due process would that be?"

"Huh?" said the boys.

"How fair would that be? We ascertain that there's a basis for your charges. Then and only then would we discuss it with Miss Batten."

"She sucks as a teacher," said Rufus.

"For the record, I hate that word," said Mrs. Mobilio.

"Can we go now?" asked Ogden.

"Let me ask you this: Are you speaking for the class? Are you three voices or fifteen?"

"Fifteen," they said in unison.

"And why did you bring this to me as opposed to, for example, Dr. Lucey or Mr. Samuels?"

Hugh, who'd made the honor roll one term, spoke for the delegation. "We talked about who to go to, and we decided you'd be the most interested." His friends nodded. "Also, we figured you'd want to help."

" 'Cause that's your job, right?" added Ogden.

Mrs. Mobilio was not popular; she was visited by students infrequently and flattered even less. "It is one of the hats I wear," she murmured.

"Are you going to do anything?" asked Hugh.

"The term is almost up. Do you think you can live with this situation for"—she turned several pages on her desk calendar—"three more weeks?"

"Then are you gonna fire her?"

"I don't have any such powers, and furthermore, I explained to you about fairness and due process here at Harding."

"His grandfather's a trustee," said Hugh, pointing to Ogden. "Plus, his father and all his uncles went here."

"They could've named the new science building after him, but he likes to give money away anonymously," Ogden said.

"You're crazy if you don't call him," said Rufus. "I think he'd love to know that a teacher called you a shithead inside the building he paid for."

"Are you gonna talk to Miss Batten?" asked Hugh.

"She's fucked," Rufus mouthed to his roommate.

Hugh added, "I mean, she's nice sometimes, but most of the time you can tell she hates us."

"No one at Harding hates anyone," said Mrs. Mobilio.

"They're lying," Sunny told her chairman, Fred Samuels, who was sporting his trademark bow tie and buzz cut.

"More than one reported it."

"Who were they?"

"I promised I wouldn't say."

"Why?"

"The usual fears—that you'd find out and they may have to face the music."

"Me?" asked Sunny. "*I'm* the music?"

Samuels picked up his pen. "I need to ask your version of events."

Sunny looked down at her lap. She'd been called out of practice and was still wearing a glove on her left hand.

"They say you called them names," he prompted. "They said epithets were hurled—"

"They used that word? *Epithets?*"

"I need to know your version of events," he repeated.

"This is not a version—this is the truth: I came into class and someone had drawn a naked man lying on top of a naked woman on the blackboard, and both were waving golf clubs in the air." She took off her glove and stuffed it into the pocket of her chinos. "Not to be confused with the man's erect, anatomically correct shaft."

"I see. And what did you do?"

"I erased it, and then I turned around and said, 'You're like real-life clichés of nasty boys in movies about prep schools.' "

"They said you swore at them."

"I called them nasty, spoiled brats."

"Is there any chance you used the words *little shits* or *shitheads?*"

"None."

"And if they reported that, they'd be lying?"

"Correct."

"Still—it's unusual for students to go to Mrs. Mobilio and complain about a teacher not having any control over the class."

Sunny said, "Mrs. Mobilio? That changes the complexion of this matter slightly, I would say."

Mr. Samuels's face reddened.

"Clearly, you grasped the significance of the golf clubs."

"Hard not to," he murmured.

"I don't know what you've heard, but I am not having an affair with Chuck Mobilio."

"I was quite sure of that," he mumbled.

"It's a stupid rumor based on the fact that he coaches varsity and I coach the j.v. and we happen to share an office."

Samuels put his pen down and lowered his voice. *"Entre nous?"*

Sunny nodded.

"Chuck may have had a dalliance or two in the past, before you came here. There may be a problem between him and Nancy in the trust department." He put his fingers to his lips. "You didn't hear this from me."

Sunny pictured the covert Mobilio gaze, the too-long and too-frank stare with which he punctuated their conversations when he thought no one else was watching.

"Here's what I'm going to do," Samuels said. "I'm going to let you off the hook as far as teaching health is concerned—"

"Are you firing me?"

"No! I've already talked to some people in the offices—development and admissions—about administrative jobs there."

"And you don't think that relieving me of my duties is the same thing as firing me?"

Samuels shook his head. "You were hired principally to coach golf and move into the varsity slot after a one-year trial. I think the students admire you for that and at the same time appreciate that you were, shall we say, untested in the classroom."

"Who's going to teach health now?"

"Chuck." He coughed into his closed fist. "Mobilio."

"Great. Perfect choice, since mine are extremely small shoes to fill."

"The school is honoring its contract," Samuels said, his voice now cool and eye contact abandoned. "Golf ends on Friday, May twenty-seventh. Finals begin the following Monday. Graduation is June the second. I'm sure you can appreciate that we're doing our best under the circumstances."

"I'll be gone on the third," Sunny said.

CHAPTER 5

King's Nite

Mrs. Peacock couldn't help looking pleased that the next of kin to a tragedy had checked into her motel. There was a connection, she explained: Her husband worked for Herlihy Brothers Fuel, and it was the two bosses, Danny and Sean, who'd fixed the fatal furnace. Volunteered. For free. Not that Miss Batten's mother was one of their accounts. Not at *all*.

"That was very kind of them," said Sunny.

"It's good public relations. They're smart in that way." She ran Sunny's credit card through her machine, once, twice, frowning. "Sometimes it's the phone lines and not the credit limit. I'll swipe it through again."

"There shouldn't be a problem."

"We have a two-night minimum starting June first," said Mrs. Peacock, whose gray hair had a pale lavender cast and whose coral beads matched her coral clip-on earrings.

"Fine."

"Don't think people weren't upset about all of this happening in King George. First, your mother and Miles Finn, then, before we turn around, we almost lose our police chief. Another few inches and a bullet would've killed him, which makes me wonder what's so great about bullet-proof vests if you consider all the parts of the body they don't cover."

"I'm in number ten?" Sunny said after a pause.

"Last unit. Don't put anything in the toilet but toilet paper. Our septic tank can't handle anything else."

"Fine," said Sunny.

"You can get a decent breakfast—eggs, toast, home fries, bacon, coffee—at The Dot."

Finally, Sunny smiled. "Do the Angelos still own it?"

"Yeah. He's sick, you know."

"Do they still make those maple sausages?"

"I eat at home. You can't smoke there anymore. Besides, I don't like paying a dollar-fifty for a fried egg."

"I'd better unpack," said Sunny.

———

At 5, 6, and 11 P.M., Joey Loach watched himself on three Boston TV stations looking worse than he realized and needing a shave. No reporter had asked him the question he feared—Why, in a one-horse town with no crime and no criminals, were you wearing a bullet-proof vest?

"Was I *wrong*?" he would have said. "Wouldn't I be dead now if I didn't arm myself every morning when I left my house?" For three years his vest had been a secret, purchased with his own money, a promise he'd made to his mother and the condition on which she had let him go to the police academy.

Elsie Loach was both inconsolable about her son's near disaster, imagining the inches in either direction that would have left him dead or paralyzed, and triumphant that she'd saved his life. She wanted him to resign immediately. No one's son should be a police officer! They should come from the ranks of orphans and middle-aged men whose mothers have passed on. He practically lived at the station, like a firefighter, like a lighthouse keeper, like a monk. She'd brought the braided rug from his room at home and a reading lamp for his bedside, which necessitated her acquiring and refinishing a solid maple night table from the rummage sale at Saint Xavier's along with a bureau scarf that wasn't frilly or stained.

Strangers assumed that she was thrilled to have Joey in uniform; exhilarated by the sight of him behind the wheel of his cruiser, pressed and clean-shaven, but she wasn't. She turned off the news when she saw reports of police officers shot, killed, sued, eulogized. And now it had happened. A crazy man had shot Joey at close range as he ambled in his good-natured fashion up to the half-open window of—as best as he could remember—a Ford pickup with Massachusetts plates. They were out there—nuts and murderers; sociopaths who thought it was better to kill someone's son than get a ticket. Marilee and her husband had safe jobs—day-care teacher at a state building with a metal detector and dairy manager at Foodland.

Worst of all, the murderer was at large. "He's gone," Joey had promised. "Even the stupidest cop killer would get out of town and not look back."

"Maybe he wasn't just passing through. Maybe this was his destination. Maybe he was out to get you."

"I pulled him over! He shot me because he must've had drugs in the car or it was stolen, or there was a body in the trunk."

"Promise me you'll let the state police handle this. Let someone else go looking for him."

"I'm not going looking for him, okay?"

"Will you spend tonight at home?"

He shook his head. She walked from the foot of his bed to one side. "Let me see."

"No."

"I want to see what he did to you."

Joey pulled the thin cotton blanket up to his shoulders. "It's black-and-blue. They told me to expect a few more shades before I'm done. But forget it. I'm not showing you."

"Is it very painful?"

"No," he lied.

She narrowed her eyes. "They said on television it was like getting beat up by a heavyweight boxer."

"Nah," said Joey. "Bantamweight, maybe."

She opened the flat, hinged carton that held his new bullet-proof vest, picked it up by its shoulders, held it against her own chest, and said, "It seems so flimsy."

"That's the point—lighter; new and improved."

"But strong enough to stop the bullets?"

"Definitely. More than ever. You're worrying about nothing. Lightning doesn't strike the same place twice."

"That's not true! If you're chief of police, you're a lightning rod."

"This is King George, Ma. This was a bad break, but it's not going to happen again."

"What if he's never caught? How do I get to sleep at night knowing he's out there?"

"You'll sleep fine. So will I. In fact I've got a prescription for sleeping pills. I'll give you one." He folded the blanket to his waist. "Now I'm getting out of bed and I'm getting dressed, so you may want to leave."

"I'll wait in the hall. I want to speak to the nurses anyway."

"About what?"

"I want someone besides you to tell me that the doctor discharged you."

Joey picked up a cord and followed it to its grip. "See this? It brings a nurse in five seconds and I'll tell her you're harassing me."

Mrs. Loach looked around the room. "Your uniform. Where is it? Can I mend it?"

Joey's mouth formed a tight, grim line. He shook his head. "The FBI gets the uniform."

Mrs. Loach backed up to the visitor's chair and sat down heavily.

Joey tried again. "I think visiting hours are just about over. Besides, it's polite to give the patient privacy when he wants to get out of bed and his ass is hanging out of his johnny."

His mother's eyes narrowed. "Why does the FBI need your pants if you were shot in the chest?"

"For lab work. Ballistics. Powder burns. You know the drill."

"I wish I didn't!" she cried. "I sit around hoping I'll never get a phone call from the emergency room, and then it happened, like my worst fear come true."

He sidled out of bed and walked backward to the bathroom. "It *wasn't* your worst fear, though, was it, because I'm fine. The vest worked. I've made those phone calls to mothers—'There's been an accident, and I'm sorry, Mrs. Smith or Jones, but your son didn't make it.' *That's* someone's worst fear. This is nothing. Day before last, I had to call the son of the man who died at Margaret Batten's house. And then Sunny. She'd have been thrilled if her mother was merely in the hospital with the wind knocked out of her."

"Margaret Batten," murmured Mrs. Loach. "What a terrible thing."

"You're right about that, and it gets worse. Her daughter heard it secondhand from Finn's son. I called him because she wasn't home. But that didn't bother *him:* He left a message on her answering machine. That's how she found out."

It had the desired effect: Mrs. Loach's features reset themselves for a new course of misfortune. "That poor girl," she cried.

Joey closed the bathroom door behind him.

"There was just the two of them," she said. "And I always admired the way her mother fought for her. I hope I told her that. I must have at some point."

"No doubt," said Joey.

"Were you nice to Sunny?" his mother called.

"Of course I was."

"Sometimes you can be brusque over the phone."

"To you."

"Did she go to high school with you or with Marilee?"

"Me."

"She was the girl who golfed, right? Wasn't there some hysteria about her playing on the boys' team?"

"They had to let her play. They didn't have a girls' team and she was better than all of the boys."

"It's because of where she lived," called his mother. "If you grow up next to a mountain, you learn to ski, and if you live next to a country club, you learn to golf."

"What?" Joey yelled.

"Bad luck, as it turned out, that house by the golf course. And you know what makes it worse? They fixed the furnace in a half hour. Maybe less."

"Who did?"

"Herlihy Brothers Fuel just showed up—not ten minutes after they read about it in the *Bulletin*. Sean and Danny both."

"Who let them in?"

"*I* did! When no one answered at the station, they came by the house."

"But, Ma—"

"No charge. They donated their services."

"What about the police tape no one was supposed to cross?"

"The door was open. They know their stuff, believe me. They wear gas masks or whatever they're called these days."

"Ma! How many goddamn times do I have to tell you that you can't let every Tom, Dick—"

"I'm leaving," she said, "but only because you sound like yourself and can walk and do your business. Just promise—"

"No promises," he yelled, followed by a muffled, "Ouch. Shit."

"What's the matter?"

"Nothing!"

"I heard you say ouch."

"I'm a little sore. It's nothing. Just go. I'll call you tomorrow. And stop making decisions about police matters. Nobody swore you in as my deputy."

There was silence beyond the bathroom. Joey opened the door.

His mother's face brightened. "Should I strip the bed?" she asked.

———

The hospital operator said that Chief Loach's condition was not a matter of public record. Could she have the name of the caller?

"Sunny Batten."

The operator gasped, then introduced herself as Danielle Thibault's sister Celeste, two years ahead of Sunny in high school. *So* sorry for her loss. Every time she picked up the newspaper, it seemed, there was a tragic headline about someone she knew. Oops. Hold on.

Celeste returned. "Everyone's calling about him since it was on the news."

"You can't say if he's still there?"

Celeste paused. "I'm not supposed to. And get this: That's a direct order from the *FBI*: 'If anyone calls asking about Chief Loach's condition, take down his name.'" Celeste's tone grew conspiratorial. "A couple of women didn't leave their names, but I knew exactly who they were."

"Who?"

"Old girlfriends of his! Linda LaDue, Patty Timmins, for sure. Or it could have been her sister. They sound the same."

After a moment Sunny said, "I did see him on the news, but I'm calling for official reasons."

"Call him at the station. He should be back by now. Or run over there. Where are you calling from?"

"King's Nite."

"The office phone or the pay phone?"

"Pay phone."

"Is there a light on in the front of the station—I mean, not just the porch light, but inside?"

Sunny turned and looked.

"Doesn't matter. He's there. Just walk over. The front door'll be open. If he's snoozing in the back, ring the bell on his desk. How long are you up here for?"

Sunny said, "Until I figure out where to go next."

"Any chance you'd stay?"

"First I need a job," said Sunny.

"Like what?"

"A change," said Sunny. "I was teaching, which I sort of fell into. I think I might try something a little more exciting."

"We have openings here," said Celeste. "In fact they just posted 'In-patient Pharmacy Technician.' Heather Machonski's taking maternity leave. Do you want me to pick you up an application?"

"Not just yet," said Sunny.

"You probably want something out of doors, right? You were the big tennis player."

"Golf," said Sunny.

"I'd try the summer camps," said Celeste. "Maybe they have camps for golfers—there's one for everything else."

"Maybe when my head is clearer," said Sunny.

"Gotta get this. You stay strong, okay? Call me if you want to bounce any job ideas off me. In any event, I'll see you tomorrow."

"Tomorrow?" Sunny repeated.

"Your wake, hon," said Celeste.

——

"Keep it on," said Sunny as Chief Loach snapped off the television and jumped to his feet. "Joe—it's me, Sunny. I made it back just in time to hear you were shot."

"Shot *at*," he said. "The bullets bounced off me." He banged a fist against his ribs. "Kryptonite." He winced. "More or less."

"No damage?"

"Plenty," he said. "I'm black-and-blue like I was worked over by an angry mob."

"Should you be back at work so soon?"

"I'm it. There's no one else."

"When do you sleep?"

He shook his head. "I'll let you in on a little secret: Nothing ever happens here—until this week, that is. I've been in this job for three years. I was on the Keene force for nine years before that, but I swear to God this thing at your mother's house is the first time I had to put up my police tape."

He stared at her hair. Finally, he pointed. "When did this happen?"

"Prematurely."

"Like, overnight?"

"Not overnight. You haven't seen me since graduation."

"It's nice," said Joey. "Gray-blond, you could say."

Sunny didn't respond.

"So where have you been?"

"College. Then various schools, teaching."

"How many?"

"Three: one in New York and two in Connecticut. Private schools, so I had to teach and coach and sleep and eat in one place, all for a pittance. I couldn't find a good fit." She backed up to the visitors' bench and sat down.

"You okay?" he asked.

Sunny shook her head.

"Want a glass of water? Or juice? I've got a refrigerator in the back. Or I can pop a potato into the microwave."

She looked up at the large, plain-faced wall clock: nine o'clock, and she couldn't remember when or what lunch had been.

Joey asked, "Anything I can do for you?"

Sunny said, "I'm staying at the King's Nite, and I don't have a phone in my room."

"Do you want to use mine?"

"I just thought you should know I was here if anything came up."

"Did you want to go to the house tomorrow?"

Sunny closed her eyes, then opened them before she spoke. "Not unless I have to."

"There's nothing there that would upset you. I mean, sure—everything would upset you—the house where you grew up and then your mother dies there. But I meant everything's in order. It's not creepy, if that's what you're thinking."

"Who put everything in order?"

"I stopped by on my way back from the hospital to take down the police tape." He shrugged. "Maybe I moved some dirty dishes to the sink."

"Have I asked you if they had been there all night? I mean, I know they were, but did anyone figure out how long before they were discovered?"

"Mr. Finn picked up their sandwich orders at The Dot, so we know they were alive the night before. They must've been overcome between dinner and when the paperboy arrived. It wasn't really important to pinpoint the exact time of death."

"I guess," said Sunny wanly, "that you only have to do that if there's a murder."

"So they tell me." Joey checked his clipboard. "Mr. Finn's next of kin? Fletcher?" He looked up. "Has he been any help?"

Sunny said, "Not so far."

"Is he here?"

"He's coming up for the funeral, but he's too busy to come any earlier." She stood up and said, "I'm sure you're busy, too."

"Busy putting ice on my hematomas," he said. When she didn't respond, he added, "No one told me to do that, but it feels better when I do."

"Did they catch the man who shot you?"

Joey said firmly, "They will, any second. Nothing to worry about." He reached for his hat, grimaced in pain at the stretch. "C'mon. I'll walk you back."

"No. I'm fine. You're working."

"When's the funeral?"

"Friday morning. The wake is tomorrow night."

"Dickie been okay? Helpful and all that?"

Sunny shrugged. "He wanted the wake at the funeral parlor, but I insisted. He said he'd need a permit for the theater, but I said, 'Give me the name and number of the custodian and I'll make one phone call.' It turned out it was his sister's husband—"

"Roland LaPlante."

"So that took all of thirty seconds."

"Everyone wants to help. The whole town feels responsible."

"Responsible?"

"Like someone should have noticed. Or if someone had invited them over for dinner that night, then when they didn't show, they could have called. . . . Or maybe we should have made carbon-monoxide detectors mandatory."

Sunny's eyes filled.

"You gonna be able to sleep? The King's Nite's not famous for its Sealy Posturpedics."

"Probably not."

Joey walked over to a wooden coatrack, patted the pockets of a navy blue windbreaker, and came back with a bottle of pills. "How about if I give you one or two?"

"Don't you need them?"

He held the amber vial up to eye level. "There's four in here. I might use one or two. But then I'll forget about them and they'll expire."

Sunny held her hand out. "It must be legal if they're being dispensed by the chief of police."

Joey laughed. "You remember what a genius and scholar I was in high school, right? Well, I went to medical school nights. Or was it pharmacy school? I forget. I'd better go check my diploma."

Sunny didn't smile. She said politely, "I think we were in study hall together but not any classes."

"Because the only time kids like us got thrown together was in study hall. Or maybe driver's ed."

"But here you are," said Sunny. "Chief of police. You probably visit elementary schools and tell all the students how to be good citizens."

"I do. I'm good at it. I can make quarters come out of their ears, and I can turn balloons into dachshunds."

"When I teach at that level," Sunny began. "Actually, when I *taught*—"

"That's it? Past tense? You're done with it?"

Sunny said, "I had a one-year contract."

The phone rang. Joey put his hand on the receiver but didn't pick up. "Does that mean *fired*?"

Sunny said, "Maybe it's an emergency."

Joey rolled his eyes. "King George Police Station, Chief Loach speaking." He closed his eyes and kept them shut as he recited, "Only in winter. After April thirtieth you can park on either side." He hung up. "That's what I do: I give directions and I answer the questions people would ask the D.P.W. If we had one."

"Then let me ask this," said Sunny. "Off the record, is there a place I could hit a bucket of balls where I wouldn't run into anyone who knew I was doing it the morning of my mother's wake?"

"Why not at the club?"

"I'm not a member, and I just want to hit a bucket of balls. Preferably within walking distance."

Joey pointed. "Route 12A North—maybe a mile past the Creamery. There's a little hut on your left shaped like a hamburger and a bun. Opens at nine A.M."

"Thanks," said Sunny.

"Seriously: I can call a half a dozen guys who are members and would be happy to take you out as their guest. Believe me, they'd understand."

Sunny said, "I know those guys. No thanks."

"I can drive you. It's not exactly next door."

"A mile's nothing," said Sunny. "A mile will feel good."

"Watch the oncoming traffic," said Chief Loach.

CHAPTER 6

The Dot

No-nonsense Mrs. Angelo, famous for adding figures in her head, who rarely climbed down from her stool at the cash register, did so to enfold Sunny in a bosomy hug. "It's a miracle that you walked in here! We were just saying that we wanted to send some platters over; some sandwiches, some pasta salad, the tricolor rotini, and an assortment of cookies—we do anise and pignoli beautiful."

"I wasn't planning any kind of reception," said Sunny.

"You have to invite people back to the house after the funeral. They want to be with each other." She led Sunny to the booth next to the cash register, despite the fact that it was already occupied by a woman in a white tennis sweater and maroon velvet headband. The woman removed her reading glasses, folded them into hinged quarters, and offered her hand.

"Sunny? I'm Fran Pope. You don't know me, but I directed your mother in *Watch on the Rhine,* and we are all just shattered."

Sunny said, "Did you say Pope?"

"Like the pontiff. As in Pope Sand and Gravel. Your mother and I—"

"Are you Randall Pope's mother?"

Mrs. Pope's face brightened. "I certainly am! You know Randy?"

Sunny inhaled and exhaled before saying, "I was on the golf team with him. He was captain the year I joined."

"Of course I knew that. Very small world. I think your mother knew the connection."

"She certainly did," said Sunny.

"I hope he was a good captain," said Mrs. Pope.

Sunny said after a pause, "He was a good golfer."

Beaming, Mrs. Pope said, "It was his spring sport, which you probably know. Football was his first love, and basketball was second. Mr. Pope was a football fanatic, but I liked the basketball games, because I got to watch them in a nice warm gym."

Sunny opened a menu and said without looking up from it, "Your son found a dead carp floating in the brook—or what was euphemistically called the brook—and put it in my golf bag." She plucked several napkins, one by one, from a dispenser and spread them on her lap. "At least I was ninety-nine percent sure it was Randy."

Mrs. Pope blinked, took a sip from her cup, blotted her lips, and asked, "Did Bill Sandvik get in touch with you? Or Bill Kaufman? Someone was going to call you and ask if we—meaning the Players— could say a few words at the funeral. We thought either of the Bills would give a stunning eulogy."

"That would be fine," said Sunny. "I'm sure my mother would love it. *Would* have loved it . . ."

"Bill S. was her leading man a number of times and has a gorgeous speaking voice, but Bill K. is a freelance toastmaster. They may still be sorting it out."

"Either," said Sunny. "Or both."

"Everyone was *rocked* by this tragedy. It touched everyone in town, directly or indirectly."

"I'm beginning to see that," said Sunny.

"Did you order?" Mrs. Pope asked her, accompanied by the snap of

Mrs. Angelo's fingers behind her. From the counter, The Dot's one waitress barked, "What?"

"Winnie! Bring Sunny a menu."

"Just coffee," said Sunny.

"What if Gus scrambles you an egg or two?" asked Mrs. Angelo from her stool. "Or we have omelets now—Eastern, Western, or Hawaiian."

Mrs. Pope confided, "When I went through this with my mother, I lost one dress size without even trying. And she died at eighty-eight. Not unexpected."

"*Still* too young," said Mrs. Angelo.

"Not in my mother's case," Mrs. Pope continued. "She was completely demented. But I know what you're saying: You think you're prepared, but you never are. And in your case, there's an extra layer of tragedy—losing your only parent before you're even . . ."

Sunny wasn't sure where the unfinished sentence was supposed to lead. Her age? Her marital or professional status?

Mrs. Pope tried, "Thirty-three?"

"No, I was two years behind Randy. It's the hair. People always think—"

"Well, of course! People are so unobservant. Your face is still the face in your yearbook picture." She patted Sunny's hand. "Mr. Pope and I take out a full-page ad in every King George Regional yearbook—Pope Sand and Gravel—so we get a courtesy copy."

Sunny could see that Mrs. Pope, whose own hair was dyed a uniform chestnut, was counting the days until she could take the younger woman under her wing and advise her that gray is for aging hippies or the occasional over-fifty model whose silver hair is the very point.

"Tell me what I can do," said Mrs. Pope. "There must be something I can help you with. Do you need a place to stay? Will the relatives need a place to freshen up?"

"I'm set," said Sunny. "But thanks."

"Randy lives on East Pleasant. You might know his wife."

"I do."

"It's one of those cute stories: They didn't like each other in high school—she thought he was conceited—three-letter athlete, tall, good-looking—and Regina was a few years younger and, from what I understand, a late bloomer. But then they ran into each other after he graduated from B.U., and she was back here from Rivier College, student-teaching—"

"I know the whole story."

"I don't know how well you knew him, but I can assure you that he's matured into a fine husband and father. He'll most certainly be paying his respects."

"I'm sure Regina will," said Sunny.

Winnie rounded the counter carrying a platter of English muffins, sunny-side-up eggs, home fries, and sausage flattened into a patty. "Couldn't help it," she said. "Gus heard you were here. He practically wept." She checked to make sure Mrs. Angelo was out of range. "He thinks you're taking a stand by coming here," she whispered. "He's really touched."

"I'm taking a stand?" asked Sunny.

"The food," Mrs. Pope explained. "Their last meal. It was take-out from here."

"It was the last time anyone saw Miles alive," said Winnie. "Until they ruled out food poisoning, we were sweating bullets around here, if you know what I mean. Even with all the hoopla about the furnace, business has dropped off—at least that's my opinion. Guilt by association."

"Then please tell Mr. Angelo that he'll be seeing plenty of me, but I'm going to insist on paying for my meals," said Sunny.

The waitress said, "Let him if he wants to. He had a lung removed and we like to give him his way."

"Cancer," Mrs. Pope translated.

"In remission," said Winnie.

"Is he okay?" asked Sunny.

"We think so. It didn't spread. Next Thanksgiving it'll be five years." Winnie knocked on the wood-look Formica, and Sunny seconded the motion.

She was waiting with her golf bag when the driving range opened at nine. After paying for the largest bucket of balls, Sunny walked past the rubber mats to the grassy area that separated the beginners from the experts. She began with short irons and worked her way up to her woods. An older couple arrived in matching cruise-line sweatshirts, stretched in tandem, then addressed each ball with their lips moving, as if reciting lessons. Even with her head down, Sunny sensed when their bucket was empty, when the husband had simply instructed his wife to watch her.

"You the pro here?" he finally called over.

"I wish," said Sunny.

As she returned her empty basket, the man behind the counter asked, "Any interest in a member-guest tournament coming up next weekend in Sunapee?"

"Can't. Thanks."

"Up here on vacation?"

"No I'm not," said Sunny.

=====

For the wake, Regina Pope dressed her two-year-old son in miniature grown-up clothes—gray trousers, white shirt, red clip-on bow tie. He owned only sneakers, which would have to do—no disrespect intended. It was too warm for the little patchwork madras sports jacket, dry clean only, that completed the outfit. He was Robert, without nicknames, and to his mother, especially in his dress-up clothes, the most beautiful boy in the world.

=====

Coach Sweet decided to skip the wake and make an appearance at the funeral. Or maybe the reverse. Milling around a coffin, he'd be obliged to speak to Sunny, while at the funeral he'd sign the book, hang back, and still get credit for doing the decent thing. He could call the guys who were still in town, and they could form a kind of honor guard—some goddamn ceremonial thing like that. Nah. It wasn't Sunny who had died. It was her mother, the ex–legal, ex–medical secretary, who could rattle off her daughter's rights chapter and verse. Mrs. Equal Opportunity. Mrs. Title Nine.

He'd send his wife.

———

When Dr. Ouimet hired Margaret Batten to fill in for Mrs. Ouimet following her gallbladder surgery, there was a conspicuous change in office routine: Margaret didn't leave early or come in late; didn't berate him for spending too much time with a patient; didn't tie up the phone while refusing to add a second line. Margaret was calm where his wife had been rattled, and forgiving to the cranky and the sick. Insurance companies reimbursed him for services the first time the paperwork went in, and patients surrendered co-payments before they left the office. Dr. Ouimet convinced his unsalaried wife—whose gallbladder had been removed through laparoscopy, and whose recovery was all too quick—that they *should* gut and remodel the kitchen the way she'd been asking for years, and, yes, she could act as general contractor, however long that took.

He was shocked that Chief Loach didn't call him personally to break the news. He should not have had to hear about Margaret across the breakfast table, his wife's mouth forming the words of the *Bulletin* headline as if they were gossip rather than personal tragedy. He cried as he reread the story himself, then dialed Margaret's home number, praying for a case of mistaken identity. He wept throughout the day to himself, in the bathroom, garage, and car. He couldn't eat. He blamed himself: Margaret, who rarely took a sick day and never brought her personal medical concerns to work, had complained of a serious headache for the past few weeks.

"Are you taking anything?" he'd asked, not looking up from his paperwork.

"No," she said.

"Well, there you go. We have a miracle drug called aspirin that you could try," he'd said with a distracted smile.

All he could think to do was run a half-page ad in the *Bulletin* announcing that the offices of Dr. Emil Ouimet would be closed for one week out of respect to his devoted and beloved employee, followed by a stanza by Robert Browning that he copied from *Bartlett's Familiar Quotations*.

"*Beloved*," said his wife. "A married man doesn't use that word about another woman, especially a divorcee."

"A widow. And I was speaking for my patients."

She rattled the paper and asked from behind a page as frivolous as Living/Arts, "How long would you close the office if *I* died?"

"Don't ask foolish questions," he answered.

———

Even though the theater was only two blocks from the motel, Dickie Saint-Onge picked Sunny up in his stretch limousine. He asked her about pallbearers and, because calls had come in, about her mother's favorite charity.

"I should know," said Sunny.

"The ladies like the homeless, and almost all the men support the Shriners."

"It should have something to do with the theater—maybe an award at the high school, a memorial scholarship."

"For who?"

"I haven't thought it through. Maybe a graduating senior who wants to study acting."

Dickie took out a pocket notebook and made a notation with a miniature pencil.

"Don't announce it yet," said Sunny.

"What about pallbearers?"

"I did that," said Sunny.

Dickie took her list and read it aloud. "Very nice," he said. "I've used every one of them before. Dr. Ouimet called me and volunteered for the job. I was hoping you'd pick him."

Dickie had a ring of keys, one of which opened the stage door after a half-dozen tries. He left Sunny in a dressing room, alone, sitting at a peeling vanity table, numbly surveying the pots of cracked makeup and dirty brushes.

"I've got to admit," said Dickie as he returned, "I had my doubts about doing this off-site. But it looks like she was a head of state. And more flowers where these came from. You ready?"

"Is anyone here yet?"

"My wife and my mother," said Dickie. "They come to everything I do."

"Do I know your wife?"

"I met her at school in Albany. Her father's a funeral director in Plattsburgh."

Sunny stood up and quickly sat down again.

"You're okay," said Dickie. "I'll be right there, moving people along, directing traffic. I've got Kleenex, Wash 'n Dri, Tic Tacs, water, whatever helps. Just nod and shake their hands. They usually do the talking."

"It's not that. I should have done this earlier. Isn't that what people do—have a private good-bye?"

Dickie walked over to the vanity stool and helped her up, a boost from around her shoulders. "She looks like she's sleeping. I promise. She looks beautiful, if I do say so myself."

"Do I have a few minutes? Before anyone gets here?"

Dickie took a diplomatic quick-step away from Sunny. "Absolutely. I'll ask my mother and Roberta to step outside."

He looked at his watch, bit his lip.

"I don't need long," said Sunny. She left the dressing room, walked between the maroon velvet curtains that her mother had patched in her pre–leading lady days.

The coffin was parallel to the orchestra seats and surrounded by potted lilies. Margaret looked small and alone. Worse than asleep—unreachable, irretrievable. Sunny moved closer. She could see that her mother's brown hair was parted on the wrong side and that her lips were painted a darker shade of red than Margaret had worn in life. The dress was out of season: black, V-necked, long-sleeved, and ending in a point at each wrist. It needed pearls, a locket, a pin, a corsage—something.

"Mom?" Sunny whispered.

The footlights and the lilies flashed white at the edges of her vision, and her knees sagged.

Roberta Saint-Onge, who'd been spying on Sunny from the vestibule, yelled for ammonium carbonate, for a cold, wet facecloth, for a chair, for help, for Dickie.

CHAPTER 7

The Viewing Hours

With a firm hand on the back of Sunny's neck, Roberta Saint-Onge repeated, "Head *down*. The head has to be *down*."

"I'm okay," Sunny murmured. "You can let go now."

"Head between your knees," ordered Roberta.

"You're hurting me."

"How long does she have to stay like this?" asked Dickie.

"However long it takes for the blood to drain back into her head."

"It's there," said Sunny. "Let *go*, for Crissakes."

Roberta did, petulantly, as if a referee had called a jump ball and re-possessed the disputed goods.

"You're still pale," said Dickie. "You might want to touch up your cheekbones with a little color."

"I'll be okay," said Sunny. "Give me a minute without the headlock."

"This isn't the first time we've encountered this," said Roberta.

"I never fainted before in my life," said Sunny.

"It's a shock to the system," said Dickie. "No matter how close you were or what kind of parent she was or how well or poorly you got along, you only have one mother."

"She was a fantastic parent," said Sunny.

"Of course she was," said Dickie.

"We grew up around it," said Roberta. "We're both third-generation funeral directors, so sometimes we lose sight of the fact that it's so much more than the corporal remains of an individual."

"What she means," said Dickie, "is that we understand very well that it's someone's mother or father or husband or wife, and we can empathize, but we're professionals and we don't have the exact same *physiologic* response to the death of the loved one as our client does. We *share* the sorrow, but at the same time we have a job to do."

"Hundreds of little jobs that have to be performed seamlessly," added Roberta. "Our goal is to be as helpful yet as unobtrusive as possible."

Sunny rubbed the back of her neck and asked what time it was.

"It's time," said Dickie.

"You stay right here," said Roberta. "Everyone will understand—"

"I don't want anyone's understanding! No one has to know I fainted."

"Technically? I don't think you actually lost consciousness," said Dickie. "I think you got woozy."

"I want to greet people standing up. It seems the least I can do."

"There are no rules," said Roberta. "We encourage our mourners to do what feels right to them and not to worry about"—she flexed two fingers on each side of her face—"doing the 'right thing.' For example, the fact that you're wearing navy blue tonight, and it's sleeveless? With dangly earrings? Well, why not? There used to be an unwritten rule that anything but black and long sleeves was wrong, but times have changed. If you'd worn red, we wouldn't have said a word."

Sunny got to her feet, gripped the back of her metal chair with both hands, and straightened her shoulders. "Unlock the door," she ordered.

Those who couldn't conjure a distinct recollection of Margaret made one up: Cora Poole, whose late husband owned Fashionable Fabrics, said she remembered, as if it were yesterday, Margaret and Sunny picking out a pattern and powder-pink piqué for Sunny's senior prom dress.

"Are you sure?" asked Sunny. "I don't think I went to the senior prom."

"Everyone goes," said Mrs. Poole. "It was a Simplicity pattern, and you trimmed it in pink and white embroidered daisies that we sold by the yard."

"It's coming back to me," said Sunny.

Janine Sopp, L.P.N., said she was on duty the night Sunny was born at Saint Catherine's and took care of her in the newborn nursery.

"But I moved here when I was two," said Sunny.

"You couldn't have," said Mrs. Sopp. "I remember you had a high bilirubin count and we put you under the lights."

"Then you must be right," murmured Sunny.

Mourners testified to being present at all of Margaret's performances, to clapping louder and longer than anyone else to spur multiple curtain calls. Endless Community Players—co-stars, seamstresses, scenery painters, ushers—formed their own receiving line. Sunny's Brownie troop leader, pediatrician, children's room librarian, the Abner Cotton board, the mayor, the superintendent of schools, and the mechanic who had serviced Margaret's car all clasped Sunny's hand between both of theirs. Invitations issued from every trembling set of lips: Would Sunny come to Sunday dinner? Care to play eighteen holes? Borrow the videotape of a dress rehearsal of *Two for the Seesaw*? Mr. DeMinico, still the principal of King George Regional, still dressed in shiny brown, still resting his folded hands on the paunch bulging above his belt, asked Sunny to attend commencement as his special guest.

Dry-eyed at last, Sunny said, "Perhaps you recall that I didn't attend my own graduation."

He squinted into the distance, nodded curtly at several alums. "Did you get your diploma? I think Mrs. Osborn mailed it the next day."

"No," said Sunny. "My mother went by herself and picked it up for me."

"We called your name," he said, "and even though we had asked everyone to hold their applause until the end, there was a lot of clapping."

"So I heard."

"In recognition, I guess you could say. If I remember correctly, your mother initiated it." He glanced toward the coffin.

"That's not the version I got. What I heard was that a couple of girls yelled, 'Yay, Sunny!' Something to that effect."

"You may be right," said Mr. DeMinico.

"Which of course meant that the boys had to boo—"

"Just the athletes."

"All I did was make the varsity," said Sunny. "All I needed was one adult to stand up for me, one adult besides my mother, who thought that maybe having someone with a single-digit handicap would be good for the team and good for the school."

"I didn't mean to upset you," said Mr. DeMinico.

"Now? Or do you mean then?"

"I can't turn back the clock. I meant now. On this occasion."

Behind him, an elderly woman in a black picture hat complained, "There's a long line. Some of us have been here since twenty to seven."

"My fault," said Sunny, and reached around to take the woman's gloved hand.

"You don't know me," said the woman, "but I had the same standing appointment as your mother did for our hair—hers with Jennifer and mine with Lorraine—side by side." Her voice quivered. "A lovely woman. Top-drawer. That's all I need to say, because you know better than anyone."

"Is Jennifer here?" asked Sunny.

The woman looked behind her, leaning left then right. "There she is. Jennifer! Come meet Margaret's daughter." She fluttered her hands. "Hurry up. She asked for you."

Jennifer had radically chic and severe hair for King George, bangs short and straight, dark roots showing on purpose, blunt orange hair to her jaw. "I liked your mother a lot," she told Sunny. "She could have switched to a Boston salon—a lot of the local actresses did that once they saw their name in lights. But not your mother. She even gave me a credit in the playbills. I'll never forget that. She was as loyal as they come."

"I know," said Sunny.

"A brick," said the elderly woman.

"I'll be moving along now," said the principal.

Jennifer reached up to touch Sunny's hair. "You don't get this from her," she said.

———

Regina Pope was hurt to see a hairdresser summoned to the front of the line ahead of herself, but she understood: She had married the enemy. Worse, the enemy commander. Mrs. Batten had had to go to DeMinico with a season's worth of Sunny's scorecards and make her case. There was a federal law, she'd said, and she knew a lawyer. Sunny showed up at the next practice—all shiny new lady's clubs and ironed culottes—to discover that no one had told the boys. Captain Randy Pope fashioned the unwritten rule: Make her life miserable. Move her ball. Drag your spikes in her line.

Sunny didn't complain. Only Regina knew about the dead carp in her golf bag. Mrs. Batten would have cried, and Coach Sweet would have pretended to disapprove and would have made the boys stand in a row, like at a military tribunal, until one confessed. Over sandwiches in the drab green basement lunchroom, Sunny pronounced Randy Pope an idiot. She'd removed the rotting, stinking, dead-eyed carp and left it on the hood of his Tercel. In world history the next day, he repeatedly turned around, his mouth annular, his lips parting and puckering idiotically. Even Mr. Cutler, usually in the thrall of varsity athletes, told Randy to face front and stop doing whatever he was doing or there would be consequences. Regina thought Randy was cute—the top layer of his hair went blond around the middle of May—but she loyally took on her friend's grudge as her own. At Senior Honors Day, Sunny received an award that a handful of women teachers had paid for themselves: a silver-plated loving cup inscribed to "Sondra 'Sunny' Batten, the graduating senior who, in the judgment of the faculty, breaks ground in the area of sports leadership." The audience gave Sunny one of those slow-spreading, person-by-person standing ovations, and even though the winner appeared stunned as she shook Mr. DeMinico's hand, her best friend knew that the look in Sunny's eye had been not one of gratitude but of irony.

Four years later, Regina ran into Randy Pope leaving the Orpheus in West Lovell, after seeing a movie that Regina thought might be emblematic of a change in his worldview. It was *Thelma and Louise,* to which neither had brought a date or a friend. He invited her to a muffin house, where he drank herbal tea and told Regina he was embarrassed when he looked back at how he had acted in high school. As soon as she got home, she called her friend.

"Did he mention me specifically—I mean, the War Against Sunny?"

"*I* did. I said, 'You certainly were a jerk when it came to Sunny Batten. What did she ever do to you besides beat you at match play?' "

"You said that?"

"More or less. A little more politely than that. But he knew exactly what I was talking about."

"And what did he say?"

"He said he was ashamed of himself, the old him. He said if there were such a thing as a time machine, he'd set it back to the first day you came to practice."

"And then what?"

"He'd say, 'Welcome to the team, Sunny. We're all behind you.' "

"It's an act! Nobody changes that much in four years, especially a jock. He thinks if he acts humble and admits to being a jerk in high school, you'll fall at his big feet."

"He looks different," said Regina. "He has a goatee and a mustache. It looks a little Shakespearean. And he's thinking of joining the Peace Corps. B.U. humbled him, and that's a direct quote."

"Meaning, he learned that swaggering around the halls of B.U. didn't get him what he wanted."

After a pause, Regina said, "I really think he's different. Or maybe he's not so different. I mean, how would we know? Neither one of us ever had a conversation with him in high school."

"For a reason!" said Sunny. "He started the deep freeze. If he hadn't started it, or if he had come around, it wouldn't have been so painful."

"Mr. Sweet should've helped. That's what Randy said: 'Too bad Coach didn't threaten to throw us off the team.'"

"Maybe he'd like to apologize to me now," said Sunny. "Maybe you could give him my phone number and he could call and say, 'I'm sorry I painted a bull's-eye on your back. Sorry I couldn't be big enough to recognize that a girl could beat me in golf. Sorry I was the biggest asshole on the team.'"

After a pause, Regina said, "You sound so bitter. More so now than when you were living through it."

"Not more bitter," said Sunny. "Just more willing to say it out loud."

———

She'd been invited to their wedding, but sent her regrets. Regina didn't mail Sunny a birth announcement, but after six months wrote a note and enclosed a photo of Robert, bald, drooling, happy. If Sunny sent a baby present, Regina didn't remember what it was. But here was her son, two years and two months, the only child at the wake, asleep on her shoulder, too heavy for a wait this long. Women in line whispered, "Look at the little angel. Look how big he is. Sound asleep. Good as gold. She was Sunny's best friend growing up, you know. Regina Tramonte. Regina *Pope*. Married Fran's boy."

The line inched forward. Warm hands and cold ones clasped Sunny's. Shapes and voices moved past her, and on to view Margaret. Some hurried by, crossing themselves, but most touched the ebonized wood of her coffin, touched her hands, mouthed good-bye, hurried down the steps of the stage and back up the theater's center aisle.

"Sunny?" said the last person in line. "I hope it was okay to come."

Then Regina folded her free arm around Sunny's neck, and the baby was squeezed between them, and even Dickie Saint-Onge felt an unaccustomed lump in his throat.

CHAPTER 8

Meanwhile, at Boot Lake

Overheard at the filling station by a jittery teenager buying nacho chips and Dr Pepper: A man had died; a man named Flynn or Fin, who lived alone on Boot Lake.

The teenager had no money for gas and wasn't going to pull any more stunts in this lifetime. "Boot Lake?" he asked the cashier. "I used to swim there. How far is it from here?"

"As the crow flies? Two miles. But you have to get back on 12A again, then west on Old Baptist Road, past the gravel pit."

"Right," said the kid. "Now I remember."

———

FINN glowed white in the dark, stenciled on the black mailbox at the head of a dirt driveway. No lights, no signs of life. He'd hide the truck first thing in the morning. No big deal. He'd switch plates first—he was in New Hampshire now, Live Free or Die—and find an empty garage, a normal place, like it belonged to some old couple who only took it out for church. He nosed the Ford down the narrow road through scrubby bushes. It was a smaller cabin than he expected from the long private driveway, but nicer than you'd think for a dead guy who lived alone. New paint on the trim, light, maybe yellow. The siding at night was dark, stained by weather, wet-cigar brown. He found the spare key under a chunk of pink granite, sitting like a stool pigeon next to the door. You're not breaking in when you use a key, he told himself. You're freeloading. Taking shelter. Resting. Like Goldilocks. He wouldn't steal anything, except maybe eat what was in the refrigerator. The guy was dead. He wouldn't mind. He could think, borrow some clothes, maybe call Tiff.

Because he wasn't breaking and entering, he'd leave things neat. He'd make the bed and wash his dishes. He could say if they found him, "Look—I didn't take nothin'. There's your TV, your computer, your VCR, your CD player, your microwave oven. I was just taking shelter. If I was going to steal anything, I'd have done it by now."

Shower. Shave. Wipe out the sink after. Hope the guy had disposable razors; too fucking creepy to shave with a dead guy's blade. Fish after sundown. Deep-six the gun. Watch TV. Hope the guy had cable.

Find out if anyone had I.D.'d him, and if the cop had died.

CHAPTER 9

The Flight

Emily Ann diagnosed Fletcher's bad mood on the flight as situational depression, richly deserved.

"Would you like to talk about your dad?" she tried.

"Absent father, lousy husband," he snapped.

Emily Ann didn't snap back. A man on his way to his father's funeral deserved some latitude. "Do you think," she began carefully, "that it's doubly hard for you because of his deficiencies? Because you held out hope that someday you might become closer—like maybe when you had children of your own—but now that dream is lost, so it's all the more painful?"

Fletcher's lip curled. His stare was more disdainful than usual. "Is that supposed to make me feel better?"

"I'm trying to be compassionate," she said. "I'm trying to provide a shoulder to cry on."

He shrank a few inches from the armrest between them. "I had no illusions about him showing any interest in me—none—let alone in my eventual children."

Emily Ann's voice brightened. "Do you think about having children? I mean, sometime in the future?"

"Way, way in the future." He reached inside his jacket for his sunglasses and put them on.

Emily Ann and Fletcher were the lone passengers on the Big John jet, its fuselage painted a brash cranberry and pumpkin, winged bicycles gilded on its tail, cream-colored leather and burled walnut within. Fletcher had declined Mr. Grandjean's first offer of his pilot and his plane.

"But Emily Ann's going with you," he had reminded Fletcher.

"Precisely. It feeds the critics. They love to hate the family's deep pockets. They'll make too much of it."

But Emily Ann hadn't traveled by public transportation since her field hockey away games at Lawrenceville, and she wasn't going to start now. Let the Tommy d'Apuzzos of the world take potshots at her corporate perks. This was not campaigning; this was an emergency— something close to a humanitarian airlift. Besides, the Grandjeans had earned these prerogatives: Claude Grandjean had come to America in—well, not exactly steerage, but in an interior cabin, and had then inhaled mustard gas for his adopted country in World War One.

"If we drive," she had pointed out, "we'd have to leave before dawn to make the funeral. And if we're going by air, why in the world would we want to fly with strangers?"

"This time you were right," Fletcher conceded. He unbuckled his seat belt and walked to the stainless-steel galley. Emily Ann heard the sound of cupboards opening and closing, then the click of the refrigerator latch.

"There's dried fruit and pretzels," she called.

"Any real food?"

Emily Ann smiled. "Check the warming oven, next to the Poland Spring dispenser."

He came back down the aisle, peering into a shopping bag of McDonald's take-out. "Hash browns!" he exclaimed. "And it looks like one of everything. Did you get extra ketchup?"

"Bret did."

"Who's Bret?"

"The co-pilot. I introduced you. He stopped on his way to the airport."

"Good man," said Fletcher, just before his teeth sank into a half-wrapped sausage biscuit. He climbed over her legs and dropped into his seat.

"It was my idea," said Emily Ann.

"One of your best," he said. He offered her the bag. "Want anything? There's tons."

Emily Ann said, "I had a huge breakfast before I left."

"Yeah," he said. "I'm sure you did."

Out the other ear, she reminded herself. Out the other ear.

"I've been meaning to try one of these," he said, unwrapping a bagel sandwich. "Looks like a Western. Or an Eastern. I never can remember which is which." He took two rapid bites, then two more without swallowing. Like an animal, she thought. Like a junkyard dog.

"I miss their breakfast burritos," he continued. "But I could drive with this. I needed two hands for the burrito."

"When I'm upset, my appetite disappears," she offered.

"Is that your way of saying I'm making a pig of myself?"

"No, I'm saying I understand that sometimes a person eats to dull the pain."

He reached deep into the brown bag and pulled out a lost hash brown, separated from its sleeve. "I've heard of that," he said.

"Do you want to talk about it?"

"Abow whah?" His mouth bulged; a green-pepper fleck was pasted to his gums.

"Your father."

"Not in the least."

"How old were you when they divorced?"

He shrugged.

"You don't know?"

"I was in eleventh grade. What age is that?"

"Sixteen? Seventeen? Depends on your school district and your birthday."

"My mother didn't want to break the news to me until after my SATs, but I caught on anyway." He crumbled his last wrapper and reclined his seat. "Wake me when we get there," he murmured.

"Wait. How did you do?"

He raised himself an inch from the headrest. "Are you asking me for my SAT scores?"

"No," said Emily Ann. "Of course not. I meant . . . the divorce: How did you take it?"

Fletcher made a grudging affirmative noise and lowered his seat another notch.

Emily Ann wanted to clean off his tray, but the dirty wrappers bore either melted animal fat, melted cheese, or smears of ketchup. And the smells.

"Will I meet your mother today?" she asked.

He shook his head.

"She's not coming?"

Fletcher said calmly, "To a double funeral? With his latest paramour? Unlikely."

"But she knows, right? You called her?"

He frowned. "Is that my job?"

Emily Ann groaned.

"Now, wait one minute," said Fletcher. "How does my father's death—the death of a total stranger—and how I've chosen to break or not break the news to my mother distress you?"

"Because! I have a mother and a father and brothers, and I consider us a functional family and . . . and yours wasn't and I'd know how I'd act if, God forbid, I got a call one night that my father was found dead."

"That's right, I forgot: your family-values plank, which makes you an authority on funeral guest lists."

Emily Ann tried to keep her voice even, her feelings unbruised. "I'm simply saying she's going to be furious. He was the father of her child, and no matter—"

"Excuse me, Dear Abby, but her rule was, Don't mention that man's name in my presence. I think that's a pretty clear guideline."

"She didn't mean life-or-death! She meant, 'I don't want to hear about his girlfriends or about'—I don't know—'the excellent cabernet you shared at Le Bec-Fin.'" Emily Ann reached into her green leather satchel for her phone. "Call her. Right now."

"You can't use cell phones on an airplane."

"That's an old wives' tale. What's her number?"

Fletcher shook his head.

"You don't know, or you're stonewalling?"

"I'm stonewalling."

"I've never heard of such a thing! Your father dies and you don't call your mother!"

"You're projecting what Emily Ann Grandjean would do in this situation, but you don't know my mother." He paused, then added angrily, "You don't even know me."

Emily Ann unbuckled her seat belt and plunked herself down across the aisle.

"Why are you pouting? I'm the one who's burying my father today. Can't you cut me a little slack?"

Emily Ann slowly turned back to face him. "Okay," she said. "I'll change the subject. I promised myself I'd be compassionate today." She yanked on the two halves of her ponytail to tighten it. "How far away is Dixville Notch? My father said it was relatively close."

"What do you want with Dixville Notch?"

"What do I want with Dixville Notch? To be seen and noted, Fletcher. Maybe shake the hands of the staff at the hotel where they vote."

"As . . . ?"

She smiled serenely. "A Republican with a future."

He jerked his sunglasses off. "Is that why you wanted to come? To position yourself in New Hampshire? Because that offends even me, and as you know, I'm not easily offended."

"This wouldn't involve you! You're in mourning. I'd hire a car and a driver while you're taking care of family matters."

"First of all, I don't think you can rent a car or a driver in King George, and second of all, you don't do something like that without an advance team. You don't just walk into a town and start kissing babies."

"Not even a car rental agency?" she repeated. "Not even at the airport?"

"It's a landing strip with a Quonset hut and a wind sock."

"Then who's picking us up?"

"Somebody from the funeral parlor."

"In a limo?"

"I didn't ask."

"What about the daughter? Doesn't she have a car?"

"I know nothing about her. Her name is Sunny. Her mother was reportedly my father's fiancée, but I don't believe it."

"Why not?"

"Miles Finn wouldn't have taken up with somebody who lived in the boonies. He liked urban women. Stylish women. Loose women."

"Maybe it's a summer colony," said Emily Ann.

"Have you ever heard of anyone summering in King George? He had a primitive cabin on a lake. No heat and no indoor plumbing. I went up with him once to fish and live off the land for a week. I hated it. He loved it—no shower, no shaving and, believe me, no women. I think he probably saw this dame when he needed to, and the only way the daughter could make peace with her mother dying with a male overnight guest was to say they were engaged."

"What if you're wrong? What if they *were* engaged, and she was the reason he kept going back there? Not the fishing; not the iron-man thing?"

Fletcher didn't answer.

"The daughter would know," prompted Emily Ann.

" 'Miss Batten?' " he mimicked. " 'I'm Emily Ann Grandjean, running in the Sixth Congressional District of the Garden State? Just being a little nosy here, but was this a long-standing affair between your dead mother and Fletcher's dead father? I was wondering if said dead mother might have been the unnamed corespondent in his parents' divorce. Oh, and please accept my deepest sympathies.'"

Emily Ann's pinched face turned a shade paler. "I didn't want to say this on your way to your father's funeral, but you can be unbelievably cruel."

"You're right. You should not be saying this on my way to my father's funeral."

Emily Ann sat perfectly still, her eyes closed, a sign of an anger-management exercise under way.

Finally, Fletcher grumbled, "I'm not cruel a hundred percent of the time."

When she didn't answer, he added, "I can be gracious when I want to be."

"We *pay* you to be gracious. A campaign manager, by definition, wants to be gracious at every turn, in every single contact—"

"I'm not an idiot. Name one time I was less than gracious in the line of duty."

"I'm talking about today. I'm saying that you and the dead woman's daughter were one wedding away from being stepsiblings—"

"I never met her in my life!"

Emily Ann hissed, "This is exactly what I mean. You have no innate social graces—"

"I have no interest in social graces."

"And no table manners!" she threw back.

Fletcher didn't flinch. He swiveled his head slowly to face her. "Then perhaps I should resign and save you the embarrassment of our association."

"I'm trying to do you a favor. I'm offering you a woman's point of view, but you have so little empathy—"

"Explain to me what the favor is if I don't care what impression I make or how much of a grief counselor I am to a total stranger who will never be my stepsister and whom I'll never see again after this weekend?"

Emily Ann said, "Why do I bother? You're beyond help."

"Cruel, rude, and beyond help. I'd fire my ass if I were you."

After a tight-lipped pause, she said, "I can't. My father says I have to stick it out."

"So you've discussed firing me with your father?"

"Maybe."

"But he nixed that?"

She didn't answer.

"Is it my payout? Too much up front? And the stock options? He's in too deep?"

"No comment."

"Just think how you'll feel when it's over," he coaxed. "No more humiliating polls. No more speeches to empty halls. No more saturated fat at street fairs."

Was he serious or was he teasing, she wondered. Either way, he was hateful. She wanted her water, but she'd left her bag across the aisle. The pilot's voice announced that they'd be landing in minutes.

"If you paid us back, you could resign," she said.

Fletcher frowned. "I can't quit voluntarily. I am contractually obligated to see you through until the last vote is counted in Tommy d'Apuzzo's landslide victory."

"Fuck you, Finn."

He smiled. "Am I fired?"

"You should be! I won the primary, and look where I am now—in single digits! Even the undecideds want d'Apuzzo!"

"It's me, then? It's my fault? Let me remind you who the candidate is: Emily Ann Marie Grandjean. I never should have signed on. I knew we couldn't win, but I didn't know I'd dread getting up every morning."

Emily Ann went white.

"I guess we both want the same thing," said Fletcher. "But you're stuck with me unless we find some loophole."

"How about insubordination? How about incompetence? How about first-degree murder of someone's political future?"

"Not good enough," he said.

"The minute this funeral's over, I'm calling my father," she hissed.

"You can always fire me for an egregious act," he continued. "Every single one of your father's lawyers will understand that."

"You just try it," she said.

He stood up and stretched—noisily, theatrically—in the aisle between them. Emily Ann batted his arm away. Two fingers of his right hand found the barely discernible swell that was her left breast and squeezed.

CHAPTER 10

Graveside

It was Regina who picked the beautiful dress from her own closet for Sunny, insisting that several cultures—give her a minute and she'd name them—considered white to be the color of mourning. Regina didn't say that her friend looked lovely or that the dress's long-waisted, pleated cotton voile suggested a garden party between the wars.

Sunny looked down at her feet in borrowed white shoes, narrow and pointed T-straps of a pearly leather. "They look like manicured fingernails," she said.

"What do?"

"These shoes. They're so . . . you and not me."

"I'm only interested in the fit," said Regina.

"A little tight. Not terrible."

"They'll stretch. They go with the dress. You can't wear black pumps, I'm sorry."

The hat came last, lifted from a round paisley box on Regina's closet shelf. "No," said Sunny, ducking out of it. "Now it's looking like a getup."

"I think you can give me some credit for knowing what's appropriate for a funeral."

Sunny allowed Regina to place the hat on her head and swivel it into its most attractive lie. "It hides my hair at least," Sunny said.

It didn't; nothing could. Regina released a few strands caught under the hat's brim. "I love your hair. You must like it, too, or you'd have dyed it."

"I don't."

"But?"

"My mother had a thing about it. It seemed to mean more to her than to me." Her eyes filled. She pulled the brim an inch lower.

"See," said Regina. "It has several useful properties."

Sunny turned around and looked over her shoulder at her reflection, smoothing the pleats over her backside and studying the length. "It seems too costumey. People will know it's not mine."

"Answer this question if you're still in doubt: How do you think your mother would feel about you dressing like a character from—if you insist—*Masterpiece Theatre*?"

"Ecstatic," admitted Sunny. She plucked a tissue from the box on Regina's bureau.

"She'll be looking down and thinking, Wow. All those beautiful dresses I made for her, the smocking and the tatting, which she refused to wear, and look what she's done for me today," said Regina.

"Or else she'll look down and won't recognize me."

"Oh yes she will," said Regina.

"I'm worried I look like a bride. Or Daisy Buchanan's bridesmaid."

"It's just right. It's for your mother. Everyone will recognize the tribute."

Sunny let Regina put her arms around her and readjust her hat.

"Here," Regina said. "A handkerchief, which I'm putting in this little beaded purse. Just hang if from your wrist. And some extra tissues just in case."

"What was your wedding dress like?" asked Sunny.

"My wedding dress?"

"Because this feels a little . . . something old, something newish . . . as if you're dressing me for a ceremony."

"My wedding dress was like a thousand others you've seen stuffed with tissue at the dry cleaner's—lace and tulle. I wish I'd thought of something original."

Sunny walked to a window overlooking the street and pulled the curtain aside. "Did I at least R.S.V.P.?"

"I'm sure you did."

"Did I give a convincing excuse?"

"I knew why you couldn't come. I should have called you and said, 'I insist you come to the wedding. I insist you walk down the aisle ahead of me.' "

Sunny said, "Be serious: The groom would have veto power over your choice of maid of honor—"

"Bridesmaid. My sister was the matron of honor in, I'm sorry to say, a plaid dress."

"No!"

"You know she's Annemarie McNab now? She's embraced the clan and its tartans. This was red and green taffeta. It looked like a Christmas tablecloth."

Sunny laughed, then her eyes filled again.

"Did I say something wrong?" asked Regina.

Sunny shook her head.

"Just this . . . everything? Your mom?"

"You," said Sunny, then choked out, "What I've missed."

"Stay awhile," said Regina.

Sunny looked at her watch.

"I meant afterwards. Stay in King George while you're deciding what to do next."

"Everyone's been saying that."

"Like who?"

"My mother's fellow thespians. All of whom have spare bedrooms."

"What about here?"

Sunny rolled her eyes.

"What about home?"

"I can't. Every time I walked down Station Street, I felt as if people were saying, 'There's Sunny Batten, all dressed up and going to the nationals. Who does she think she is?' My mother made the best of it, stayed in that pathetic little house, as if to prove it wasn't so unworthy and embarrassing in the first place. And look what it did to her. It's probably out to get me next."

Regina rubbed Sunny's back in circles. "No," she said. "It's not. Sean and Danny fixed the furnace, and everything's right as rain now. Besides—it's ninety degrees outside. You certainly won't be needing the furnace anytime soon."

Sunny felt her scalp prickle under the hat. "It was June earlier in the week, too," she said. "Why would my mother need heat in June?"

"An unseasonably chilly night?" asked Regina.

"We always set the thermostat for sixty-two at bedtime. Could it have fallen below that?"

"It was broken," said Regina. "It could have done anything."

"I'm going to call Joey Loach," said Sunny. "I have to know if my mother had the heat on or if there was foul play."

"He won't be there. He'll be directing traffic outside the cemetery. Anyway, hon, this isn't a good time to be playing detective."

"I could dial 911. Someone has to answer."

"It's a regional system. An operator in Grantham won't know what you're talking about."

Sunny picked up the phone next to Regina's bed and intoned, without dialing, "This is Sunny Batten. Perhaps you heard about my mother. She died before her time, of carbon monoxide poisoning, which I think sounds a little fishy. I'm about to bury her around noon today, but what if she died of something else? I'll never know."

Regina took the receiver and replaced it in the cradle.

"Not fishy. There was an autopsy—you know that. We'll ask Joey when we see him. Okay? You all right?" Regina's dress and shoes were pale, too, in solidarity. Her eyes were red.

———

Joey took off his sunglasses and crouched down to the level of the limo's back window. "We looked into this," he said. "Don't think it wasn't the first thing I thought of."

"And?"

"More bad luck," said Joey. "There was an air conditioner cranked way up. It got cold enough in the bedroom to kick on the heat. The thermostat was set for sixty-five."

"My mother hated air conditioners," said Sunny. "She thought she caught colds from them."

Joey looked in both directions at the traffic backing up. "It was purchased the day before by Miles Finn. At Aubuchon Hardware. A gift, apparently. Didn't think you'd particularly need the fine points of what caused the heat to go on."

"He bought her an air conditioner and turned it up so high that it made the heat go on. Which killed her."

"And him, too," said Joey. "Completely and totally an accident, without a shadow of a doubt."

"Miss?" said the driver. "We're causing a major bottleneck here."

"He killed her," said Sunny.

"Not under any statute we have on the books. And you're just going to make yourself miserable thinking like this."

"I'm not talking about murder or manslaughter. I just mean . . ."

"Reckless endangerment?" offered the driver.

"Sunny? Realistically?" said Joey. "The heat would've gone on in the fall or on the next cold summer night. So let's not get litigious over the fact that Finn wanted to cool off your mother's house. Okay? It's not a productive road to take, and there isn't one single thing I can do about it. I'm sorry. It was a freak accident and lousy luck, but I have to get this traffic moving." He took a step away from the limousine and touched the brim of his hat in a salute.

"You're not a lawyer," called Sunny hoarsely. "I'm blaming him." She raised the electric window, then lowered it halfway. "I have to blame someone."

"Miss?" said the driver.

"Nobody killed anybody," said Joey.

Approximately one mile behind Sunny's limousine was a buffed and gleaming black Town Car driven by Dickie Saint-Onge himself, who liked to do the honors when it concerned a V.I.P. But plans had changed somewhere. Now the Town Car's backseat held only Fletcher Finn, the son of one of the deceased. The gal running for some national seat, the promised V.I.P., had turned her plane around and gone home.

Dickie had arrived at the airfield in the middle of their squabble. After expressing his condolences, he explained that if Mr. Finn had arrived earlier, he could have arranged for a few private moments with his loved one, but this was cutting it too close. The hearse had left the funeral home promptly at eleven-thirty.

"No big deal," said Fletcher.

Emily Ann, smoking a cigarette ten yards away, her back to him, harrumphed.

"That's my boss," said Fletcher. "She just fired me."

"You have my deepest sympathy," said Dickie.

Fletcher called to Emily Ann, "How the hell am I supposed to get home?"

"Walk. Hitch. Steal a car. That's what criminals do."

"She's pissed at me," Fletcher translated.

Emily Ann strode over to him and Dickie. "You thought I'd fly you in our private plane back to—where?—campaign headquarters? My parents' house for dinner? Forget it! Let the punishment fit the crime: Sexual assault of the plane owner's daughter results in the perpetrator being grounded."

Dickie blotted his forehead with a large white handkerchief and replaced his chauffeur's cap.

"No one would question my using the return half of my figurative ticket," said Fletcher. "Nor would anyone have to know you gave me a ride."

"You don't think they keep records?" She pointed to the two men standing inside a corrugated metal lean-to in Big John windbreakers and Big John baseball caps. "Like the F.A.A. wouldn't know that

Fletcher Finn was on this flight? With my luck, we'd crash and no one would ever file a complaint."

"You're making a scene and you're only punishing yourself: You've started smoking again and you're cheating yourself out of a listening tour of Dixville Notch."

Emily Ann yelled to the pilot and co-pilot, "Alan! Bret! Can you come over here?"

Fletcher handed his suitcase to Dickie and held up both hands. "She doesn't need protecting. I'm harmless."

"He is *not* harmless. Quite the opposite."

Fletcher lowered his voice. "I think you and I both know that what I did was a deliberate act of civil disobedience to get myself off the payroll and to get you out of an embarrassing campaign."

"Civil?" she repeated shrilly. "Civil disobedience? How about sexual harassment? When was the last time you read a newspaper?"

Fletcher said, "Em—"

"He assaulted me," she told the pilots.

"I did not assault her. It was consensual in the sense that she and I entered into a conspiracy—"

" 'Consensual'? Are you insane? He grabbed my left breast!"

Fletcher, with Dickie in step, moved back a few feet. "I'm not discussing this in front of your henchmen. I thought we had a deal. If I misunderstood, I'm sorry. I am not interested in your breasts. And if you'll excuse me, I'm off to bury my father."

Emily Ann shouted after him, "I knew you wouldn't work out. You never had any faith in me. And now I know why! You saw me as an object."

"I assure you—" Fletcher stopped. "Guys? C'mon, back me up here. Tell Ms. Grandjean that that's ludicrous."

"Why is it ludicrous? Men see me as an object all the time. It's why they don't vote for me. It's why they can't see me as their congressperson!"

"Take your belongings and scram," said one of the men.

"Find your own way back," said the other.

"We don't want to miss the service," said Dickie.

"Like they'd start without the guest of honor," snapped Fletcher.

———

Dickie hustled Fletcher across the spongy grass toward a girl in a white dress and picture hat, who stood still and silent on the edge of the buzzing crowd. "You two haven't met: Miss Batten, Fletcher Finn. We should start right away—the bagpipers have already done a graduation this morning. Please follow me to your seats."

Fletcher liked the way she looked—dignified and a little fierce. Not a bad outfit for the boonies. "Sorry I'm late," he whispered. "Just landed." He offered his hand, which Sunny didn't take.

"Sorry about your mom," he tried.

"Let's get this over with," she answered.

They both pretended not to stare. Her hair had properties he recognized: It rose and floated as if magnetized. His was backlit and almost invisible—filaments of silver she had to squint to see.

The bagpipers tuned up, then played "Pomp and Circumstance." Sunny and Fletcher took their seats, and the minister cleared his throat. The citizens of King George lifted their gazes from the ebonized coffin and its mahogany mate to study the next of kin. Later, the topics of their gossip would be these: the propriety of a white dress at graveside; the son's chewing gum, his red tie, his argyle socks, and the flagrant display, wherever one looked, of Miles Finn's genes.

CHAPTER 11

After the Service, No Mourners Are Invited Back

M ind if I hitch a ride?" Fletcher asked Sunny. "I assume that's the way it works? The next of kin get the limo?" He had stayed by her side since their introduction, had even put a comradely arm around her shoulders as the first few spadefuls of dirt trickled onto the coffins.

Sunny said, "I believe there's one car for each family." Fletcher opened the rear door a step ahead of Dickie. "Slide in," he said. "What's the next event?"

Dickie said, "Sunny's decided to call it a day. Understandably."

"Fine with me," said Fletcher.

Sunny removed her hat and stepped into the limo. Fletcher climbed into the backseat next to her. After playing with the buttons that raised and lowered the windows, he said, "You understand, of course, that I'm contributing to the cost of everything."

"Contributing?"

"My father's share."

"Which I consider to be half," said Sunny.

"Fine, half. That seems fair. Sure." He moved his gaze to her shoulders.

"What?" she said.

"How old are you?"

"Thirty-one," said Sunny.

"When's your birthday?"

"Why?"

"I'm thirty-one, too. What month?"

"April."

"I'm August."

"So I'm older," said Sunny. After a minute, after the limo had finally left the cemetery roads and turned onto Route 4, she asked him what he was staring at so intently.

"Did either of your parents have insanely premature gray hair?"

"My mother didn't."

"And Mr. Batten?"

"Moved away before I was born."

"And where is this father today? Why isn't he at your side as your sole surviving parent?"

Sunny murmured, "He couldn't cope with being a father. Or so the story goes."

"My parents eventually got divorced because Miles fooled around a lot."

"A lot of times? Or with a lot of women?"

"My guess would be both—frequent affairs, with hordes of women."

Sunny said, "You're sitting on my dress," and wrenched a few inches of a wide voile pleat out from under him.

"Not that my mother is a reliable source," Fletcher added.

"And you are? You didn't even know your father was getting remarried."

Fletcher turned away to look at the scenery. "Cows," he said. "What's it supposed to mean when they're lying down? Rain or no rain?"

"Don't patronize me," said Sunny. "I don't need to walk my mother down the aisle to make her respectable. I'm just telling you what everyone else knows."

After a few moments, Fletcher turned back. "It isn't just the hair."

"What isn't?"

"You. The resemblance. There's more to it than that."

"I just met you," said Sunny. "Isn't this a topic someone should lead up to gradually?"

"Not my style," said Fletcher. "Okay, here's what I'm thinking: You look uncannily like my father's mother. He looked like her, but you look even more like her. It's spooky."

"I look like a lot of people," said Sunny.

"Au contraire."

"Then it's the outfit. You probably have a picture of your grandmother in her youth wearing a dress like this."

"I'm a little more observant than that," said Fletcher. "I spotted my grandmother in you from the other side of the cemetery."

Sunny put Regina's hat back on her head and pulled its brim down over each ear.

After a minute Fletcher asked, "Can I touch yours?"

"No you may not."

"Have you found any product that makes it lie down?"

"No."

"I don't buy the stuff, but sometimes I'll try a cream rinse in a hotel bathroom."

"You're a guy. You can cut it short and forget about it."

He smiled. "It's my signature. I think it makes me look dignified. Prematurely so."

"Or mad-scientistish." Frowning, she reached over and rubbed a few wisps between her fingertips. "Some products work better than others. The weather is the main factor."

"Were you blond to start with?" he asked.

"Very."

"Was your mother?"

"No."

"What about the putative father?"

"He lives in Arizona."

"Sorry, that's not responsive. What I'm getting at is the paternity issue—do you resemble him? If you don't know, why not? Don't divorced fathers, even lousy ones, see their kid once a year? Once a decade?"

Sunny opened Regina's beaded purse, fished out a roll of mints, peeled back the foil, and took the top mint without offering one to her seatmate. "What would make a total stranger drill someone he's just met at a funeral about her parents' divorce and her paternity?" she asked.

"No social graces, or so I've been told."

Sunny asked, "How do you know it isn't the most sensitive topic in the world to me? Or that you aren't dropping a bomb on my head?"

"Am I?" he asked mildly.

"Assaulting me with questions is bad enough, but highly personal—"

"It's highly personal for me, too. It would be a lot easier all around if I were making small talk instead of tackling issues like identity and paternity and, and, adultery."

"Well, good for you. Congratulations on not taking the easy way out, on not just maintaining a respectful silence on the five-minute ride from the cemetery."

"I know what you mean, though, about getting assaulted with questions," continued Fletcher. "I had a roommate in college who worked for the school newspaper, and the only way he could carry on a conversation was to interview you—where you grew up, your major, your minor, sisters, brothers, pets, secondary school." He paused, then asked, "Where'd you go to school?"

"Maryland."

"How come?"

"Golf," said Sunny. "Mid-Atlantic Conference."

"Now, that is interesting," said Fletcher. "Very interesting. More than you know."

Sunny said, "And why is that?"

"Because—and this astounds me—my grandmother played golf. I mean, really played. She was a scratch golfer and a club champion."

"Is this the grandmother I'm supposed to resemble?"

"Exactly."

After a minute, Sunny asked, "Do you know if she was on the tour?"

"She was an amateur, I know that much. And she once gave Eleanor Roosevelt a golf lesson."

"People competed as amateurs unless you were a big, big name, and even someone like Babe Didrikson—"

Fletcher asked, "Have I isolated the strand of DNA that piques your interest?"

"Golf isn't an inherited trait," said Sunny. "In my case, it was geographical. My mother rented a house that sat on the edge of a golf course. Still does. I played because it was my backyard. We couldn't even afford to join, so I caddied."

"I like that," said Fletcher. "Very Abe Lincolnesque. Sportswriters love that rags-to-riches stuff. Did my father know you golfed?"

"Your father didn't know I existed."

"Literally?"

"We met once. She introduced us."

"As?"

"As 'Sunny Batten, my daughter; I'd like you to meet my friend Miles Finn.' "

"How old were you?"

"Thirteen? Fourteen?"

"And did you look then like you look now, only with blond hair? Because if you did, he couldn't have failed to notice—denial aside—the resemblance."

"Which begins and ends with the hair," said Sunny.

The limo was slowing down for King George's only stop sign. Fletcher looked out the window. The King's Nite appeared, and Dickie pulled into the loop in front of its office. "This is where you're staying?" Fletcher asked.

"It's the only option."

"In that case, so am I."

"No vacancy," said Sunny.

He peered through the tinted glass, then lowered the window. "It appears that the NO in the sign is not illuminated. I would read that as VACANCY."

"I've yet to see both words lit up," Dickie said over his shoulder.

"You won't like it," said Sunny. "No phones in the room. No air conditioner."

"What's my alternative?"

"To go back home."

"You've got the wrong guy," he said. "Maybe yesterday I was thinking in terms of a round-trip ticket, but that was before I had my graveside conversion. Now I'm convinced I'd be abandoning a sister, not just some alleged future stepsibling. Besides, I have to close up the cabin and pack my father's things."

"I'm not up to fraternizing," said Sunny.

"Here we are," sang Dickie. He scurried out from behind the wheel and around to Sunny's door. Fletcher leaned over to ask, "Could you get my bag out of the trunk? I'm checking in."

"You'll be very comfortable here," said Dickie. "Mrs. P is a stickler for cleanliness. Her husband did the squirrel cutouts on the shutters himself. He's got a little workshop out back."

"Fascinating," said Fletcher. He stepped out of the car and swiped at the wrinkles in his suit.

"If you need anything at all during your stay . . ." offered Dickie.

"Really? Because I don't have wheels. Any chance you can give me a ride out to Boot Lake tomorrow? Say, eleven? Doesn't have to be the limo."

"He's an undertaker, not a taxi service," said Sunny.

"He asked, though. Right, my man? Eleven good? If not, you name the time. What is it? A couple of miles?"

"If I do drop you off, how will you get back?" asked Dickie.

"He can charter a plane," said Sunny.

"She's in major denial," Fletcher confided to Dickie. "I'm trying to convince her that we're related. I mean, look at us." He stooped to line his jaw up with Sunny's, but she moved away.

"Hey! Why not? He was the last person to see my father. He's not the worst guy to consult."

Dickie's face was composed and professional. But what a day this had been; what bald revelations he'd collected to pass, in strictest confidence, to his wife, sister, mother, aunt.

"Dickie—please don't repeat any of this nonsense," said Sunny. "Not even to Roberta."

"Look at his expression," said Fletcher. "I know what he's thinking: 'You mean to tell me no one's noticed this before? Everyone in town suspected as much.' "

"I assure you—" Dickie began.

"The valise, the briefcase, and the clubs, old sport," said Fletcher.

CHAPTER 12

How Long Has This
Been Going On?

When she served Chief Loach his Polka-Dot Pancakes, Mrs. Angelo asked if he would mind leaving his gun in the cruiser from now on. "How come I never noticed it before?" she asked, refilling his coffee, dropping two more plastic thimbles of cream onto his place mat.

"Because it's new. I mean, carrying it is new. Before, I just carried a nightstick."

She asked how he was healing.

"I'm still sore. And turning every color of the rainbow."

She leaned closer. "Are you wearing it now?"

" 'It'?"

"The new vest? The free replacement they gave you on TV."

He touched his chest and shifted inside the padding. "It's why I'm hanging around in air-conditioned comfort."

"I bet. Like wearing long underwear, huh?"

"Worse," said Joey.

"Scoot in," she said, and perched herself on the edge of his bench. "Did you go yesterday?"

Joey nodded from behind his coffee cup.

"I could've done without the speeches from the leading men," she said. "One eulogy is enough in my book. They said the same thing twice—the same thing any one of us would've said: 'sweet, sweet woman. Unselfish. Always thought of others first. Worked so hard to give Sunny advantages.'"

"I liked what the doc said."

"That poor man! I think he's taking it worse than anybody."

Joey cut a vee into his pancake stack. "Not worse than Sunny."

"Was that her boyfriend, the fellow with the gray hair?"

"That was Finn's son. He flew up on a private jet just for the funeral."

"No one introduced him. But I guess I should've figured that out myself. . . . You'd have thought he would've said a few words about his father. It was kind of a lopsided service. I got the feeling that they tacked on the remarks about Miles at the end but that nobody really knew him."

"Did *you*?" asked Joey.

"He ate breakfast here a couple of days a week, closer to nine. My second shift—the retirees and the tennis players. Once in a while Margaret would join him. He was a health fanatic. We had to change the menu because of him."

"How so?"

"We serve oatmeal from October through May, but he wanted it year-round. And he didn't want whole milk in it. I started buying a half-gallon of skim to keep on hand just for him. I remember the days when it was considered a classy thing to serve cream with oatmeal. Not anymore! Today if you want to put sour cream on top of a baked potato, you have to ask first."

"I still like sour cream on my baked potatoes."

"'Cause you're a kid!"

"Still, I've got arteries. I can't ignore them forever."

"And here's the funny thing." Mrs. Angelo paused. "I shouldn't use *funny* in this case, because it sounds coldhearted. But here was a guy who looked after himself and counted his calories and jogged all the way to the lake and back and—boom! Fit as a fiddle and he dies anyway! He could've been eating eggs and bacon and half-and-half every day of his life for all the good it did him."

The door chime sounded, and both looked up. It was Sunny, wearing Bermuda shorts, a pale pink sleeveless blouse, sunglasses, and Regina's big-brimmed hat. "Sweetie," cried Mrs. Angelo. "Here, sit. What're you doing up at this hour on a Saturday?"

Joey stood up and snatched his napkin off his tie.

Sunny backtracked to pick up *The Valley Shopper.* "I'll just sit at the counter."

"I'm breaking the law," insisted Joey. He pointed to the hand-lettered sign that said TWO TO A BOOTH DURING PEAK HOURS. "I'm going to get busted."

"Okay," she said. "Sure. Just coffee to start."

"Such a lovely service," said Mrs. Angelo.

"Do you think so? I don't remember much."

"You know what I liked best?" asked Joey. "Besides the bagpipes? I liked the fact that people added their two cents, even if they hadn't planned on saying anything. Like Regina. That stuff about your mother being your biggest ally and fan, giving you lessons with the pro even though she'd rather have been taking you to DeCastro's Dance Academy."

"What's his name?" asked Mrs. Angelo. "The boy? The son?"

"Fletcher."

There was a silence until Sunny said, "He's still here."

"He seemed perfectly nice," said Joey.

Sunny met his eyes and said with a half smile, "Well, he didn't slap me or steal my wallet."

"Uh-oh," said Joey. "That bad?"

A man in a Red Sox cap left the counter stools and stood by the cash register. "I gotta ring up Richie," said Mrs. Angelo. "I'll be back in a jiff."

Sunny waited until she and Joey were alone. "There's me, who feels like I was hit by a truck, sharing a tragedy with someone I've never met, who acts as if some casual acquaintance inconvenienced him by dying."

"Sometimes that's just the way guys act. We don't show how we feel in front of a townful of strangers."

"He isn't shy, if that's what you mean. He now knows more about me than my best friends do."

"How is that possible?"

"He grilled me in the limo. About all things professional, personal, and genealogical."

"You're not gonna stop there, are you?" asked Joey. "I've got good manners, but now you've got to give me the grilling specifics."

Sunny took a lock of her hair between two fingers and flipped it toward Joey. "This. He claims everyone noticed."

Joey said, "Go on."

"He seemed to think that we have the same gene pool."

"Because of the hair?"

"Which apparently is identical to his father's. And which he seems to think is unique in all the world. And that the whole town unanimously leapt to the same conclusion."

Joey murmured, "Only the ones at the service."

"The whole town was at the service!" said Sunny. "And the dozen who stayed home have now received telegrams from Dickie Saint-Onge."

"It'll die down," said Joey. "Finn Junior is probably alone in the world now and wants to make you an honorary sister."

"I'm not turning this into a search for some hypothetical birth father. I'm not that interested." She looked over her shoulder to ascertain Mrs. Angelo's whereabouts. "I think he happens to be right, but so what? If my mother had a fling with Miles Finn thirty-two years ago and that's why her husband divorced her and that's why she kept me and Finn separate, even when they got engaged . . . so be it."

Joey began shaking his head before she finished.

"You disagree?" she asked.

"First of all, no one's *not* interested when they find out that a whole new guy might be their father. And second, I don't think it's true, because Finn Senior had been coming to Boot Lake as long as she was here, and I just think at some point she would've taken you aside and said, 'It's time you knew the truth.' "

"Do you mean this as a character reference? That Miles Finn would have done the honorable thing and acknowledged I was his?"

Joey said, "I didn't know him. He was just a face and a set of legs jogging to and fro on Old Baptist Road. I knew he and your mother were an item, but I didn't know the details."

"Neither did I. Neither did Fletcher."

"Maybe—" he began. "I don't know. Was that the kind of thing you and your mother talked about, woman to woman? Did you tell her about your dates and your romances?"

Sunny's pale cheeks turned pink.

"What I meant was," said Joey, "were you close these past few months, or whenever it was that Miles Finn became a year-round resident?"

"Obviously not close enough," said Sunny. She slid Regina's hat off her head and onto the seat next to her, leaving a crown of static floss.

He watched it settle, then said, "There's something to be said for the hair argument."

Sunny allowed a faint smile.

"What's your argument on the other side? I mean, who do you think your father is?"

"John Batten."

"What happened to him?" asked Joey.

"He moved to Arizona and married a faithful woman."

Joey smiled. "And how do you know that? You visit him?"

"Never."

"Child support?"

"Not for a long time."

"Did you ever ask him?"

Sunny blinked.

"Don't you think he'd tell you the truth? Because it would make him look like a decent guy rather than a deadbeat dad."

"I went through a phase in high school when I wrote him letters and he answered them, but all we talked about was golf clubs."

"It was different back then," said Joey. "Let's just say Miles Finn got your mother pregnant while she was married to John Batten. She wouldn't have admitted that—not to her husband, not to her best friend or her doctor; maybe not even to Miles Finn."

"Or herself," said Sunny.

"And if it hadn't been for the appearance of, well . . ."

"Me looking like Fletcher in drag. Say it. It's what everyone's thinking, right?"

Joey took a menu from behind the napkin holder and handed it to her. "When did Sunny Batten or her brave crusader of a mother care about what King George was saying? If you did, you'd have played field hockey in high school." He looked at his watch. "Are you going to eat anything?"

"Why?"

"Because I would consider it official business to escort you to the Abel Cotton House and ascertain that everything is shipshape."

"That isn't necessary."

"You can't even make that sound convincing. Someone's gotta do it, and it might as well be the chief law officer and ghostbuster of the town of King George."

"I might have blueberry pancakes first." She opened the menu. " 'Fresh wild blueberries in season.' Is this in season?"

"I eat what they give me. They taste the same twelve months a year." He called to Mrs. Angelo, "A short stack of Polka Dots for Sunny." He smiled at her across the table. "Extra fluffy."

"Comin' right up," Gus called from the grill.

———

She asked him to wait outside. No escort needed. In fact he might as well go back to the station.

He touched his transmitter. "I take the station with me. Besides, my secretary gets in at nine."

"It's Saturday," said Sunny.

"It's my mother," said Joey. "I'll wait. I've got reports to fill out right here."

"On a day like today, I wouldn't leave a dog in the car, even with the windows rolled down. Really, I'll be fine."

"I'll stay on the porch. And if you need me—"

"In case I come screaming out with my hair standing on end?"

He smiled. "As opposed to what it's doing now?"

Sunny made a face. "Let's get this over with," she said.

———

He waited on the glider, which squeaked with each skid of its rusty runners. The cushions smelled of mildew, and left pollen on his dark blue trousers. After what felt like a polite interval, he went to the screen door and called, "Mind if I come in?"

He opened the door when she didn't answer. "Could I use the phone?" he tried. He was in the room where they had died. The walls were a funny color, like knockwurst. A black velvet loveseat split the parlor in half and faced a new television sitting on top of a chest of drawers. His first thought was, A guy's TV, state-of-the-art—Miles Finn's contribution, how he passed the time while she was rehearsing. There were dying flowers in a pewter vase, and a dusting of dead fronds below it. He wished he'd thrown those out so Sunny didn't have to. He recognized them—the daily special from the bucket outside the Century Market—the cheap stuff: a carnation, two daisies, a mum, and something exotic that they rotated daily. He'd bought a couple of them in a pinch.

"Sun?" he called.

"In here."

The kitchen was past a curtain that hung on a suspension rod in a doorway. Like a dressing room, he thought. As if the actress in Margaret wanted a little mystery between her kitchen and her parlor. Sunny was standing in there with an address book open in her hands. The kitchen was yellow in every possible way—the linoleum, the appliances, the checked oilcloth on the table, the speckled Formica, the curtains. She looked up. "I don't know why I came in here first," she said, raising the address book a few inches. "I don't know what I'm looking for."

"People, maybe? Friends of hers you wanted to call to tell about her?"

"A little late for that," said Sunny. "They'll ask about the funeral and I'll say, 'Oops, sorry. It was yesterday. Didn't know you existed, so how could I contact you?' "

"You could say, 'I'm sorry. We had a private graveside service.' They won't know that the whole town turned out."

"I wish it were annotated," said Sunny, leafing ahead a few pages. "It would be so nice if it said, 'Haven't seen her since we moved here.' 'Old friend from secretarial school.' 'Sunny's baby-sitter.' "

"What does it say for Finn?" asked Joey.

Sunny turned to the F's: "Just 'Miles.' Two numbers crossed out, then a local number."

"What exchange?"

"Two-eight-seven."

"That's the cabin."

Sunny handed him the book. "Look at my listing. She's had this book my whole life." Under "Sunny," Margaret had written in ink and then crossed out with each relocation an address and phone number. There was her mother's helper job at Hampton Beach when she was fifteen; each year of college as the dorm room changed; a camp-counselor summer; her first job; her second job. The Harding School was not crossed out. Recorded proudly were "dorm" and "office."

"Your whole life is flashing before me," said Joey.

"She had no more room," said Sunny. "After this, I'd run into the other B's. I wonder if that should tell me something."

"Like what? Other than your mother should've written in pencil?"

"I meant, 'End of the road, Sunny. Stay here.' "

"You keep bringing that up," said Joey. "I'm no psychologist, but you've said this to me a couple of dozen times. So stay. Live here. Or at least have a little stopover."

Sunny took the book back and closed it. "I'd have to get permission from the landlords first."

"Done," said Joey.

Sunny, walking to the sink, turned around. "How is it done? Are you on the committee?"

"I'm the chief of police."

"I know, but—"

"I got the 911 call. I spoke to the reporters. I did not remind the citizens of King George that they were your mother's landlords. And then I got shot. People felt bad. I survived. They were happy." He placed the flat of his hand over his midsection and took a deep breath. "And did I even miss a beat, except for one night in the hospital? No. This town is feeling pretty fond of me these days."

Sunny turned around, ran the cold water, with her hands braced on the edge of the sink.

"Sunny?" Joey asked. "You okay?"

She nodded without turning around.

"Just letting the water get cold?"

She nodded again.

"Can I have a glass, too?"

She opened the cupboard to her immediate right, which held only dishes. "She changed things," she murmured. In the cupboard to her left were glasses—tall frosted ones and short ones with fruit-shaped bumps blown into their surfaces. She took one, looked at it, took a second one. "New," she said. "Pretty."

"They're yours now," said Joey.

Sunny shut off the water without filling either glass, and slumped into a chair.

Joey said, "You know what you should do? Play nine holes. Just go out the front door at dusk, slip onto seventeen and then play your favorites."

"I don't belong. I'd be sneaking on."

"You'd be my guest. I'll sign you in."

"You belong?"

"Not exactly."

"But this would be another example of everyone feeling fondly toward you these days?"

"Correct."

"Why does everyone think that whatever's wrong with me can be cured by nine holes?"

"Not cured. Helped maybe."

Sunny opened the window above the sink. "It's going to be a scorcher."

"On days like this, you don't have to wait until dusk for the course to be deserted."

"I know," said Sunny. "I know all the loopholes. All the best times to sneak onto the King George Links, virtually invisible."

"Not you," said Joey.

CHAPTER 13

Checkout

Mrs. Peacock noted that her chief of police, whose salary, overtime, and gas-guzzling Chevy Tahoe were paid for by her tax dollars, was devoting his morning to Sunny Batten.

"Mrs. P," he said, lifting his cap.

"I would've thought you'd be on disability," she answered in greeting.

"Doing nicely," he said. "Thanks for asking."

"I heard he got away."

"Imagine that," said Joey. "What kind of perp would shoot a cop, then not get out of his car to help him up? What's this world coming to?"

"Did you get his license plate number?"

"Part of it."

Mrs. Peacock tsked. "Any witnesses?"

"Not so far."

"He's probably in Canada by now. Probably drove straight through and didn't even get stopped at the border. How would they know what to look for?"

"I managed to alert the proper authorities," said Joey.

"How's your mother doing?"

"The way you'd expect. Thrilled I'm not dead, then a basket case over what might've been."

Mrs. Peacock looked past him to the cruiser. "I saw you gave Sunny a ride."

"That's correct."

"From The Dot?"

"No. Not from The Dot."

She reached below her counter for a feather duster and swiped the desktop absentmindedly. "Is she in some kind of trouble?"

Joey laughed, which caused Mrs. Peacock to frown. "I don't see what's so funny about that."

"What kind of trouble could Sunny Batten get into between her mother's funeral and breakfast?"

Mrs. Peacock said smartly, "She brought the Finn boy here."

"Good! More business. You must be happy."

"He paid cash," she said.

"Cash is good."

"Cash is highly unusual. How many people carry enough money to pay for a hotel in cash?"

Joey said, "Correct me if I'm wrong, but wouldn't one night run him around seventy-seven dollars?"

"It's June," she said. "High season."

"Eighty-five dollars?"

"Ninety-nine, with a two-night minimum."

Joey walked back to the foyer's only chair and sat down. "No special bereavement rates?" he asked.

Mrs. Peacock stared as if he'd uttered something incomprehensible. "Are you suggesting I have special rates for different occasions? Because I've never heard of such a thing."

"I guess I was thinking you might let folks stay one night in cases of . . . like this—a tragedy," said Joey.

"I'm not a homeless shelter," she said. "Besides, I can't tell you the number of calls that came in from her mother's friends offering her a place to stay. But it seems"—and she looked accusingly at Joey—"that she wants her privacy."

"Can you blame her? Here she doesn't have to discuss her business or defend her decisions or make small talk or take calls. Or, God knows, watch cable."

"We're getting cable," said Mrs. Peacock. "We might even get HBO." She glanced at her watch. "Checking out at nine-fifteen. I wonder what her rush is."

Joey shrugged.

"Is she catching a bus?"

"I don't believe so."

"Are you giving her a ride?"

He sighed and stood up again. "She doesn't have a car, Mrs. P."

"I wonder how she thought she'd get around," she murmured. She flicked her feather duster at a few more patches of wood. "Will you be chauffeuring Mr. Finn as well while he's in town?"

"If I feel like it, I will," said Joey.

"There's work to be done," she grumbled.

"Yours, you mean?"

"Theirs! Two houses to pack, clean, sell—on his part, at least. I don't know who they think is going to do that for them."

Joey coughed into his fist. "I can't speak for him, but I believe she's staying put for a while."

"How long?" Mrs. Peacock asked sharply.

"Until she's ready to move on, would be my guess."

"Not anytime soon, judging by how long it takes her to pack one suitcase."

"Do you have someone waiting for her room?" he asked.

Mrs. Peacock's nose and upper lip twitched. "Just my mop and pail, my ammonia, and my bleach. I think you know how I keep my units. You'd never believe how some people leave a place. Like an animal—like a *pack* of animals slept there."

"Hard business," said Joey. "I'm so glad I do something easy."

Mrs. Peacock stared, then produced a strained smile. "I'm not deaf to your sarcasm, Joseph. You may be the chief of police—"

"But that doesn't give me the right to give someone a lift in my cruiser?"

"Don't put words in my mouth," she snapped.

Joey leaned across the counter. "Her mother *died,* Florence. She doesn't know whether she's coming or going. She's never had a father. I'm driving her a half mile to the pathetic little excuse for a house that killed her only living relative, okay?"

Mrs. Peacock lifted her chin. "I've heard you speak to your mother like that and maybe she's impressed by that title of yours, but I know how many men turned this job down before your name came up."

"Nice," said Joey. "Very nice." He rapped on his chest. "Good thing I'm wearing this today." He walked to the door. "I think I'll go stand in the burning sun and wait."

"What about him?"

"Finn?"

"Do I wake him up and tell him his ride is here?"

"Me? I'm not his ride."

"He got a phone call this morning." She shuffled pink message slips. " 'Emily Ann. Call her cell phone.' Want to run it over to unit two?"

"I don't think a guy needs to be awoken by a uniformed police officer for a simple phone message. I'll give him a heart attack."

Mrs. Peacock was looking past him, at the view through the screen door. "What's she doing with those?" she murmured.

Joey turned to see. Sunny had her golf bag over one shoulder and her other arm around a glass bowl containing large, crisp white lilies. They'd dripped or sweated—he couldn't help but notice—leaving wet spots on the front of her pink blouse.

"The flowers or the golf clubs?" he asked.

"The clubs."

"Just like high school, I guess. Wherever she goes, they go."

"The flowers came this morning."

"A day late," said Joey.

"They're for her, not Margaret. The card specifically said 'Sunny.' They're from someone out of town. F.T.D. But that's all I know."

With his hand on the doorknob, he asked, "Is she all square with you? Can I take her away?"

Mrs. Peacock squinted out the window. "Probably a boyfriend. Evette wouldn't tell me—some kind of confidentiality oath they take as florists . . . or so she said."

"Very good to know," said Joey.

———

"One last thing," Sunny said to Joey, handing him the lilies. "I need to give Fletcher directions to the house."

"Why?"

"We're splitting the funeral expenses. I want him to know where he can find me."

"Tell him he's got a phone message in the office: An Emily wants him to call her on her cell phone."

Sunny headed for the path to the cabins.

"I thought you couldn't stand him," Joey yelled.

"I can't. I need the money. It'll just take a sec."

Joey held the bowl. It still bore a card, in an envelope, perched on its plastic stick. He watched Sunny knock on the door of unit two, wait, knock again.

Joey slipped the card out of its prong and read quickly, "With deepest sympathy from your freinds at Harding," Evette had transcribed to the best of her ability. The school. Just teachers. A group of them.

Fletcher appeared in blue jeans but no shirt, flabbier at the waist than his funeral suit revealed, feet bare, hair crazy. He smiled at Sunny. No wonder, thought Joey. Her hair was up in a twist with pieces flying out of it and curling down her neck. Fletcher went back inside, returned with a pen and a piece of paper. Sunny wrote something. Fletcher asked a question, got an answer. Fletcher put the slip of paper in his jeans pocket. Sunny nodded.

Joey watched carefully. Yesterday the guy was lobbying for kinship.

Today he's taking a second look at his new sister, noticing that when she's not wearing a dress down to her ankles and a hat over her eyes, it's something else altogether. Bet he wishes he hadn't started the brother campaign. Bet he wishes he never opened his big mouth.

Keep it up, thought Joey. Fall for your half-sister. Fall as hard as you want. I don't know New Jersey law, Fletcher boy, but in this state, it's a sin.

CHAPTER 14

Fletcher and Billy

The teenager had gone to bed hungry after finding only pizza with soy cheese and filleted raw fish in the dead guy's freezer. None of the cereals were normal, and none tasted sweet. On the plus side, he reminded himself, everything was hooked up—cable, electricity, gas. Who knew from the ratty outside that the inside would be excellent: The wood floor was shiny, as if it was newly laid. The air smelled like paint. The ceiling had floodlights that were sunk right into it. He'd decided not to turn on the lights at night, but now he fiddled with everything, slid the dimmers up and down, figured which remote control worked the television, which premium channels the dead guy got. It was great—a bachelor pad hideout, if only there were chips or Pop Tarts in the cupboard and some beer in the fridge.

The phone worked, too. What the hell. He had good news; the TV said the cop was saved by a bullet-proof vest and was back to work. So he hadn't killed anyone. He was innocent. He dialed Tiff's number. She didn't know any of it; didn't even know he'd borrowed the truck, or why he was so relieved now, but he felt like telling her how cool things were.

Tiff's mother answered. "Is this Billy?" she asked coldly when he didn't speak. "I know it's you." After a longer pause she asked, "Where's 603?"

Shit, Caller ID. He'd forgotten. "Is Mike there?" he asked in what he hoped was a stranger's voice.

"There's no Mike here. And if this is Billy, don't call back."

"Sorry, wrong number," he mumbled and hung up.

═══

Fletcher remembered the cabin as being such a depressing dump that he was heartened by what he saw at the end of the dirt driveway. Shingles not yet weathered to match the burnt-toast look of the original homestead announced an addition. "I remember it as a hell of a lot more ramshackle," Fletcher said to Dickie, next to him in the driver's seat.

"He never told you he was renovating?"

"He probably said something. I should've figured he couldn't have lived here year-round the way it was."

"The lake's gotten kind of fashionable," said Dickie. "All it takes is a couple of New Yorkers buying tear-downs and hiring architects to get the market moving."

Fletcher got out of the car and walked across the grass to the water. He looked left and right, and came back shaking his head. "So Boot Lake is hot," he said, grinning. "Ain't America great?"

"Two words," said Dickie. "Fly-fishing. Some outfit is building a lodge on the northeast shore, and since that was announced, the flatlanders have been sniffing around. Doctors and lawyers who get four, five weeks of vacation a year and like to vary their fresh and salt water." Dickie hit the button that unlatched the trunk, but he didn't spring out of the car as usual.

Fletcher was squinting up into the trees. "I don't see any phone or power lines. I was hoping for that much."

"Underground," said Dickie. "Everything went in at once when they laid the fiberoptic cable. The whole lake. There were hearings, and people testifying to how the big bad outside world was ruining their pristine surroundings and their chosen lifestyle. It went on for months. Front-page coverage in the *Bulletin*." Through the open car window, he extended his hand to Fletcher. "I've gotta get back. Roberta's beeping me."

"What a business, huh?" said Fletcher. "You guys on call twenty-four/seven? No fly-fishing vacations for your team."

"The relatives always want a human being at the point of contact. Imagine losing a loved one and getting our voice mail?" He paused and said pointedly, "Your bags are in the trunk."

"Sorry," said Fletcher. "I'm a little stunned by all of this. I didn't even expect electricity, let alone a deck and a bug-zapper." He turned back toward the lake. It was not a body or a view that would inspire anyone to forsake the Poconos. He thought about the Grandjeans' summer home—three acres on Nantucket Sound—an aerial view of which was enlarged and framed behind the boss's desk.

"I assume you have a key," said Dickie.

"Do I need one? It never even had a lock."

Dickie put the Town Car in reverse and backed out without answering. Just before turning onto the paved road, he waved into his rearview mirror.

Fletcher waved agreeably. "Fuck you, too," he said through his smile.

———

Billy watched the drop-off and the retreat of the fancy black car. Shit. He'd have to run out the door, past the guy, into the truck and take off. Keys? Where had he left the keys? Just like at home, just like a million searches a day he had to make for whatever crap he'd misplaced in the five minutes between coming home and going out again.

The guy in the driveway, meanwhile, didn't seem to notice that there was a truck parked behind the house or music coming from inside. He couldn't be a cop; no cop arrives alone to apprehend a dangerous criminal at his hideout, and certainly not with luggage and golf clubs. He must be a relative. He looked like the dead guy, who had pictures of himself in every room.

The doorknob turned left and right like a horror movie where the girl is home alone and the mass murderer is trying the door before slashing his way inside. In one second, Billy decided to fake it—to be as charming and clueless as he knew how to be. He'd make something up. He went to the door and opened it with a perplexed but welcoming smile.

Fletcher jumped and put his hand over his heart. "Jesus! You scared the shit out of me."

"I didn't mean to," said Billy. "I saw you coming up the stairs, so I opened the door."

"Who the hell are you?"

Billy grinned sheepishly. "I'm so friggin' embarrassed," he offered.

Fletcher handed this stranger his golf clubs. "Here. Make yourself useful. I take it you're not the caretaker?"

"I was just . . . the door was open. I thought my friend lived here."

"Bullshit." What an annoying complication. Fletcher looked around. Where there once had been cobwebs were air and skylights, and where there had been cracked linoleum was pale, polished wood and an Oriental rug.

Billy said, "Okay. I'm not gonna lie to you. I told my parents I was sleeping over a friend's house, and my girlfriend told *her* parents she was sleeping over a friend's house. . . ."

"How long has this been going on?"

"Just this once," said Billy. "I swear."

"Where's your girlfriend?"

"She left early. She had to go to work. She's a nurse."

Fletcher brushed past the teenager and went down a new hall, where the one bedroom used to be. "Hey, not bad at all. You should've seen what it was like last time I came." He returned back and said, "It was my father's house, but he died."

"I heard that," said the teenager. "That's how come I knew to stay here."

Fletcher waved him off. "Look. Don't do this anymore. If you want to fuck your girlfriend, go find a minivan. This is off limits. I'm not going to report you to your parents—" He stopped. "What's your name?"

"Billy."

"Look, Billy—strip the bed and throw the sheets in the washing machine. If there is one."

Billy said, "We did it on top of the bedspread, on a towel. We didn't even touch the sheets."

Fletcher sighed. "Look, just get lost, okay? I'm not that interested."

"I didn't take anything," said Billy. "You can check. I'll stand here and wait while you see if anything's missing."

"How would I even know? It was a hole when I was last here. You could've fenced an entire home entertainment center and I wouldn't have a clue."

"But I didn't," said Billy. "I swear. I only spent one night here and I was real careful. I cleaned up after myself, and I even picked up a little."

"Am I supposed to thank you?" asked Fletcher. "You break into my house—"

"I thought you said it was your father's house."

"It's mine now," said Fletcher.

Billy lay the golf clubs carefully on the floor. "Any chance I could sleep on the couch? In the loft upstairs?"

Fletcher shook his head. "You've got balls, I'll give you that much. I catch you squatting in my house and you ask if we can be roommates?"

"I don't have anywhere to go," said Billy.

"What about home?"

"I can't. They threw me out. They don't like my girlfriend." He thought for a few seconds. "She's a Gypsy, and my parents are prejudiced."

"You're wasting your breath, kid. I have a heart of plutonium, okay? I don't care who threw you out or why."

Billy said, "It's actually my mother and stepfather who don't want me around. My real father died, just like yours did. If he was still alive, I wouldn't be homeless."

"Too bad! I'm not a social worker. Go sign up for a Big Brother. Go cry on the doorstep of some sympathetic aunt or uncle. Everyone has one of those."

"They're prejudiced, too," said Billy. "Everyone in my family is, except me."

Fletcher frowned. "Can't you turn yourself over to Children's Protective Services or whatever it's called around here?"

"I'm eighteen. I'm too old for that."

With the leather couches, the stainless-steel appliances, and the Italian tiles beckoning, Fletcher was losing interest in the subject. "Hold on. I want to look around. Don't bolt."

"Check out the lights," Billy advised. He walked to the wall switches and demonstrated. "The bulbs move inside their sockets. See: left, right. Separate controls for each fixture. They're halogen."

"Cool," said Fletcher.

"You're just checking it out, right?" asked Billy. "You're not moving in or anything?"

"I didn't know it was an option," said Fletcher. "Now I'm thinking, Why the hell shouldn't I stay here? It beats the King's Nite Motel." He pointed toward the kitchen window. "Is that your truck out back?"

"It's my uncle's," said Billy. "He's in a nursing home, so he lets me use it when I go out on dates."

"That's a break, huh? He has wheels *and* he isn't prejudiced against Gypsies?"

Billy hesitated. "That's because he's an Indian."

"Really? What tribe?"

"It's one of the big ones—Apache, I think."

"Not one of the tribes indigenous to New England?"

"Like what?"

"If he's lucky, one that owns a big casino."

"I forget. He doesn't like to talk about it."

Fletcher said, "Bill, I'm not an idiot. What's the real story here? You stole this truck and you're on the lam?"

"No fucking way."

Fletcher said, peering through the blinds, "Why does it have Massachusetts plates?"

"That's where my uncle's from. I told you it was his."

"What town?"

"Boston," said Billy. "Sort of near Boston."

"What's his name?"

"Mike. Uncle Mike."

"Uncle Mike what?"

"Why?"

"So I can check his name against the registration."

"I'll stay out of your way," said Billy. "I could do odd jobs around here to pay for room and board. Whatever you needed."

"Look, I'll tell you what I'll do out of sheer boredom: a huge favor, generosity personified. I'll stay here, and I'll give you my motel room back in town. I had to pay for two nights, but I'm not going back. I'll call the dragon lady in charge and tell her I'm lending my room to a guy who came up for the funeral."

"Could you say brother, or nephew so she wouldn't be suspicious?"

"Suspicious of what?"

"That you didn't mention it before. Or maybe she was at the funeral and didn't see me."

"It's paid for. I'll give you the key and you won't even have to check in. Just go to unit two, sleep there, and leave before eleven in the morning."

"What if she knocks on the door?"

"Bill! Were you born yesterday? You say, "I'm Fletcher Finn's nephew. He's loaning me the room because he's staying at the lake. Or better still, say, 'Miles Finn's nephew.' That's my father."

"What if she asks me stuff about you or him?"

"Say, 'I haven't seen Uncle Miles since I was a little kid.' "

"After that? After I sleep there for one night, can I come back here?"

"Forget it! You are *not* coming back here." Fletcher sat down on the couch and raked the fingers of both hands along his scalp and up to the ends of his hair. "Let me describe a scenario, and you don't have to admit or deny anything. If you stole the truck, you could drive it back to where you took it. The owner would have to call the police, and say he made a mistake; it wasn't stolen after all. Run it through the car wash first for extra points, like you're paying for the joyride."

"Are you a cop?"

"Would I be harboring a criminal if I were a cop?"

"You could be a crooked cop."

"I'm a political consultant."

"Are you rich?" asked Billy.

"That's a rude question. Why are you leaping to that conclusion?"

"You have this camp, and you're giving me your motel key."

"So? I paid for two nights. It'll serve the old lady right."

"Did you bring any food with you? Or CDs?"

"No. Look. Stop bugging me. Take it or leave it. You broke into my house and now you're asking for references. Just tell me I'm not an accessory to any crime if I shelter you for a night."

"I didn't do anything," said Billy. He looked fifteen, and his T-shirt read MAY 12–14, TOUR DE CURE.

"I'm not going to find an underage Gypsy in a shallow grave out back, am I?" Fletcher grumbled.

Billy walked into the kitchen, touched his forehead to the refrigerator, then retraced his path. He stood before the screen door and surveyed the yard. "I thought I might've got into some trouble, but I found out I didn't."

"Such as?"

Billy turned around. "This sounds really bad, but everything turned out okay, so I'm not guilty—"

"Just tell me what you didn't do."

"Nothing. I already told you. No one got hurt."

Fletcher walked over to the phone and put his hand on the receiver. "What didn't you do, Billy? Besides breaking, entering, trespassing, and/or statutory rape?"

Billy smiled nobly. "I didn't kill a cop," he said.

CHAPTER 15

Bungalow Blues

Gone were the twin beds with the flimsy headboards, the whitewashed rattan night table, the pagoda wallpaper. Every surface was a shade of gold now—burnished, lacquered, or spun with metallic threads. Margaret had turned their mother-daughter barracks into a boudoir, with tassels and Chinese influences, red lightbulbs, and a wide, outspoken bed.

Sunny had intended to start the packing with her mother's clothes but changed her mind as soon as she opened the closet door. It wasn't just the sight of the flannel dusters next to the chiffon or the satin mules alongside creased patent-leather pumps that paralyzed her but the unexpected smells of her mother's cologne and sachet, the stray brown hairs on lapels, and the Styrofoam heads holding her First Lady wigs. Least bearable was a long white zippered garment bag, advertising, in gothic letters, FAYE'S BRIDAL FINERY. It was set apart, given pride of place on the crowded rack. Sunny didn't look inside; didn't slide the zipper down to see what weight of silk, what length of train her mother had picked without a daughter's intervention or her maid-of-honor vote.

She closed the closet door and lay down on the green-gold iridescent bedspread. Matching pillow shams and bolsters lumped under her neck and crowded her elbows. When had this interior decoration happened? She closed her eyes. A conversation returned to her: Post-Christmas, half listening and uninterested, she had approved a new color scheme before her mother described a chemical that could be painted on old wallpaper to make it peel off like an omelet cooked on Teflon.

Sunny sat up and turned down the edge of the bedspread. Sheets. Pillowcases. Sooner or later she'd have to change them. Or should she? Was it wise to wash away the last molecules of skin and fibers and hair that linked this bed to her mother? She thought of calling Joey Loach and asking if the town or the state or the FBI wanted these percale striped forensics, but knew he'd only talk of unambiguous autopsy results, of acceptance and denial.

She moved to the kitchen, where the refrigerator presented its own set of heartbreaks: the last dozen eggs; a carton of low-fat pineapple cottage cheese; a foil-covered form that was surely a chicken leg attached to its thigh; two brown bananas, a quart of buttermilk, an open can of cling peaches, a six-pack of V-8, a box of baking soda dated 1/1/96.

She walked over to the sink and parted the curtain above it. Through dead-headed lilacs were the small, ragged backyard and ancient aluminum clothesline. The outdoor thermometer registered ninety degrees. On the other side of unkempt bushes was the seventeenth tee. Sunny could hear voices, the good fellowship of a male foursome. She used to stand at those bushes, waiting for a break in play before slipping onto the course. "You're lucky," the diplomatic members used to say as they waved her through and complimented her swing. "Wish I lived on the course," as if it were a luxury to sneak onto a private club from the grounds of a pauper's cottage. She'd always pictured that if one day she won a major, she would look directly into the camera and thank the pro of the King George Links, King George, New Hampshire, for pretending she was invisible throughout her formative years.

She turned back to the kitchen. As soon as she'd moved one set of glasses back to their original shelf, she lost interest in the task. Regina would want to know that she was home and staying for a while. She looked up Randall Pope and dialed. Whoever picked up the receiver on the first ring spoke no words. Sunny heard noisy breathing, then a smacking of lips against the mouthpiece.

"Robert?" she said. "Is this Robert? Is your mommy there?"

"Mummy," he repeated.

"Can you get your mommy?"

"Mummy car."

Sunny sighed. "Did Mommy go out?" she tried.

"Mummy car."

"I'm going to hang up now," Sunny said. She heard the painful blare of numbers being pounded. "Robert! Hang up the phone," she commanded into the din.

"Hello? Sorry," said an adult male.

Of course Robert wasn't home alone; of course she should have expected an adult to take over, yet the sound of Randy Pope's thirty-three-year-old voice unnerved her. After a pause, and over the sound of the toddler yelling, "Nana!" she said, "This is Sunny."

She heard Randy say patiently, "It's not Nana. Nana's taking a nap. This is Mummy's friend Sunny. Let *go*. We'll watch the tape when I'm off." Then: "Sorry. He thinks it's his grandmother."

"Could you tell Regina I called? I'm at my house."

"For how long?"

"Till about dusk. Then back by dark." As soon as she'd said it, she knew Randy would decode her answer: two hours, nine holes.

"I haven't expressed my sympathy yet. I hope you know how sorry I am for your loss."

"Thank you."

"I couldn't make it to the funeral because I had a case I couldn't postpone. But I wanted to. I think you know that our mothers had become friends."

"I know. Through the Players."

"It had already been postponed once—the case, I mean. I couldn't get a continuance." He waited. "I'm a lawyer now. Maybe Regina told you."

"Your mother did."

"I'm a litigator. Mostly criminal."

"How nice for you," said Sunny. She could sense the effort at his end, his search for something effectual and diplomatic.

"Regina's hoping you'll stick around for a while. She wants you to come over for dinner. She seems to remember that you liked her mother's salmon croquettes."

Sunny couldn't answer; her throat was closing around any response, because it was not Mrs. Tramonte's but her own mother's salmon croquettes that Regina had liked and remembered, consumed in the bungalow kitchen with canned peas and mashed potatoes.

Randy said, "I guess I'd better go see what Robert's getting into. Does Regina have your number?"

"It hasn't changed," she said, and hung up. Ten seconds later the phone rang.

"Sunny? Randy again. After Regina gets back, I was planning to run out and play nine holes."

"And?"

"Well, I don't play eighteen all at once, because it leaves her alone for the whole day. Which isn't fair to her. I mean, she has him all week.... I'm encouraging her to take up the game. Maybe when Robert's in school. I gave her a set of lessons for Mother's Day. Which she hasn't used yet ..."

"Are you asking me to play nine holes with you today?"

"Look. I know. Terrible timing. But you wouldn't have to make conversation. You could just get a feel for the old backyard. Front or back nine, your choice. And you don't have to have a beer with me in the clubhouse afterwards, either."

Phrases formed that would revive dead carp and balls kicked into the rough by teenage feet, but she didn't want him to think that the old grudge trumped her grief. "There may be a thunderstorm," she said.

"I didn't hear that," said Randy.

"I heard a few rumbles," said Sunny.

After a pause, he repeated, "I'm really sorry about your mother."

"Thank you," she said stiffly.

"Another time? I know Regina would like that." He waited. "I guess I'll try to put Robert down. Catch you later ... maybe on seventeen if the storm holds off."

"I'll keep my eye out for you," Sunny lied.

———

She couldn't predict which drawer or cupboard held the land mines disguised as grocery lists or recipe cards in her mother's neat hand. Even an envelope of expired coupons made her weep in memory of Margaret's brand loyalties: Ivory Snow, Fig Newtons, Lestoil, Aunt Millie's Marinara, Loving Care. She went back to the window, looked toward the green.

What kind of regression would a summer in King George represent? she asked herself. I'd feel the same compulsion I had as a child to entertain myself with golf. I'd play every day. I'd keep score. The dreams would start up again, first about club championships and then state championships, then bigger dreams, until I was seeing sponsors—a line of clothing, Sunny irons, Sunny woods.

And then I'd have to remind myself: I tried this for a long time, and I failed. I'm not fifteen. I'm not a prodigy. It's a hobby, not a career. I've not only closed the book on that, but I've retired—if one can retire from an amateur activity—and I'm a healthier person for it; possibly a happier person, if only I could remember, as I sit here in the kitchen of the house that killed my mother, what happiness felt like.

Sunny heard a car, saw highly polished black through the trees, and thought, Oh no—Dickie again. But it was a Volvo sedan instead of a limo, and its M.D. plates announced Dr. Ouimet. Sunny had always known him as portly, with a pale round face, no angles or bone structure visible, and in suits that suggested a big and tall–shop purchase. But this week's red-eyed mourner was trimmer, and his dark suit looked almost fashionable. He had sobbed throughout the service, propped up on one side by his noticeably unmoved wife and on the other by a grown son, who programmed computers in Rhode Island. Now, Dr. Ouimet's composure lasted only until his eyes met Sunny's. Dressed in a starched plaid shirt and khakis, he bobbed his way up the porch steps, tilted forward, arms outstretched, and wrapped her in a damp hug, patting the back of her head awkwardly with his soft, immaculate hand. "It's hit me so hard," he explained. "It's almost embarrassing. I knew I wouldn't have to hold everything back with you."

"I know," she said. "I know."

"I'm not a child. People die. I lose patients. I've lost friends, parents, grandparents. But this breaks my heart. And here I am putting you in the position of having to comfort me. I'm ashamed of myself. But I couldn't keep away."

"It's fine," said Sunny. "I wasn't doing anything."

"There was such a mob," he said. "I wanted to talk to you. I couldn't even get close enough to ask if you were all right. And at the wake, I'm afraid my wife did all the talking. Well, of course, she had to, with my blubbering."

Sunny flashed back to her disappointment in Mrs. Ouimet, who'd shaken Sunny's hand and murmured stock phrases that would have fit anyone's mother, anyone's wake. "I'm touched that you felt this strongly about your administrative assistant," Sunny told the doctor, who had finally detached himself from her.

"I did," he sniffed. "I do."

"Several people said to me, 'Dr. Ouimet is taking this harder than anyone.' "

"Which I hope didn't offend you. I never meant to challenge your position as most heartbroken or most visibly affected."

"You didn't," Sunny said. "And if it looked that way, maybe I deserved it. I hadn't seen her since Christmas. I thought we were close even if I was an absentee daughter—"

"You worked in another state. She understood that. She had your pictures all over her desk, and when patients asked about you, her face would light up. It was a lovely thing to see. I'd egg her on a bit. People would ask in passing, 'What's new with Sunny?' and she'd give a short answer, because she was not someone who chatted with the patients, and I'd say, 'And ... tell them the rest,' and then she might tell them about some new trophy or a new job at a new school."

"I didn't mean there was a falling-out or anything, but I didn't call enough and I came home even less. And now ..." She bit her lip to keep from crying again, but didn't succeed. She rummaged in the pocket of her shorts for a tissue.

"I'd give you my handkerchief, but it's soaked," he said.

Sunny stood and said she'd find some tissues. Would he like anything? A glass of water? A can of V-8?

"I could use a shot of cognac."

"Cognac," she repeated.

"The Courvoisier Millennium. It's in the cupboard below the china closet."

"I'll see if you're right," said Sunny. She went into the kitchen and found not only good and better cognac, but single-malt scotch, dry vermouth, gin, vodka, and a boxed set of martini accessories. She poured an inch of cognac into two juice glasses and returned to the porch, where Dr. Ouimet was squeaking the glider back and forth, his lower lip protruding. He thanked her for his glass, took a sip, and began his oration. "We always feel guilt when a loved one dies—the time wasted, the calls we didn't make, and the visits we cut short. But that's because we don't know in advance. When your mother's in her mid-fifties, you don't think, I'd better call daily and visit weekly, because I won't have her around much longer."

"It never once occurred to me that my mother *could* die," said Sunny. "Isn't that idiotic? I'm sure I would have started worrying when she was seventy-five or eighty, but not this early. Not while my back was turned."

"But that's the nature of an accident—the unexpectedness of it, and the shock."

"What about the shock of her secret life? I shared a bedroom with her for eighteen years, and I always knew where she was every second. Now I'm discovering that she told me nothing."

His voice wobbled when he asked, "Secret life? In what respect?"

"Taking up with Miles Finn. Getting engaged. I had to hear from her cleaning lady that they'd set a date."

Dr. Ouimet blinked hard. "I knew she was busy outside of work and that her nights were taken. As for her announcing an engagement or showing me a ring . . ." He closed his eyes and shook his head.

"Had she asked you for any vacation time for a honeymoon?"

His chin quivered. "No," he whispered. "She never told me. I had to learn it from the newspaper."

"Maybe—I don't know—she thought you wouldn't approve."

"I didn't know the man! No one in King George did. I mean, I saw him running through town in his skimpy outfits, but I never had a conversation with him. He certainly never came to the office, socially or professionally."

"Dr. Ouimet," Sunny began. "I don't think you should take it personally. I'm her daughter and her only child and she didn't tell me. I think for whatever reason, she wanted it to be very private. She hated being the center of attention."

He said gravely, "I think we both know that your mother had a taste for the spotlight, Sunny."

"Only recently. Only since the Players brought her out of her shell."

He took a sip and coughed. "It's very hard for me to accept her death. Harder than you know. And I'm sorry if that sounds presumptuous."

"It doesn't."

"I closed my office for two days. It wasn't an empty gesture. Do you understand what I'm saying? I composed the ad myself. I quoted Robert Browning. I referred to Margaret as a beloved employee. But she was so much more than that. Do you understand what I'm trying to tell you?"

Sunny took a gulp from her glass.

"—And why a secret engagement and a diamond ring would shock me to the core?"

Sunny fixed her stare straight ahead, over the porch railing and down the driveway. "I think I'm starting to."

"I have no one to confide in," he whispered.

She knew he expected her to say, "You have me. Anytime you want to talk about my mother, I'm here." What she said instead, briskly, was, "I appreciate your condolence call. I know my mother was very fond of you. She often said that you were the best boss she ever had."

"Did she? Were those her actual words—'best boss'?"

"I'm pretty sure they were," said Sunny.

"Well then ... I should be flattered. Familiarity did not breed contempt in our case, and I should be grateful for that."

The doctor nodded, once, twice, as if affirming something he didn't say aloud.

"I think I should probably unpack my stuff," said Sunny.

He forced a weak smile. "You're staying, then?"

"I can't just abandon her things. I have to go through every drawer, every closet, every cupboard."

"There's a box outside First Church," he said. "Although I couldn't bear it if a patient appeared one day wearing an article of Margaret's clothing."

"I know," said Sunny. "I'll probably take them with me and donate them to a more far-flung charity."

"Take them with you where?"

"To my new job," she said. "Which I'll know about as soon as I print out my résumé and make some follow-up phone calls."

Dr. Ouimet stood up and handed Sunny his empty glass. "If you *are* staying and if you need work, my door is open."

"Which door?" asked Sunny.

"My office! Your mother's desk."

"You're offering me my mother's job?"

"A fallback," he said. "That's all I was thinking. Not this minute. But perhaps when the dust settles. Temp work. That's how your mother started with me."

"That's awfully nice of you. I'll certainly ... think about it."

"I know you're overqualified and that you have talents and career goals. But so did your mother. And dreams. She was a very intelligent woman, and she applied her people skills to my office and ... really, in a few short years"—he groped in a trouser pocket for his handkerchief and passed it across his eyes—"she turned my life around. She found an outlet in her acting, and I tried to be flexible about her schedule. Because two thirds of Margaret"—he swallowed a sob—"was better than a hundred percent of someone else."

Sunny felt it was only good manners to hug him one last time. He nodded formally in response, walked down the steps, then stopped. He reached into his shirt pocket and took out an envelope. "I almost forgot. This was why I came to see you this afternoon, even if it appeared that I came about more personal matters. This is for you—your mother's last paycheck."

Sunny took the envelope. Where her mother's name had been typed on a computer label, he'd crossed it out and written, *Sunny Batten.*

"It's made out to you," he said, "so there wouldn't be any difficulty cashing it or tying things up in probate. You don't have to open it now."

She did, then looked up. "This can't be right."

"It is."

"I've seen my mother's paycheck, and it never came out to an even number, and certainly not to an amount like this."

"Because this includes comp time, overtime, and vacation time. Plus her next Christmas bonus, which is completely at my discretion, so you have no basis for disputing it."

"But ten thousand dollars?"

"Every penny of it wages and benefits."

"I didn't expect this," Sunny said.

"She earned it. Sooner or later you would have called me up and asked if there were any payroll checks due your mother, and I would have been embarrassed that I hadn't attended to my bookkeeping." He started toward his car, then returned to the steps again. "One favor, Sunny: I didn't feel there was any need to discuss this matter with Mrs. Ouimet, so if you should run into her on Ladies' Day this Tuesday—"

"I won't," said Sunny.

"Or anytime."

"I understand," said Sunny.

"Not just the money. The conversation, too—my personal reflections on your mother."

"Maybe she knows," said Sunny. "Wives pick up on things. And you haven't been the most stoical soldier in town."

His face crumpled again.

"Don't cry. I didn't mean it as a criticism."

"She doesn't know. When I told her I was making a house call, she didn't even look up."

"Because she's so used to it?"

"Because she doesn't approve. She thinks I should have banker's hours. And because there was a time when she came along. Of course she stayed in the car, but it still gave her a sense of connection to my patients. Sometimes, if it was nothing contagious, she'd come in afterwards for tea or coffee."

Sunny hoped that the phone would ring or the skies would open. "I'd love to talk longer," she said, "but I have to get back to work."

"Of course. As do I."

"Thanks again," said Sunny. "And if it's appropriate, please send my thanks to Mrs. Ouimet."

He shook his head primly, eyes shut. "It's not," he said.

CHAPTER 16

Nobody Slips Anything
by Winnie

With his seat belt buckled and his hands glued to the steering wheel like a model for a driver's ed diagram, Billy crawled toward the King's Nite at twenty miles per hour. After today, he wasn't going to do another criminal thing in his life—big, small, premeditated, or fucking retarded. *Ever.* God had spoken: If He'd put a bullet-proof vest on a cop in this bumblefuck town, it was a sure sign that He didn't want Billy to go to the electric chair. He'd return this shitbox to the gas station, where the stupid owner had left it running, lie low, and get his license the minute he turned sixteen and a half.

Maybe he'd head back now. On the other hand, one more night wouldn't make a difference to God, who would surely understand that he was tired and didn't want to miss his chance to sleep in a motel. He'd seen the commercials: In every one, the maids treated you like royalty and the swimming pools were shaped like Nutter Butters.

He depressed his left blinker, turned carefully into the motel parking lot, and backed into the space farthest from the street. He had hoped for something fancier, maybe two stories, with carports. This was like the places he'd seen up and down Route 6, a string of cabins with lame names and no pool. Just like Fletcher had drawn on the directions, there was a diner across the street. BREAKFAST ALL DAY, it said out front. He liked that. He had two twenties he'd found in the dead guy's kitchen drawers: definitely bacon or sausages with his eggs.

Maybe he'd eat first and then watch a movie, if the motel had Pay-Per-View. He didn't unlock the door to unit 2 but peered through the rear window, hands cupped around his face. Not bad. A double bed all made up and a clock radio next to it. No TV visible from his angle. It could still be somewhere, attached to a wall. That's what he would do if he owned a motel: Buy the cheap stuff and bolt it down.

—

At the diner, he took a stool at the counter and ordered a large root beer. The food listed on the blackboard was lunch stuff—meatloaf, pork pot pie, fried haddock, hot turkey sandwich. "Are you still serving breakfast?" he asked the waitress, then added courteously, *"Winnie,"* with a nod to her name tag.

She checked her watch. "Do you know what you want?"

"Steak and eggs with pancakes. Do you have that?"

"Believe it or not, we do," said Winnie.

He stretched toward the closest napkin dispenser and came back with a menu. "Lemme check one thing first."

"Five ninety-nine. We're not talking filet mignon here," said Winnie. "It's cube steak."

"No problem. Home fries come with that?"

"You want home fries?"

"Is it extra?"

Winnie said, "I think we can do home fries. How do you want your eggs?"

"Fried. On both sides."

"What kind of toast?"

"The regular."

"White?"

"Yeah, white is good. With jelly."

She yelled the order to Gus, then turned back to the teenager. "Where you from?"

Billy met the waitress's stare. "Why?"

" 'Cause I know everyone who comes in here. Are you passing through?"

"Yeah."

"On vacation?"

"Sort of."

"Heading north?"

"South."

"By yourself?"

"Yeah," said Billy. "But I'm not sure where I want to go next." He brightened and said, "Maybe the Basketball Hall of Fame. That's south. I may go there next. To Springfield. I have my uncle's truck. . . ."

"Nice uncle," said Winnie. "Wish I had one."

"He's in a nursing home, so I get to use it anytime I want. As long as I pay for the gas."

"What kind of truck?"

"A Ford F100."

"New? Old?"

"Medium."

"What's your name?"

"Mike."

"Yours will take a little time, because the steak's frozen, Mike."

"No problem," said Billy.

———

When Gus called from The Dot saying Winnie was waiting on a kid wearing the late Miles Finn's Rolex, Joey groaned. Winnie watched *America's Most Wanted*; it wasn't the first time she'd fingered an innocent tourist at the counter.

"What do *you* think?" Joey asked Gus.

"Want me to put her on?"

"Not really," said Joey.

Seconds later, without preamble, Winnie hissed into the mouth-piece, "I wouldn't have suspected anything if it was just the watch, but he's wearing a T-shirt that Miles wore all the time."

"A T-shirt?"

"Penn State. Faded pink, with bleach spots. Believe me, it's his or else I'm living in the Twilight Zone."

"Did you say anything?"

"No! I asked him where he was from, but I didn't want him to think I was on to him."

"No one's reported break-ins at the lake," said Joey.

"Dead guys don't call 911! You interested or not?"

"You know I can't do anything official without backup. How much longer will he be there?"

"Long enough. He ordered the Presidential, and I'm giving him free refills on his root beer."

"Look. Tell Gus to stall on the order. I'm radioing Claremont."

"And then what?"

"Then I'll check it out."

"Couldn't you just pretend to drop by for a cup of coffee? Then if you noticed something fishy, it would seem like you just stumbled across it."

Joey closed his eyes, reclined his desk chair back as far as it would tilt. "Is he alone?"

"Alone and half your size. Mainly hungry. He's got the ketchup and the A-1 Sauce all lined up. You could just slip in next to him and start a conversation."

"Any sign of weapons?"

Winnie said, "He's sitting here fishing for ice cubes with his straw and staring at the Sof-Serve."

"Lots of people went to Penn State," said Joey, "and lots of people own Rolexes."

"Not in this joint," she said.

———

He jogged the two hundred yards to the diner, removed his hat, smoothed his hair, and opened the door. The teenager, drumming at the counter, didn't turn around. " 'Morning," Joey sang in his pleasant-est off-duty voice. "Or I guess I should say good afternoon?" He swung his leg over the stool next to the kid, who flinched at the sight of the uniform.

"Whoa," said Joey. "Take it easy."

"No big deal," the kid managed. He looked down at Joey's gun. "My father's a cop. So I'm used to them."

"Really? For what town?"

"Not around here. In California. Hollywood."

Joey didn't respond, except to stare at the teenager's thin, familiar face.

Winnie came over, pencil and pad in hand. "The usual?" she asked.

Joey barked, "No"—odd for him, no *please* or *thank you*.

She retreated to the far end of the counter and watched. The look on Joey's face—fury and hatred combined—was one she'd never seen be-fore. His hand shook on its way to his water glass, and his lips moved silently.

The boy swiveled a quarter-turn away from the police officer, then glanced skittishly back to his neighbor. "I just remembered—" he called to Winnie. "I gotta meet someone."

Joey jumped to his feet and, in a tone no one at The Dot had ever heard him use, ordered the teenager to sit the fuck back down and put his hands flat on the counter.

The boy steadied himself, hands gripping the edge of the coun-ter.

Joey was behind him now, holding him by the belt, his right hand drawing his gun. "You're under arrest for the attempted murder of Chief Joseph Loach"—he yanked the belt hard, causing the boy to yelp—"which is *me*, you little prick."

Billy's eyes darted back and forth between Winnie and the door. A whimper escaped each time he exhaled.

Winnie was torn between delight at being right and dismay at inciting Joey's overkill. She hadn't said anything about murder; the kid had stolen a watch and a T-shirt from an empty house.

"Ronnie! Get over here," Joey yelled. A tall, round-shouldered man in gray work clothes rose from a booth, wiping his mouth with a napkin.

"I'm deputizing you right now, under my authority as chief, to be my special assistant. I need you to pat him down."

"Really?" said Ron. "You don't want to?"

"I'm asking *you* to, okay? Like now."

Ron came to Joey's side. "Sorry . . . can you walk me through it?"

Joey said through clenched teeth, "You ever watch TV?" He pulled Billy off the stool by the belt and kicked his legs apart. "You start with the chest, go down his body, up the legs. Okay? You're looking for guns, knives, anything. I'll cuff him when you're done."

Ron traded places with Joey. After every few inches, he looked toward Joey for approval.

"Don't just tickle him," said Joey. "Squeeze."

Winnie felt a stab of pity for the teenager, who was too stupid not to have left town once he'd burglarized a dead man's house. Ron's search stalled along Billy's right jeans pocket.

"Anytime today," said Joey.

Ron reached gingerly into the pocket and brought out a plywood squirrel that was attached to a key.

"Where'd you get this?"

"It's mine. For the hotel across the street."

Invigorated, Ron resumed his search. "Spread 'em," he growled, then checked with his audience—two guys in the farthest booth. They waved.

"That's good enough," said Joey. "Can you get between him and the door? I'm cuffing him."

"What'd I do?" the boy cried. "I have money. I was going to pay for my breakfast."

Joey smacked the kid's elbow with the back of his hand. "You stupid asshole. You didn't think I'd remember who shot me? *That's* what you did, dickhead. You tried to kill me, and now you're under arrest."

"What's he talking about? I didn't try to kill anyone. I didn't do anything. He must be crazy."

"One block away! And then you stick around for a couple of days? Are you retarded or what?"

"It wasn't me," cried Billy. "And whoever it was, he mustn't have killed you."

"Whoever it *was* is looking at attempted capital murder. I don't care how old you are or how retarded."

"Joey, easy," said Mrs. Angelo.

"Maybe you should just go without a fuss," Winnie said to the boy.

"It wasn't me. I was never here before. I was with my girlfriend."

"When was that?" asked Winnie.

Joey glared at the waitress, who pursed her lips and retreated another foot.

"Do you have to use the gun?" said Mrs. Angelo from the cash register. "He's only a kid."

"You might want to consider leg irons," said Ron. "He can still run in cuffs."

"He's not running anywhere," said Joey. "He knows what I'll do if he moves one inch."

"You need a real deputy," clucked Mrs. Angelo. "I don't know how one police officer is supposed to do everything in this town."

"Need any more hands, Chief?" asked one of Ron's booth mates, whose ten fingers remained wrapped around a lumpy pita.

"Don't I get a lawyer?" asked Billy.

"Call his parents," said Mrs. Angelo. "They're probably frantic."

"My parents! That's a laugh."

"Ron," Joey said impatiently, pointing with his gun.

"What?"

"The door?"

Ron pressed his back against the glass panel to open it, sucking in his stomach as they passed.

"Stay here and watch for the Claremont cruiser," Joey told him.

"Joe—I'm already late. Leo was covering for me just so I could get an iced coffee."

"Okay, *go*. Jesus. Can I trouble you to find another volunteer?"

"I'll keep an eye out for the cruiser," said Mrs. Angelo.

"What're you gonna do to me?" asked Billy.

"Shut up!"

Billy flinched, grew smaller. Two wet streaks shone on his cheeks.

Winnie walked out to the top step holding a Styrofoam container. "Should we send over his steak and eggs?"

"Do you understand what he did?" Joey yelled, giving Billy a shove for emphasis. "Because your consorting with the enemy is getting on my nerves."

"He's got rights," said Winnie. "Anyone who watches TV knows that."

"Maybe you'd like to bring him take-out in prison," Joey grumbled.

"You didn't even want to *come,* Joey Loach," Winnie threw back.

"Prison!" wailed Billy.

"Do you know if there's a reward?" Winnie asked.

CHAPTER 17

Happy Hour

Sunny stopped by the bar to thank Chester Gobin for the beautiful spray of American Beauties and the lovely sentiments on the card. "It was Evette's idea to make it look like one of her opening-night bouquets," he said. He had shaved his veiny head and sprouted a stiff, red mustache since Sunny's last visit to the clubhouse. His hug was huge, unself-conscious; he filled a wineglass to the brim as Sunny slipped a five-dollar bill from her pocket onto the bar.

"Put that away, Sun. It's the least I can do. Want anything to eat?"

"No thanks. I'm going to make it quick."

"Plans?"

She shook her head. "I don't think it looks right to be hanging around a bar the day after your mother's buried."

"Not to argue with you, Sun, but you're not in any danger of looking like a disrespectful daughter. You have a pretty long way to go before you'd give off that impression. Besides, we're alone."

"Where is everyone? Isn't this happy hour?"

He shrugged. "People listen to the weatherman talking about the heat index and they stay inside."

"It's nice this time of night," said Sunny. She smiled. "Or maybe it was the easiest time of the day to sneak on—now and sunup. But then I'd have to dodge the sprinklers."

"How about some mozzarella sticks? Or some salsa and chips?"

"Maybe chips and salsa," she said. "Thanks."

Chester ripped open a bag of taco chips with two hands and poured its contents into a plastic basket. "How's your game?" he asked.

"Good."

"Are you getting close to scratch?"

Sunny said she didn't know; didn't want to know; didn't think it mattered in the great scheme of things.

"Your mom, you mean? It puts hazards and double bogeys into perspective? I wish more people saw the big picture."

"Actually," said Sunny, "I've been doing this for a while—where I just get out there and enjoy nature."

"No you don't. This is Chet you're talking to. I've seen you break an iron against a helpless tree after you hit one off the hosel."

"That's what I'm fighting," said Sunny. "Who needs those demons anymore?"

Chet had worked his way down the bar, replenishing the peanut dishes, but returned to stand squarely in front of her, his arms crossed. "Go on. I'm interested. When did you stop trying to win trophies?"

"Really? You want to hear this?"

"It's my job," said Chet. "Maybe I'll pick up a little golf psychology I can apply to someone else."

"My senior year in college," said Sunny. "I couldn't do anything right—after doing a lot right for three solid years."

"I don't think you mean 'a lot right.' I think you mean All-American."

"Okay, All-American. But I lost it and I decided I didn't need it back."

"Mental," said Chet. "I guarantee it—strictly between the ears."

"Whatever it took to ruin my round, I'd do it. I'd get home in two on a par five, then miss six- and seven-inch putts. I started dreading everything. Even before I teed off, I'd start thinking about how and where

I was going to get snakebitten. The payoff was that Maryland made it to the nationals that year and that year only, and I didn't make the team."

"Ouch," said Chet.

"I took a break. A long one. When I graduated, I had no time, no money. I went to New York, so I had no land, either—which turned out to be a blessing." She checked to see if anyone had entered the room. "After a whole spring and summer without picking up a club, I said to myself, You're pouting. You're a sore loser. Find another way to play, or you'll lose something you really love. So I took the train up to a public course in Connecticut. First, I'd walk the course with a couple of clubs and no ball. It made me something of the course crackpot."

"Not that Zen-of-golf thing?"

"My own version," she said. "Something like: Sunny stops thinking of herself as a prodigy and stops striving for perfection because she recognizes that she peaked at fourteen. Now I try to think, Good shot, and be satisfied. Like it's for me, not for a gallery or a match."

"You're a better man than me," said Chet. "*Plus,* I have to listen to these guys come in here bellyaching about how they missed by this much, and if only they had a Big Bertha or a better lie. The real good ones don't bellyache. They go out to the driving range and the putting green and they practice."

Sunny asked who was in that category these days.

"Some new, some you know."

"Any of my old teammates?"

Chet lowered his voice. "He didn't make it to the quarter-finals of the club championship last year—first time since he was about thirteen. He wasn't thrilled, believe me."

"He used to cheat in high school," said Sunny. "I don't know why I was so afraid to tell people that."

Chet said, "Like we didn't know."

"It was another way of ganging up on me. They all did it—I'd see their scorecards after practice rounds, and it didn't match what I saw playing behind them."

"Tough couple of years," said Chet.

"It wasn't the Dark Ages. It wasn't like girls had started playing sports the week before."

Chet grabbed the wine bottle and poised it over Sunny's glass. "Refill?"

"Sure."

"Relaxing a bit?"

"Might be." She smiled.

"And you're not driving, right? Just ducking back through the bushes?"

"Not today. I came around and played the front nine."

"*You?* Back-Nine Batten?"

"I'm a little old to be sneaking on. Everyone used to look the other way, but at my age it's not cute anymore."

"You know why we didn't complain? Because we thought you had the stuff. If you were out there hacking around, sooner or later they'd have complained to your mother, God rest her soul."

"I guess it didn't hurt to be the charity case next door, either."

Chet stopped what he was doing—clanging cups and saucers in soapy water—to say, "What does that mean, 'charity case'?"

"You know: the house—that arrangement. Abner Cotton?"

Chet shook his head. "I hate to burst your bubble, but I never thought anything like that. Did you ever see where I grew up? Plastic sheeting instead of storm windows? I always thought of you as this girl with nice manners and a beautiful swing. I never thought any of that other stuff. And as far as I'm concerned, you put us on the map. You can play whenever you feel like it. I'll mention it to Sid."

"Who's Sid?"

"Bushey. The starter—all day every day since he retired."

Chet looked up. His smile changed, became more formal. He nodded, acknowledging someone behind Sunny.

She turned around, and quickly back again. She murmured, "Shit," then, "I should go." But there was only one exit, and it was the door through which Randy Pope had just entered, still handsome and cocky, still with creases in his chinos and blond streaks in his hair. His firm hand guided her back to the bar.

"I missed you on the course," he said.

"She played the front nine," said Chet.

"Will you stay for another round? Drinks, I mean?"

"I can't," said Sunny. "I'm already late."

"For what?"

When she hesitated, Chet supplied, "She's going to the cemetery. It's nice this time of night."

"I wouldn't," said Randy. "The mosquitoes are bad enough by day, but they'll eat you alive at this hour." He patted the stool she'd just vacated. "Please. Let me buy you a drink. Everyone in town would like the chance to sit down next to you and say how sorry we are . . ."

Chet nodded a wary approval.

Randy laughed. "Very nice. I'm the town counsel, and people are worried about having a drink with me at their friendly neighborhood country club. Good thing I'm not easily wounded."

"Good thing," said Sunny.

"The usual, counselor?" asked Chet.

Randy nodded. Sunny said okay, maybe she'd have something ice-cold, too. A lemonade?

"A virgin margarita," said Chet. "My specialty."

"How *are* you?" Randy tried again.

"How do you think I am?"

They sat in silence until he asked if she would mind sharing the taco chips. She sent them off to her right with an ungracious shove.

A minute later he asked, "You know who would be happiest of all about us having a friendly chat at the bar?"

"Don't say 'my mother.' "

"No—although I could make a case for that. I was going to say Regina."

Her voice caught when she said, "Regina and I are doing just fine."

"And that doesn't tell you anything? There isn't a syllogism here? If you and Regina are so compatible and if she thinks I have some redeeming qualities, wouldn't that suggest that I'm not an entirely worthless human being?"

Sunny shrugged.

"That's your position? Even though I'm not the same person I was in high school, and I'm sure you're not, either, you're unwilling to let bygones be bygones?"

"This isn't a good week for me," she said. "I buried my mother less than twenty-four hours ago, so your bygones are very low on my list of priorities."

Randy took a swig of beer and blotted his mouth. "Your mother's death was a tragedy. Absolutely. No argument there. But doesn't that put things in perspective and beg the question What did we do that was so unforgivable?"

Sunny asked evenly, "Are you talking about my tormentors?"

"Tormentors! My point exactly. What did we do other than tease you? Maybe gang up on you a little? Do that announcer thing—'Now teeing up for King George Regional in sparkling white'—to rattle you, but it was all good clean fun. We were teenage guys, and we had a girl foisted on us who knew every rule, chapter and verse, and who did her math homework on the van. Maybe it wasn't very mature, but if you were totally honest with yourself, you'd realize we were egged on by your getting so bent out of shape at the slightest joke."

Sunny gasped. "Did you think it was a joke to clink the loose change in your pocket, and give gimmes to everyone but me, and grind my ball into the muck and pretend the embedded-ball rule wasn't in effect?"

Randy turned his face away, but not fast enough to conceal his smile.

"*Was* it?" Sunny demanded.

"My point exactly—that Sunny Batten can throw some ancient grievance back at you, like whether or not the embedded-ball rule had been called on some muddy spring day fifteen years ago."

"This isn't going to make her feel any better," said Chet.

"I'm not trying to criticize you or say we didn't make your life miserable, but—"

"I'd be down to a six-inch putt," she railed to Chet, "and one of them would say, 'I think there's a little meat left on that bone, don't you?' "

Randy smiled.

"You loved it! Every one of you. It was part of the golf season—

torture Sunny. There wasn't one guy on the team, including Coach, who treated me like I was an equal."

"Because you weren't! You were better." Randy paused. "Even if you did drive from the ladies' tees."

"You know Coach made me, and you know I hated that."

"Look: I didn't measure your drives. If you got a few yards' advantage, that wasn't our major complaint. Some people are more fun to tease than others, and you made it very rewarding."

Chet brought Sunny's margarita. "I'm not taking sides," he said, "but one thing I've noticed is that guys rag on each other and make up names and do gross things and girls aren't made the same."

"You let it rule your life," Randy said to Sunny. "For us, golf was just one of two or three sports we played—"

"Without begging. Without having to circulate a petition."

"That's what I'm saying—it was a very big deal to you. I understand that. Especially now."

"Why especially now?"

"As an attorney. And an officer of the court."

"Then don't blame the victim. Don't say, 'If only Sunny could take a joke, if only she could have enjoyed our teasing and our conspicuously urinating behind trees, she'd have had a great couple of seasons.'"

"She didn't have any brothers," Randy explained to Chet. "That might have been part of the problem. My sisters can give as good as they get."

"Remind me," Chet said to Sunny. "Who were the other guys on the golf team?"

Sunny reeled off, "René Fournier, Jackie Buckley, Ray-Ray Goyette, Punchy Ryan, both Bettencourts—"

"Every single one's a member here," said Chet.

"And this was the ringleader."

"Of course," Randy said proudly. "I was the captain."

"And wouldn't you think they'd fake even the slightest display of team spirit at matches? If we won—thanks to me on most days— wouldn't you think there would be some high fives or some cracks in the united front?"

"Yes I would," said Chet.

"Unh-uh. No one ever said anything remotely like 'Thanks.' "

"What about 'I'm sorry'?" asked Chet.

"Least of all that," said Sunny.

"Never?"

"Why should he? He thinks it was my fault."

Chet moved a dish of peanuts closer to Randy. "C'mon, counselor. You're a grown-up now. When we tease the ladies, we apologize."

"Some ladies roll with the punches," said Randy. "Some even laugh instead of carrying a grudge."

"What if the punches landed? What if she got scarred for life? What if she just lost her mother? What do we say then?"

"Don't bother," said Sunny. "It's fifteen years too late."

"Counselor?" prompted Chet.

Randy swiveled his barstool to face Sunny. "I'm willing," he said.

"Wrong approach," said Chet. "She doesn't have to meet you half-way."

"In that case: I apologize, Miss Batten."

"Say it like you mean it," said Chet.

"I sincerely apologize for all the unconstructive and insensitive things I did, and for making your life miserable."

"How's that?" Chet asked Sunny.

"He's a lawyer," said Sunny.

"He's married to your best friend. He turned out okay. And what's that thing about one door closes and another opens? This could be it."

"Meaning, I lose my mother and I gain Randy Pope as a friend?"

"Not him," said Chet. "Regina."

Randy put his hand out first. Reluctantly, Sunny shook it.

"Cold," they said at the same moment.

"My fault," said Chet.

CHAPTER 18

Fletcher Inherits the Bug

After all that—after the shock of finding his own would-be killer on the adjacent stool and practically getting booed in the process—Joey was disgusted to learn that the near assassin was a juvenile. Barely sixteen years old; learner's permit and no license. Eager as the boy was to confide every sin he'd ever committed, Joey couldn't even question William Thomas Dube or call his parents or do anything but give him Kleenex and, in the end, the Presidential steak and eggs. The kid prattled just the same—about sleeping at the dead man's house, about how the dead man's son was cool with everything.

The self-deputized Mrs. Loach refused to go home, and threatened to give the cowering boy the back of her hand. "He's a cold-blooded killer," she spat out, then louder, to the boy, "Murderer!"

"*Attempted,* Ma," said Joey. "Not to mention *alleged.*"

"When are you turning seventeen?" she demanded. "Because that's when the law catches up with people like you. I'm going to send you a birthday card in prison that says, 'Now you're an adult. Now you're in for it.' "

"Knock it off, Ma. You know better. You've gotten it out of your system, and he's getting picked up soon."

"Do you have a mother?" she asked the boy.

"Stop it," said Joey.

"Read him his Miranda rights so I can question him," she ordered.

"Ma, no. It's different. He's a juvenile. I can't ask him anything."

Mrs. Loach pinched the starched sleeve of Joey's uniform for emphasis. "This is my son you tried to kill! Do you have any idea what it means to take another person's life?"

"Ma, save it. If it goes to trial, you can stand up at the sentencing and deliver a victim's statement."

"Is there something wrong with you?" she asked Joey. "Are you such a cool customer that you can sit in the same room with your own killer?"

"I'm alive, Ma. By definition—"

She waved off his nonsense. "I could be marching in a parade today in a black mantilla, with your fellow police officers from all over New England holding me up and paying their respects to their brother slain in the line of duty. If it wasn't for the vest, I'd have buried you." Mrs. Loach's voice broke.

Dutifully, Joey patted her back.

"I'm just saying, hon, that if ever a police chief had the right to put his fingers in his ears and let his mother yell at his prisoner, it's you."

Joey looked at the wall clock, then out the window. "The transport van's going to be here any second, so make it quick."

"Thank you," said Mrs. Loach. She stepped toward Billy, but Joey caught her arm. "Stay back. I don't want you laying a hand on him."

She closed her eyes, opened them, then said in a shaky voice, "Because my son survived, I don't think you'll be put to death, but I hope you rot in jail. And just in case they put you in a boys' home instead and you escape, I want you to promise me that you'll never go near a gun again, and you'll learn to think before you act and, most important—"

"Ma, forget it. He's a dope."

"I am *not*," said Billy.

"We're not having a dialogue," said Joey. "My mother's reading you the riot act, and I'm allowing it because you shot her kid and she's only human."

Billy wiped his nose, sniffed, then said in a small, choked voice, "I'm sorry."

"Don't say you're sorry!" Joey yelled. "Jesus! Don't say another fucking word. Save your confessions for the attorney general."

"Sorry is as sorry does," said Mrs. Loach. "Of *course* you'd feel sorry now, sitting here in handcuffs, waiting for the sheriff to come get you. Do you think he's going to be as nice to you as my son is? You'll be lucky to get a grilled cheese sandwich." She turned to Joey. "You need a jail here. I don't like the idea that a criminal just sits around the office with us."

"I'm not a criminal! I'm not gonna hurt anyone."

"How often would I use a jail?" Joey said quietly. "The occasional drunk and disorderly? The annual domestic dispute?"

"You need a separate police station," she hissed. "This is a disgrace! It doesn't make the right impression—a paneled room in the basement of the town hall."

He signaled with his eyes: *Enough.*

"How come I hear on the news all the time about juveniles being tried as adults for murder, and this delinquent gets turned over to the state without a whimper?"

"Where are they taking me?" Billy asked.

"Concord. The youth detention lock-up facility," said Joey.

"I have A.D.D.," said Billy. "I get into trouble, but I can't help it."

"A.D.D.?" repeated Mrs. Loach scornfully. "You don't think we hear that all the time? From every mother of every kid who throws a rock through a window?"

"It's true! I used to have to go to the school nurse to get my medicine during the day." Billy jiggled each leg separately, then both together.

"Keep it up," said Joey. "I may not be able to ask you questions, but I can hog-tie you if you keep twitching."

"And I'll help," said Mrs. Loach.

"Why are you being so mean to me?" Billy cried. "Nobody got hurt. I was on my way home to return the truck. I didn't even get a scratch on it. I was even thinking of filling it up with gas."

"You're an idiot, you know that? You think you can erase whatever you did because your victim didn't die and the truck you stole didn't get wrecked? Attempted capital murder and grand theft auto don't work that way. That's what the word *attempted* means. You're in deep shit, junior. And stop wiping your snot on the upholstery."

Billy sniffled miserably.

"You only have yourself to blame," said Mrs. Loach. "Although I'm wondering what kind of parents raise a boy who breaks several commandments in one night."

"Assholes," said Billy.

"Don't be fresh," said Mrs. Loach.

Joey laughed.

"What's so funny?" she asked her son.

"Ma—he stole a truck and he tried to kill me. Fresh is the least of his problems." He turned to Billy. "If you have one brain cell in your head, you'll throw yourself on your parents' mercy."

"What does that mean?"

"It's advice: Let them help you. You're in a lot of trouble, and you're going to need them."

Billy looked away, defiantly, as if no conciliatory tone could make up for the previous insults.

"Eat your steak," Joey said.

"How'm I supposed to eat with my hands locked behind my back?"

"Stop being a crybaby. You said you were hungry. They could've sent bread and water."

"I'm starved," he whimpered.

Joey came out from behind his desk and Billy shrank. "I'll unlock you for five minutes, but no funny business."

Freed, Billy lifted the entire cube steak to his mouth on a plastic fork, gnawed off two mouthfuls in quick succession, and swallowed them in a gulp.

"Steak!" tsked Mrs. Loach. "Ridiculous!"

"Chew it, you moron," grumbled Joey.

———

Just after five o'clock, Joey rapped on Finn's front door, frowning at the stained-glass panel—milky pink tulips swathed in blue leaves. Fletcher answered, smiling hospitably, wearing that morning's blue jeans, a white dress shirt, tails out and sleeves rolled up. "What's up?" he began, but his smile faded at the sight of the plywood squirrel swaying at eye level.

"Did you give William Thomas Dube your consent to stay in unit two of the King's Nite Motel?" Joey asked.

"William who?"

"William Dube of Agawam, Massachusetts."

"Why?"

"Why am I *asking*? Because I arrested him this afternoon, and he had very flattering things to say about you."

"Arrested him on what grounds?"

"Attempted capital murder and grand theft auto."

"Whoa," said Fletcher. "I never met the kid before noon today. I'm not a party to anything, if that's the implication."

Joey's expression remained neutral. He asked if he could come in.

"For what?"

"A friendly little chat."

Fletcher rolled his eyes. "Do I need a lawyer for this friendly little chat?"

"I wouldn't bother," said Joey. "All I'm interested in is how you and Billy know each other and whether you freely gave him certain items in his possession—"

"Such as?"

Joey took a small notepad from his breast pocket and read, "A watch. A Penn State T-shirt, pink. The aforementioned room key."

Fletcher opened the screen door, and Joey walked past him into the sky-lit room.

"Beer?" asked Fletcher.

"Can't."

Fletcher sat down glumly on a gray flannel couch and motioned for his interrogator to do the same.

"Mr. Finn—"

"Fletcher. And are you forgetting something? My Miranda rights?"

Joey said, "Did someone arrest you? Because all this is, is a friendly conversation."

Fletcher slumped deeper into the couch.

"Fletcher, it's not against the law for an adult man to give a teenage boy gifts—"

"Me? I'm the man? What gifts?"

Joey repeated in a monotone, "A Penn State T-shirt, pink. Forty dollars in cash. A gold Rolex. Engraved with the initials M.H.F." He looked up.

"Miles Howard Finn," Fletcher murmured.

"I'm sorry," said Joey, "but I have to ask: Were these gifts a form of advance payment or incentive to the juvenile for a prospective assignation at the King's Nite Motel?"

"Jesus!" Fletcher stood and began pacing. "I'm not talking to you without a lawyer. Christ! I'm being accused of what? Solicitation and . . . and God knows what because some punk robbed me?"

Joey shook his head. "*Motel* has a ring to it, Fletch. An adult man gives a boy his room key—"

"To get rid of him! I didn't want him around. He seemed like a nice enough kid. A little stupid, but harmless."

"What he is," Joey said, "is a suspect in a capital murder case—*not* harmless. On the contrary: armed and dangerous." He took a pen out of his breast pocket. "Start from the beginning."

Fletcher flopped back down on the couch. "I got here around noon, and he answered the door. He told me he had sex in the master bedroom with his Gypsy girlfriend but didn't soil the sheets. I said, 'Get out of here and don't come back; and on your way out of town, could you drop this key off at the King George Motel, please? On the main drag . . . such as it is.'"

"King's Nite," Joey corrected.

"Whatever. I had to pay for two nights, but when I got here and saw what my father had done to the house, my plans changed."

"So you sent him off, without asking to see his driver's license or registration or taking down the license plate or calling the police?"

"Why would I?" said Fletcher. "I didn't call the police because he was a good liar and he told me his parents had thrown him out, and I felt sorry for him." Fletcher picked up a red film-processing envelope, thick with pictures, from the coffee table and nervously sorted through them.

Joey reached into his pants pocket, took out a single key, and tossed it on top of the photos.

"What's this?" Fletcher asked.

"Ignition key. Your father's Volkswagen."

"No kidding," said Fletcher. "What model?"

"A Beetle."

Fletcher's face fell.

"It was parked outside his fiancée's house the night of the accident. I'm using my discretion in terms of releasing it."

"What year?"

"New. You'll sign a release saying you're the next of kin and that you received it from me. Meanwhile, it's taking up my only visitors' space."

"Automatic or manual?"

"Automatic, I believe."

Fletcher looked further deflated.

"Life is tough," said Joey. "Your father dies before his time and doesn't leave you a Lexus."

Fletcher recovered enough to say he agreed: It had gotten rave reviews in all the car magazines, it would get him where he wanted to go, and it was certainly small potatoes—especially against the broader canvas of loss and unemployment.

"Not to mention your more immediate legal problems," said Joey.

"The kid? Like I was supposed to intuit that he was a felon?"

Joey smiled and stood up. "A guy's gotta ask. We pick him up wearing your father's watch and T-shirt, babbling on about his cool son and his cool house, carrying a motel key to a room registered to Fletcher Finn. What kind of detective would I be if I didn't make a beeline for Boot Lake?"

"There's no crime in being clueless," said Fletcher.

Joey said, "I take it you have a driver's license?"

Fletcher reached for his wallet.

"Slowly," said Joey. "No sudden moves." He grinned. "Just kidding, Fletch."

"You're enjoying this," said Fletcher. "I haven't figured out why yet, but I don't appreciate it."

"I'm just doing my job. Did I mention that it was me your friend shot at point-blank range? And when someone tries to kill me, it makes me a little testy."

"Did he miss?" asked Fletcher.

Joey rapped on his stomach. "Vest."

"No shit," said Fletcher. "And you just walked away? That is so awesome. You must be in great shape."

"Don't use psychology on me," said Joey. "Or flattery. Because I'm immune."

"I'm serious."

"Let's go. The Beetle's in town."

Fletcher put out his hand. "We're okay with everything? You know I'm a lousy judge of character but not a pedophile?"

Joey grunted a halfhearted maybe, and didn't return the handshake.

"Let's get the car. Sunny wanted me to come over. We have some settling up to do."

"I don't think she's up for a social call," said Joey.

"She asked me to drop off a check."

"I'll drop it off for you. Her place is hard to find, especially in the dark."

"It won't be dark till eight or nine. It's one of the longest days of the year."

"You can say that again," said Joey.

"Thanks anyway, but I'd rather do it without the escort. She'd see the cruiser pulling up and she might think it's more bad news."

"No," said Joey. "Just the opposite. She's in a pretty isolated area. She'll look out the window, see a strange car . . ." He shook his head regretfully.

"I'll call first."

Joey pointed to the telephone, but Fletcher hesitated.

"Are you thinking she might say 'Don't come'?" asked Joey.

"I'm thinking I don't know her number. Which wouldn't be a major obstacle . . ." He squinted and tapped his forehead.

"If only you could remember her last name?"

"I know it: Sunny and Margaret . . . it's on the tip of my tongue. And it's probably on my father's speed dial."

"Let's just go," said Joey. "We can drop your check off on the way to the station."

Fletcher said okay; what choice did he have? He wasn't going to cross the chief of police. Give him a sec to take a leak.

From the bathroom, raising his voice to be heard, Fletcher called pleasantly, "I'm sure Sunny told you that she's my half-sister."

"Your *theory* that she's your half-sister, you mean?"

The toilet flushed, but Fletcher took another minute. When he appeared, his hair was newly leavened and the scent of Old Spice deodorant drifted toward Joey. "I'm going to ask Sunny to take a DNA test," Fletcher said, tucking his shirttails into his jeans. "I think they can swab the inside of our mouths, and that's all there is to it."

"I hope to God you're not going to propose that tonight."

"We'll see. I'm playing it by ear."

"Can I give you some advice? It's too much for her now. You're coming on way too strong with this brother thing."

Fletcher smiled. "*Half*-brother. And you know this how?"

"She's my friend. I'm the one who broke the news about her mother to her."

"Sorry, Chief. *I'm* the one who broke that news. You gave me her phone number. *I* called her."

"You told her machine! Who tells someone her mother died on an answering machine?"

"Now I get it." He nodded smartly. "You think I'm moving in on her. Well, you can relax. Where I come from, men don't date their sisters."

Joey set his hat back on his head. "I'd watch the insults, pal. You're in enough trouble—"

Fletcher opened the front door, smiling confidently, waving the police chief through. "We both know I'm not," he said.

CHAPTER 19

Company

From the passenger seat, Fletcher complimented Joey on his Chevy Tahoe's digital scanner, asked if he could point the radar gun at a passing vehicle, then confided, "I was wondering how much a town this size puts together for a cop's salary package."

Joey shook his head, smiling in disbelief.

"It's public record, correct?"

"Let's just say I'm paid in line with what surrounding communities pay their chiefs."

"Decent benefits?"

Joey shrugged.

"Dental?"

"Why do you want to know?"

"Just trying to get an idea of what makes King George tick. For example, how do people make a living here? Farming?"

"Yeah, right. Farming. We all live off the land."

"You have subsistence farming up here? I've seen some orchards, but I wouldn't have guessed—"

"What century do you think we're living in? People do the same things here that they do elsewhere: They pump gas and fix cars. They teach school. They commute to Concord and work for the state, or to Hanover and work for the college. They plow roads. They groom ski trails. Some are lawyers and doctors. My father was a fireman who hung wallpaper on the side."

Fletcher popped a Tic Tac in his mouth and crunched it loudly. "Much high-tech?"

"Not in King George proper. Why?"

"Just trying to get an idea of what your tax base is."

"We scrape by," said Joey. "The summer homes on the lake help."

"What's the year-round population?"

"A thousand-plus."

"That's who employs you? A town of a thousand?" He whistled. "You're not getting rich in this job, my friend."

"Which isn't why I chose this job. *My friend.*"

Undeterred, Fletcher asked if he was married or single, homeowner or renter. Joey didn't answer, but continued to nod in greeting at each passing motorist, each walker, each dog on a leash.

"Do you know *everyone*?" Fletcher asked.

"They know me."

"What do you do for housing?" he tried again.

"Look: I pay my mother room and board to help her out, but I have a little setup in the office—bed, bureau, TV."

"Full bath?"

"You think I live in a place that doesn't have a shower?"

Fletcher shrugged. "I wouldn't want to live above the store, so to speak."

"It's not forever. I moonlight on weekends."

"As what?"

"The family business. Word-of-mouth." He smiled. "If you clean up after yourself and you match the seams and the grass cloth doesn't peel off in a year, you're a genius." He depressed his left blinker as they passed a sign announcing KING GEORGE LINKS, 200 YARDS AHEAD.

Fletcher straightened up from his slouch and complained, "I thought we were going to Sunny's."

"We are. This road bisects the course."

"That's not it?" Fletcher asked as they passed an imposing stone-and-timber house.

"That's the clubhouse. She lives farther back, tucked away."

Fletcher tapped the box to dislodge a Tic Tac into his open mouth. "What's with this town?" he asked mid-crunch. "The chief of police lives in the station and the golfers live at the country club?"

"Just her. It's a little house her mother rented. It was here way before the club was built, and the historical commission wouldn't let them tear it down."

"No wonder she plays," said Fletcher.

"Sunny's good," said Joey. "I mean *really* good. A scratch golfer. I don't know how much she told you."

"Not much."

"She was the only girl on the varsity in high school, and she got plenty of shit for it. People didn't like it. And the coach was a jerk."

"Were you her boyfriend?" Fletcher asked.

"I don't think she had a boyfriend in high school."

"But you thought about it, am I right?"

Joey said, "I'm interviewing *you*, remember? About sheltering criminals and molesting underage boys. I'm the one asking the personal questions."

Fletcher smiled. "I can't help it. A generation ago I'd be one of those reporters in a brown suit and a fedora, licking my pencil point. In today's world, I'm a consultant."

"Unemployed, you said."

"On purpose. I took the job solely for the money, but she had no business running, and I hated every minute of it."

"Who's 'she'?"

"Emily Ann Grandjean, Esquire. Hopeless."

"So you quit?"

"In a manner of speaking." He smiled. "I wasn't allowed to quit. I could only be fired for cause, so"—he tapped Joey's forearm—"you might appreciate this: Her old man paid me an exorbitant retainer up front, so my only out was doing something egregious that would get me fired on the spot."

Joey turned onto an auxiliary road lined with mathematically spaced overhanging trees. "I'd just as soon not hear this," he said.

Fletcher said, "Off the record, then: I copped a feel. No sexual content, of course—just a means to an end."

Joey stepped on the brake and smacked the gearshift into park. "You sexually assaulted a woman on purpose so she'd fire you?"

"Look, I reached over and tweaked her nipple—"

"And this nipple belonged to a *lawyer*? Running for public office?"

"Believe me, the whole thing was staged. She knew I had to do something to be terminated, and this was the most attractive option." His tone changed. "I certainly wasn't going to embezzle from the war chest or party hearty before driving the campaign bus off the road."

"And you think that's the end of it?"

Fletcher patted his shirt pocket, then removed a pink message slip. " 'Emily Ann called. Try her cell phone,' " he read.

Joey checked his rearview mirror, put the car back into drive, and proceeded slowly toward the little box of a house ahead. "I don't know why I'm giving you advice," he said, "but it's so obvious I can't help myself: Be nice to this Emily woman, even if you're faking it. Best-case scenario: She knows it was a kamikaze act, and she's willing to play along with you as long as you don't ignore her. I'm a cop. I know how things work. I see what makes people sue their doctors or shoot their foremen, and it happens when they get mad. And they *get* mad when they're ignored or insulted or stepped on. I'm not kidding—I've known people who died in bungled operations, then the surgeon goes to the funeral and hugs the widow, and she never calls the malpractice lawyer."

"I see your point," said Fletcher. He studied the pink message, lips pursed. "Good advice," he said. "Good to have you on my team."

"The hell I am," said Joey.

———

"Sunny?" she heard from downstairs—a male voice, startling and silencing her. She waited, didn't answer.

"It's Joe Loach. Sunny?"

"Stay down there," she called. She pulled the bathtub's white rubber plug and reached for a towel.

"You okay?"

"I'm just getting out of the bath. Give me a sec. I'll throw some clothes on."

She wrapped the towel around herself and ducked across the hall to the bedroom. The contents of her mother's closet instantly deflated her: What had felt consecrated at first glance now looked crammed and rummage-ready. She closed the door quickly. A red swatch of something stuck out, caught. She opened the door again, followed the silky hem to its skirt, then up to its padded hanger.

No, she thought. I couldn't.

But the red slip-like thing had a robe and the robe had a belt. Opaque, she reasoned, and there was no time to find a more suitable garment. She slipped the nightgown over her head, then closed the matching kimono with a firm cinch of its belt. "You still there?" she called from the top step.

"Yup," Joey answered. "Didn't meant to—"

"Me too," said an only slightly familiar male voice. Halfway down, she saw them both, two soldiers posted at her door.

"Hey," said Fletcher. "How goes it?"

"Sorry for barging in," said Joey. "I knocked a couple of times, and when you didn't answer—"

"Visions of carbon monoxide danced in his head," Fletcher supplied.

"I was in the tub," said Sunny. "I just grabbed the first thing I could find."

"Nice outfit," said Fletcher. "Are you going out?"

"I can't go out," said Sunny. "I have no car. I was just going to get started on the thank-you notes."

"He said he had to drop off a check," said Joey, "so I thought I'd better help him find your place."

"Got a pen?" asked Fletcher. "I'll take care of it right now."

"Dickie hasn't sent me a bill yet."

Fletcher said, "No problem! Just let me know when you've done the math, and I'll hop over in my—get this—new car." He walked to the black velvet love seat and sat down.

Joey cocked his head toward Fletcher. "The terrible loss of his father has been somewhat cushioned by his new Beetle and his refurbished waterfront property."

"The cabin?" asked Sunny.

"I would *not* have recognized it if the undertaker hadn't dropped me off there," said Fletcher. "I would have thought I had the wrong address. Have you seen it lately?"

"No," Sunny said.

"I'm guessing," said Joey, "that Miles was fixing up the place so that it would be their principal domicile after they married."

"I hadn't thought of that," said Fletcher.

"Because you can't believe your father was going to marry someone you hadn't met, who lived in a place you wouldn't have deigned to visit," said Sunny.

"This is charming!" Fletcher protested with a wave of an arm. "And I heard it has historical significance."

"I meant the town—a place like King George. Population practically nothing."

"Not true," said Fletcher. "I'm beginning to get a feel for it. Especially when I sit on my deck and look out at the lake. There's something quite Thoreauvian about it."

"Don't you have to get back to New Jersey?" Sunny asked.

"I don't. I'm a free agent. I'm going to relax for a few days—"

"And reflect, no doubt," said Joey.

"Of course reflect. And mourn. It's a mourning period. I think thirty days is traditional."

"Thirty days," Joey repeated. "That sounds like a good idea for you, too, Sunny: a month to regroup and—"

Fletcher interrupted to ask, "Anyone else dying in this heat?"

Joey muttered, "Jesus."

Fletcher said, "Sorry. Unfortunate choice of words. I meant was there any air-conditioning. I thought New Hampshire would be cooler than Jersey, but whew."

"Open another window," said Sunny.

Joey said quietly, "Everything's been checked and double-checked. You can crank it up as high as you'd like."

Sunny said, "I'll bring down the bedroom fan."

Fletcher pointed across the room. "Isn't that an air conditioner?"

"Sunny has some reservations about it," Joey said.

"Then let's go find an air-conditioned restaurant. Is anyone else starved?"

Joey said yes. Sunny said no.

Fletcher said, "The chief here could drive us to my car, and we'd go from there. You and me; his mother is expecting him."

Joey said, "No she's not."

"You're contradicting yourself," said Fletcher.

"You're misinformed: My mother does *not* hold dinner for me on Saturday night. Or ever."

"You pay her room and board."

"We'll all go," said Sunny. "What's open on Saturday night?"

"We could go to Lebanon, to a real restaurant," said Joey.

"Do they let you leave your jurisdiction?" Fletcher asked.

"Don't you worry about me," said Joey.

"He moonlights as a paperhanger," Fletcher told Sunny.

"I didn't know that."

"Painting, too," Joey said quietly. "Interiors only. It pays the bills."

"What bills?" Fletcher asked. He ticked off on his fingers: "You live with your mother. The town pays the rent on your office, leases you a vehicle, buys your uniforms. And correct me if I'm wrong, but policemen don't usually have college loans to pay back, do they?"

Joey crossed the room, sat down next to Fletcher, and said, "Mr. Finn and I will wait while you get dressed, Sunny. Take your time. He can look through my wallet while we're waiting."

"I'm simply being direct. It's an urban thing. I don't get high marks for tact—"

Joey's bark of laughter cut him off.

Fletcher smiled a patronizing smile. "I'm not insensitive. I just don't like to waste my time, or anyone else's." He gestured to Sunny. "Like us. I could have waited for the perfect moment to say, 'I think Miles Finn sired us both,' but who's to say that in the long run that would be a better way to approach a potentially traumatic subject? I put my cards on the table. You seem to be handling it okay."

"You don't know how I'm handling it! *I* don't even know how I'm handling it. And nothing is confirmed. It's only a theory based on a superficial impression." Reflexively, she tucked her hair behind her ears. "This weather doesn't help, either," she grumbled.

"Better run a comb through it before it's too late," said Fletcher. He turned to Joey. "We're pooling our hair tips. Which reminds me of the idea I had earlier—the kits where you prick your finger or scrape some cells from the inside of your cheek and send them to a lab."

"Look at her face," said Joey. "Does she look like she wants to be discussing DNA?"

Fletcher held his hands up as if warding off a blow. "Okay, all right. Sue me. . . . So where do we eat? Can you get decent Chinese up here?"

"Not up to your standards, I'm sure," said Joey.

"What about sushi?"

"You'll have to go back to New Jersey if that's what you want," said Joey.

"Hey, I can eat Big Macs and Whoppers very happily," said Fletcher. "Or I can order groceries on-line. Does UPS deliver up here?"

"Yes. We also have something called a supermarket," said Sunny.

"And you can always fish in your front yard," said Joey. "Going back to that subsistence thing we talked about. And the land is pretty fertile—not sandy at all."

"Sand's good for some crops," said Sunny. "Leeks, I think. And potatoes."

"A guy could live on leek-and-potato soup," said Joey.

"I hope you're planning to compost," said Sunny.

Joey laughed.

"Compost?" Fletcher repeated. "Is that a verb?"

"It's when you collect your potato peels and your coffee grounds—"

"I know what composting is," said Fletcher disdainfully. "I just don't see myself doing it."

"I don't see you doing much of anything in King George," said Sunny.

He smiled and said, "*You're* here. My baby sister."

"I'm not your baby sister. I think we've established that I'm older than you are, correct?"

"A technicality," said Fletcher. "I think you need protecting. Here, even. This"—he gestured around the room. "Who signed off on your sleeping in a house that asphyxiated our parents?"

"The board of health," said Joey.

"I don't like it," said Fletcher. "I'd prefer if you didn't sleep here until there's been some serious testing."

"There were tests galore," said Joey. "And we put brand-new carbon monoxide detectors in every room."

" 'We'?" said Fletcher.

"The town. King George. The landlord."

"What do they get for rent for—what is it?—two, three rooms? If you don't mind my asking."

"I do mind," said Sunny.

"He asks whatever he feels like asking," said Joey. "He has no sense of what's off the record."

Fletcher beamed.

"He was just bragging to me on the way over here about . . . well, let's just say, questionable behavior—never mind that I'm obliged to report illegal acts."

Still grinning, Fletcher asked, "Did you tell your friend here that you caught the guy who shot you?"

Sunny's eyes widened.

"Would you believe at The Dot?" Joey said. "He was just a kid. I recognized him, and the rest was pretty routine."

"I was inadvertently dragged into it," said Fletcher.

"You were there?" Sunny asked.

"I was caught in the figurative crossfire."

Sunny put her hand over her mouth.

"Don't listen to him," Joey said. "There was no crossfire. The kid was on the next stool, and I cuffed him, and that was that. The county sheriff took him away to Concord."

"I meant I could have been a hostage. He was using my father's house as a hideout. Luckily, we hit it off, so I wasn't in any physical danger." He stood up. "C'mon, Sun. Get some shoes on. I'm starved. I'll regale you with my version on the way."

Sunny said, "What amazes me is how you could regale anybody about anything the day after your father's funeral."

Fletcher tried to look gloomy. "You're right. Absolutely. I only meant I was going to supply the details. But then again, I am very resilient."

"Does that mean shallow?" asked Joey.

"Resilient means the ability to—"

"I know what it means."

"It was an insult," said Sunny. She said she'd have to change into real clothes. Please excuse her. "If I don't come down in ten minutes, you two go without me."

"If you don't come down in ten minutes," said Joey, "Fletcher will call the rescue squad." He smiled and touched his shirt. "Me."

With Sunny upstairs, neither spoke until Fletcher said, "She's really taking all this pretty hard."

"Most people do."

"Then again, I never knew her in happier times. Maybe this is the real Sunny." He shrugged. "Reserved. Cautious. One might even say joyless."

"Or maybe she doesn't like you," said Joey.

Fletcher stood, and walked over to the television. There was a framed picture of Sunny as a little girl in a school uniform, front teeth missing, hair springing out of an unsuccessful ponytail. "Cute kid," he said. "Too bad I missed all those years."

He perched the picture on his shoulder and managed to reproduce Sunny's uncertain smile. "Pretty close, huh Joey boy? Separated at birth or what?"

Joey said, "Could you lower your voice? She doesn't want to hear any of this right now."

"I don't get it: Who wouldn't want a ready-made brother? Without me, she's all alone in the world, which is all I'm trying to remedy."

"She has friends," said Joey.

"*You?* You're everyone's friend. Every person you pass waves like they have a parking ticket that needs fixing. You're spread very thin. I meant someone she's connected to, like me. A brother, who's in it for the long haul."

Sunny yelled from upstairs, "Fletcher? Do you think I'm deaf?"

Fletcher yelled back enthusiastically, "I'm showing the chief a school photo that could be of me. I was just saying you're pretty much alone in the world and isn't it nice that I came along—someone who's in it for the long haul."

"And what did the chief say?" Sunny called.

"Nothing. He's turning colors down here. It must be the heat."

"No it's not," said Joey.

"I'll be down in a sec," said Sunny. "Don't leave."

"I'm not going anywhere," boomed Fletcher. "That's precisely what I've been trying to tell you. I want to make amends for not only my father's—"

"Shut up, Finn," said Joey. "She wasn't talking to you."

Finally, Fletcher lowered his voice. "I'm not the enemy, pal. I'm her blood relative. I'm not going to date her, for Crissakes. I'd just like an hour alone with her where I'm not made to look the fool."

"Fine. Ask her. I'm not her social secretary."

Fletcher walked to the bottom step. "Sunny? Can we have, like, fifteen minutes alone? He could drive us to my car, then we'd have time on the ride to Babylon. The sheriff could even join us for pizza."

She came downstairs wearing that morning's Bermuda shorts and pink sleeveless blouse. An enameled butterfly—attached to a bobby pin, and obviously Margaret's—nested incongruously in her hair. "What haven't we discussed?" she asked Fletcher.

"Us. The intersection of the Battens and the Finns. I don't think you believe me yet. Maybe you're still in shock, but I think you're being very impassive about the possibility of having a brother. I would think, under the circumstances, you'd welcome me with open arms."

"Ha," said Joey.

"You can see her anytime," Fletcher said. "I'm in town for an indeterminate stay. I think it's only fair that I buy her dinner tonight. You can have her tomorrow night."

Joey stood and faced her. "What do you say to that—Mr. Finn tonight and me tomorrow?"

"Separate, correct?" she asked. "Pizza with him tonight and dinner with you tomorrow?"

"Sure. Not pizza. Not at The Dot. Not at my mother's."

She smiled. "Some other spot in Babylon?"

He laughed. "Babylon. It's been a while."

"If ever," said Sunny.

CHAPTER 20

The Missus

Mrs. Ouimet asked Dr. Ouimet if he wanted company on his after-dinner walk, generously allowing that her tender big toe would probably slow him down.

"Either way," he said in the listless voice he'd been employing since Margaret died.

"I know you're upset," she said, "but you can't bring her back. And you'll find another secretary."

"Not like Margaret," he answered.

It was one prayerful reference too many for the doctor's peevish wife. "The irreplaceable Margaret!" she sputtered. "Your little miracle worker—part nurse, part insurance whiz, part actress . . . oh, and I forgot: part surrogate wife. As if I didn't know what was going on."

He was tying the laces on his running shoes. "What did you say?" he asked from his crouch.

"That paragon! Irreplaceable! Well, now you're back where you started. Poor you. You seem to have forgotten who found that office for you, and decorated it, and who used to sit in that chair and pack your two sandwiches and kept your patients from walking all over you. Your wife! That was my job. You don't think I know you *fired* me and that you preferred her company to mine? I had to make up excuses when every single friend asked, 'Christine? How come you're not at the office? Did Emil fire you? Ha ha ha.' And I had to smile and say, 'No. Someone had to be here while we were doing over the kitchen.' Or, 'I'm a contractor now, didn't you hear? Very creative. Very *fulfilling.*' Or, 'Emil felt sorry for Margaret, who certainly needed the job more than I did.' "

Emil stood up. "And now she's dead! Your precious chair is empty. I'll bring it home for you!" His voice rose. "You and your fat ass can sit on it until hell freezes over."

The rip of insults in his own voice stunned him. Never had such rude words been spoken or even contemplated inside these walls—slurs stolen from the unwashed and uninsured.

He'd never dreamed he could sound so coarse-fibered, so cruel.

Christine's lips parted. Her left hand, with its collection of wedding and anniversary rings, flared across her bosom. Like a cartoon, he thought; like a woman on the verge of an ugly scene.

He felt rational again, and a few notches less despondent. Cleansed. He'd better spit it out while she was flabbergasted, silenced, before she returned the fire.

Dr. Ouimet stood up, put on his baseball cap with something resembling panache. "I hate you, Christine," he said.

CHAPTER 21

Life Is Simpler
Than You Think

Not until they were seated at Pizzeria Roma and had negotiated separate his-and-her toppings did Sunny state, "I think, without putting too fine a point on it, that you're probably right."

Fletcher, frowning at the wine label, looked up. "About?"

"About your paternity campaign. About Miles Finn."

He raised his juice glass of Chianti and said solemnly, "This is truly great news."

"As long as you know that it doesn't change anything."

Beaming nonetheless, he asked, "What did I say that convinced you? The grandmother who golfed? I thought I hit that one out of the park, not to mix metaphors."

"It wasn't you. I knew what Miles looked like. The possibility crossed my mind a hundred times. You just happened to be the first person to say it aloud."

"Which *fascinates* me," said Fletcher. "The whole idea that the father of your mother's—forgive me—bastard child is right under her nose and, if one believes the wedding rumor, about to make an honest woman of her. Yet nobody, not one goddamn person until I came along, was willing to say, 'Excuse me? But isn't it obvious to all concerned that Miles is the father of the wispy-haired Sunny with the low handicap?' Hel-lo?"

Sunny shook her head. "If you knew my mother, you wouldn't find it strange. She was very conventional, and very worried about what other people thought. Above all else, she wanted to fit in."

"What fabulous irony," he said, "that it was so important for her to fit in, even in a place that's barely on the map." His gaze ended at their arriving pizzas, which absorbed and silenced him.

"What's the matter?" she asked.

He called back the waitress, a woman in a red Pizzeria Roma apron and nurse's shoes, who had the no-frills manner of someone related to the owner. "I ordered the Deluxe Carnivore, which is billed as having five meats," said Fletcher. "I'm not sure I got them all."

The waitress flexed her pinkie above each item: "Pepperoni, sausage, meatball, prosciutto, and salami."

"Salami! Mystery solved. It looked like the pepperoni. Excellent."

"Anything else? Your mushrooms all there?"

"Looks great," said Sunny.

"You two related?" asked the waitress.

"No," said Sunny.

"We're working on it," said Fletcher.

Sunny waited until the waitress walked away. "Must we discuss this with everyone?" she hissed.

"Life is simpler than you think," said Fletcher. "When a waitress in a pizza joint innocently asks, 'Are you two related?' she's looking for a yes or a no. She's not trying to trace your roots or out your mother."

"Like your father didn't keep it all a big secret? He could have stepped forward. He could have asked for my birth date and done the math. He also could have paid for my college education."

"I thought you went to Delaware on a golf scholarship."

"Maryland. I did. I meant the gesture. He could have helped with the bills, helped with rent on a real house. I hope it's true what Joey said this afternoon, that Miles renovated the cabin for her, because I know how much she wanted her own home."

Fletcher said, "It has a certain updated rustic charm, but believe me, it's no place for a woman."

"And why is that?" asked Sunny.

"It's too secluded. Too far from civilization."

"I'm sure it's all yours, if that's what you're looking so distressed about—sharing your spiffy new lakeside property and your apple-green Volkswagen."

"Don't take it out on me," said Fletcher. "I love the idea of a half-sister. You're all I have now, except for one completely annoying mother. I would have encouraged Miles to do the right thing decades ago if I had had an inkling that you were out there." He leaned in to confide, "I think I always assumed he had some shady dealings rather than some big personal secret. I mean, there *was* something slippery about him—some holes in his various stories. Annoying, but at the same time mysterious."

"And now you know why," said Sunny. "Me."

Fletcher pried coins of meat from a slice and rearranged them as he talked. "My mother always suspected there was a woman up here, but he denied it."

"Are you going to tell her about me?"

"Interesting question." He squinted into the distance. "It's not like she's his grieving widow. I mean, she claimed to hate him. I wasn't allowed to mention his name, which of course I dropped all the time."

Sunny noticed, as he turned his head, that no light glinted off his fashionable eyeglasses, small ovals of black wire. "Are you wearing frames without any glass in them?" she asked.

He answered by sticking his index finger, to the first joint, through the frames.

"Did the lenses break?"

"No. I just like them. I think I look good in them. They're titanium. Here. Let me see them on you."

Sunny took them. The earpieces were pliable, and hooked around her ears.

"Wow," he said. "Amazing."

"Don't say it."

"What? 'Separated at birth'? I wasn't going to. I was merely going to suggest that you go into the ladies' room and take a look in the mirror."

Sunny removed the glasses and held them up for inspection. "You know what they remind me of?" she asked. "The prop closet at the theater, which had lots of eyeglasses—on the theory that the right pair could turn an ingenue into a librarian, or a real-life furniture salesman into a college professor."

She was twirling them absentmindedly by one stem. Fletcher reached over and took them back.

"Seriously," said Sunny. "Were you thinking a touch more intellectual? Professorial? What effect were you going for?"

"I'm nearsighted, and I have a prescription," he grumbled. "I just haven't had time to fill it. I saw these in a mall, and I bought them before I saw the eye doctor, so don't go looking for any symbolism."

Sunny smiled. "Interesting. People who need glasses are paying for laser surgery, yet you're moving in the opposite direction: fashion accessory."

"The only direction I'm moving in is better eyesight. These are my training wheels. I'm getting using to wearing glasses at the same time my audience gets used to me in them."

Sunny lowered her voice. "It's a little strange, Fletcher. If you want to wear glasses but don't need them, you might consider nonprescription lenses."

"Do you see what's happening? You're getting sisterly: criticizing me and giving me advice. Which I think is great. Keep doing it. It's *your* orientation, *your* training wheels toward full-fledged siblinghood."

"That is exactly the kind of fake fraternal declaration I was afraid of. I'm not in the market for *siblinghood*—"

"With *me*! I'm the stumbling block here. I know it. I'm hard to take. In a mate, you don't want someone who's hard to take. But that's not a fatal flaw in a brother."

"And it doesn't take any getting used to for you? No seven stages or twelve steps? No old scars? What about your parents' breakup? Nobody comes through a divorce unscathed."

Fletcher shrugged. "In the beginning I was told it was mutual and amicable and all that crap, because I was in high school when Miles left and they didn't want to damage my delicate adolescent psyche, not to mention my SAT scores. But I wasn't blind. It was clearly my father's doing."

"So you must have hated him, too."

"I took my mother's side, but at the same time she was such a pain in the ass that I wondered how he could stand her as long as he did."

"Give me an example," said Sunny.

Fletcher drummed his fingers on the table, then grabbed a laminated menu. "Okay—this: When she orders in a restaurant? She has to read back every word. So she'll say, "I'm having the 'crisp-tender rings of ocean-fresh calamari, served with our own tangy marinara.' ""

Sunny took a sip of wine, then another. "If she died tomorrow? You'd give anything to have her back, even parroting adjectives from a menu." She looked down at his shirt pocket, where a red light was flashing through the white fabric. "I think your phone's ringing," she said.

He followed her gaze down to his chest. "Oh, right. Shit. I shut off the ringer for the funeral. No wonder I haven't gotten any calls." He snapped open the phone, barked, "Finn!" then mouthed a few unrecognizable syllables to Sunny. Next he pantomimed "pen," which she produced from her pocketbook. Fletcher scribbled on his place mat, "The cand.!!!"

Then back into the phone, approximating concern: "Seriously. I *do* want to talk. I'm at a restaurant and will be finished in . . ." He looked at Sunny, who ignored the cue.

"An hour," he said confidently. "Our pizzas just arrived, looking surprisingly good, I might add—thin crust, with those nice charred blisters you get on the real stuff?—and then I'm driving her back to town . . . *Sunny* . . . no, *I* am. I inherited a VW Bug—apple-green. Granny Smith with a touch of lime." He shot Sunny a look that apologized for his feminine parsing of exterior hues. Then, "You remember—the one whose mother died with Miles?"

"His fiancée," said Sunny.

Fletcher put a finger to his lips. "I'm really glad you kept trying. . . .

Em, you're breaking up. I'll call you from my father's house as soon as I get there. You on the cell?"

Fletcher looked startled. He grimaced, waited it out; Emily Ann was, apparently, uninterruptable. "Okay," he said. "Okay. Fine. Same plan. I'll call from my father's."

He returned the phone to his breast pocket.

Sunny said, "You were looking positively robotic—a red light blinking where your heart should be."

"You won't believe this," he said, "but Emily Ann didn't go home. She went as far as Boston, then apparently came straight back here this afternoon."

"Where was she calling from?"

"That stupid motel!"

"And why is this so terrible?"

"She fired me yesterday! So if she's back, she wants to discuss it or rehash it or, God forbid, reinstate me."

"And that's not what you want?"

"Not at this juncture. Unh-uh. No thank you." He asked if she was merely resting or was she going to finish her pizza.

"Help yourself. I'm done."

"It's not that I don't like mushrooms per se, but I once heard that mushrooms were grown in manure and that killed it for me. These look washed."

Sunny pushed the tray toward him. "Why do you think she returned if she already fired you?"

"Truthfully? The woman has feelings for me—of an erotic nature, I believe."

"And?"

"I have to finesse it. I don't want any public fallout, so I'm trying to be as nice as the situation dictates."

"What's she running for again?"

"Congress."

"Do you like her at all?"

"*Like* her? No, I do *not* like her. I purposely fucked up so she'd fire me, and I had every confidence that she'd drop out of the race. And now she's back with her . . . her *issues* and her wounded feelings and her feminine problems." He grunted his disapproval.

"What feminine problems?"

"Like I care? If she put some meat on her bones, she'd get her stupid period."

"Why in the world did you take this job?"

"Money."

Sunny laughed.

"It's true. I wasn't exactly supporting myself in the style to which I'd hoped to become accustomed." He glanced at his watch. "Want to escort me? It'll be a huge favor, because she'll be stunned by the resemblance and she'll want to know what that's all about, and second, if she's still ballistic, she'll be restrained in the presence of two grief-stricken survivors. Because after all is said and done, Emily Ann Grandjean is a very well brought up young lady."

"What did you do to get yourself fired?" Sunny asked.

Fletcher said, "Trust me. You don't want to know."

"Did you embezzle campaign funds?"

"Absolutely not."

"Were you a spy for the opponent's camp?"

"Nope. Nothing like that. Nothing big-time. Nothing disloyal."

"Then what?"

Fletcher stared at what was left of the pizza. "First, let me put it in context."

"It can't be that bad if she's back in town waiting for you at the motel, unless of course she's waiting with a loaded gun."

"One of my hands brushed one of her breasts," Fletcher said simply. "The left one, I think."

"Accidentally?"

"You mean as opposed to romantically? Because it was neither. It was pragmatic. A means to an end."

Sunny motioned to the waitress—*we're done; a box*—then asked, "Why couldn't you just quit, like a normal person?"

"Contractually, the only way to quit the campaign was to be fired. And I couldn't do something merely inept because I am the only one in the Grandjean camp who recognized ineptness. And I didn't want to do something criminal. I mean, more criminal than a little randy act."

"Can't she sue you? Or at the very least prevent you from ever getting another job?"

"I don't want any more shoestring jobs running losing campaigns. I want to do something completely different."

"Like?"

"I'm going to decide. Here." He pointed toward the floor. "At my father's house, feet up, gazing out over the lake, such as it is. Make some decisions. Scribble some notes. Collect my thoughts. *Our* thoughts. I'm not contemplating a career that involves getting letters of recommendation from angry employers. And if I do? I'll simply leave the Grandjeans off my list of references."

"Collecting thoughts and scribbling notes sounds like you're writing something."

"I might. Everyone else is. People eat up memoirs. I think we have a story to tell—"

"Not 'we.' Your father died. You came to the funeral. You found a reluctant half-sister. She didn't want to argue, so she went out for pizza with you. End of story."

"Nope. Wrong. I like my version better: Two people died before their time so that their children could form an alliance. *We're* the happy ending: you and me. Orphans for about forty-eight hours, and then we find each other. If I were the slightest bit religiously inclined, I might think they're up there pulling strings and enjoying the dance onstage."

Sunny picked up the check and stared at it, still frowning.

"Hand that over, kid. I invited you. And I hope I've convinced you to accompany me to the showdown at the King George Motel, where you can make friends with Emily Ann and stand up for your little brother."

"And what exactly would I say in your defense? 'He fondled your breast, but he's still a fine person'? Or, 'He fondled your breast, but it was an accident'? Or, 'He fondled your breast, but don't worry—he does it to everyone'?"

"First, 'fondle' is way off base. Second, she practically signed off on it ahead of time. What I'm hoping to hear is 'No hard feelings. It won't go beyond this room. I'll fudge it with Daddy. Now I'm getting the hell out of here. Let's keep in touch.' "

"Forget it," said Sunny. "Especially if she harbors feelings of an erotic nature for you."

"And you think that's why she's back—I mean, you think she's asking me over for *sex*?"

"She came back," Sunny said with a shrug. "She called from the motel."

"See. You're just what I needed: a confidante and a reader of women's minds."

"Keep me out of this. All I want is to go home—"

"And crawl into bed? Because that would be depression talking. C'mon. It's only ten minutes to eight. I'll have you home by nine. And tomorrow I'll do you a favor—you name it. You can come over to the lake for a swim or we'll play a round of golf. The cart's on me. And I'll have you home in time for your dinner date with your boyfriend."

"Boyfriend?" said Sunny. "Don't be ridiculous."

With his eyes fixed sternly on hers, Fletcher said, "Men have let you down. That's my sense. I'd like it if you gave this one a whirl. Seriously. It takes one to know one. No. That's backwards. It takes someone unreliable like me to be a good judge of character, like the thief who gets out of jail and becomes a burglary consultant to police departments."

"I'm surprised. I didn't think you liked him."

"I don't *dis*like him. I mean, I think he's a yokel, but not in any objectionable way. Maybe just categorically or occupationally: New Hampshire, a cop, a big fish in a one-horse pond. None of which I see as a barrier."

"To what?"

"Your dating him!"

Sunny said, "Since when does dinner automatically mean a date? Especially two days after my mother's funeral. He's being accommodating—he knows I don't have food in the house."

Fletcher patted her hand, plucked the check from it, and said in a near incantation, "You're right, Sunny. I forgot. Life has stopped.

Life is dangerous. Dinner couldn't possibly mean a date. Men are invisible; men in uniform exist only to direct traffic outside cemeteries. . . . Mourning becomes Sunny."

"No it does *not*. I resent that."

"Look: Mom is gone. Dad is gone. It's you and me. If you help me out with Emily Ann, I'll return the favor." He pushed back his chair and stood. "And don't say 'No favors,' because you haven't begun to know or appreciate the full range of my talents."

Sunny felt twin surges of exasperation and annoyance, then wondered if this was how a sister reacted to brotherly offenses: not anger, not hatred, not storming away from the table.

But no, she thought. That took years. That kind of indulgence was only possible when there was a shared childhood; when an older sister knew her baby brother in overalls and little striped jerseys that snapped at the neck. This was the wine talking, and the occasional angle of Fletcher's face in restaurant light that reminded her of herself.

"I'll lend you my car," he offered suddenly.

"For what?"

"Your date! You won't have to be seen riding shotgun in his cruiser again."

She picked up the take-out box. "Thanks anyway, but we'll do just fine."

"He could leave the Tahoe at my place. He might even leave his keys."

"I wouldn't count on driving it," said Sunny. "But maybe Chief Loach would let you sit behind the wheel."

"I'm not a child," he scoffed.

"He might have a regular car," said Sunny. "I don't know what he drives when he's off duty."

Fletcher shook his head. "It's about you. It's about symbolism: that I'm here for you; that for once in your life, someone puts you in the driver's seat."

Sunny took a dollar from her wallet and added it to his tip. "How annoying you are," she said.

CHAPTER 22

Advice

R egina spotted Dr. Ouimet power-walking toward her house, elbows pumping, hips swiveling, a marked improvement over his funeral slouch. Since he'd started exercising, he'd never once interrupted his aerobic pace to chat or averted his eyes from some mathematically determined distant point ahead of him. The baby was asleep in the stroller, which Regina was bumping up her front stairs backward, one wide wooden step at a time.

"Let me," Dr. Ouimet called out, breaking stride and hustling to the stairs.

"Maybe if you grab the front we can just get the whole thing onto the porch."

Together they lifted the stroller. Robert stirred but didn't wake. "I remember a time when mothers could leave their babies in their carriages outside stores without a care," the doctor said. "Just a little mosquito netting to protect them, but no one needed to stand guard; not like today, with car thieves and murderers on the lam."

"I think he's okay on the porch," she murmured. "I can get dinner started and hear when he wakes up."

The doctor hesitated, looked troubled.

"Okay, bad idea," said Regina. "Let's hoist him inside."

"What a picture," the doctor clucked. "Such angels when they're asleep. Makes me wish I'd gone back for another residency, in family practice."

Regina said politely, "I take him to Dr. Kazaras in Claremont, but it certainly would be nice to have someone right around the corner."

"Good man." Then: "Is Randy home perchance?"

"He's playing golf."

"Do you expect him soon?"

Not Dr. Ouimet, she thought. Not my heartbroken internist, new to small talk and nylon running shorts. "Any second," she said.

"May I wait?"

"Because . . . ?"

"I was hoping to have a professional word with him. Something akin to an emergency. I mean, I know it's Saturday, and I respect the fact that this is his home. But I guess it's my own old-fashioned notion of the work ethic. If I make house calls, doesn't everyone?"

Regina hesitated. "I was just going to park Robert in the living room while I start dinner."

With each step she took toward the kitchen, Dr. Ouimet kept pace. It was not her habit to ask potential clients of Randy's what their legal problems were, but here was Dr. Ouimet in her house, legs white and hairless, clucking over her firstborn. "May I tell him what it concerns?" She asked.

The doctor shuffled his feet, frowned at his shoes. "It's of a personal nature," he said.

"You know that Randy does mostly criminal law?"

"My understanding is that he's a general practitioner."

"That's true—"

"And of course it may be awkward for someone to represent his own doctor, in which case he may want to refer me to one of his partners."

"They're all your patients," Regina reminded him. "But he refers people to a lot of different firms, depending on their particular problem."

He looked around the kitchen and expressed admiration for her child-safe cabinet closures. When she didn't answer, he tried, "I can sit out front if you'd prefer. On the steps, if I'm in your way."

"Don't be silly," said Regina. She took an open bottle of white wine from the refrigerator and poured them each a glass. She waited a few seconds, trying to find the words for her toast. "To Margaret," she said. "May she be playing opposite Sir Laurence Olivier now."

Dr. Ouimet forced one sip, then moaned, "This has been the most agonizing few days. But I'm not going to fall apart again. Apparently I've been making quite a spectacle of myself."

"According to whom?"

His face lost its shaky, apologetic look and grew hard. "My dear *wife*. I'm a man married to a woman who ridicules me for my feelings." He pulled out a kitchen chair and sat down heavily. "And now I've lost all sense of propriety and discretion. Here I am, crying on the shoulder of a patient!"

Regina brought a brown bag of corn to the table and sat down across from Dr. Ouimet. "Maybe doctor-patient confidentiality works both ways," she said. "Just in case you felt like talking."

He meticulously shucked one ear of corn, then two more. Finally, he asked, "Have I ever been inside your house before?"

"Not since we've been here. Maybe when the Patnaudes owned it."

"That's it. I remember a party, a large one. A buffet dinner. Several Christmases ago. They had waiters circulating with canapés on trays, which must have been a first for King George—in a private home, that is. I think it gave Christine ideas."

"We haven't done much," said Regina. "We painted the kitchen and wallpapered the baby's room, but that's about it. I was pregnant when we moved in, so I had no interest in doing anything."

"And why should you? It's lovely."

The noise of a car approaching made him look to Regina for confirmation.

"That's him," she said.

"Do you want to warn him? I mean, it might give him a fright if he thinks I'm here on a house call."

"Not when he sees you shucking corn at his kitchen table in your running clothes."

Dr. Ouimet was on his feet, right hand outstretched, when Randy came through the back door.

"Dr. Ouimet needs to speak with you," Regina said.

Randy gestured toward the living room.

"Try not to wake the baby," said Regina. "I'll start the burgers."

"Do you know what a compassionate wife you have?" asked the doctor.

———

Twenty minutes later, Dr. Ouimet fluttered his paper napkin out to the side as if it were heirloom damask, then said halfheartedly, "Nothing like a juicy burger once in a while."

"With a glass of red wine, right?" said Randy.

"You've read the literature," the doctor said.

"Speaking of which," said Regina, "will Mrs. Ouimet think you dropped dead on your walk if you don't show up for dinner?"

"I don't think she expected me back."

"At a specific time, you mean?"

Dr. Ouimet looked to Randy, who said, "Hon? Maybe the doctor just wants to relax with a glass of wine and doesn't want to hurry home."

"Fine," said Regina. "I just meant please feel free to use our phone."

Dr. Ouimet turned toward the baby with a professional smile. "You eat like a big boy," he boomed. "I can't say that I've ever seen a two-year-old eat a hamburger with the works."

"Hubbuggah," said the baby.

"He can digest the onions?" Dr. Ouimet asked Regina.

"Apparently."

"Is he toilet-trained?"

"No interest whatsoever."

"It's early," said Randy.

"He's obviously doing beautifully," said the doctor. "And if you don't mind changing diapers, why rush him?"

"His father minds," said Randy. He grinned at the baby, who was licking his ear of corn.

"Is it delicious?" asked Regina.

Robert raised his eyes, but didn't take his lips off the grizzled cob.

"I'd just as soon not see undigested kernels in your diaper," said his father.

"Dipe," said the baby, and patted his waist.

Regina noticed that Dr. Ouimet had taken one bite of his hamburger and put it down. "Can we put that back on the grill?" she asked.

"I hate to trouble you . . ."

"No trouble. It'll give it another minute or two," said Randy.

"I've recently become a convert to the well-done school of chopped beef," he apologized.

Randy said, "Not a problem. Be right back."

"He likes it rarer than most people," Regina offered when he'd gone outside.

"I used to like it *bleue,* myself, but even medium these days . . ." Dr. Ouimet began, his voice fading.

"Are you okay?"

He raised his chin and said, "I stopped by Margaret's house earlier today."

"Did you see Sunny?"

"I did. I didn't get to talk to her at the funeral."

"Except for your beautiful eulogy."

"My 'beautiful eulogy,' " he repeated disdainfully. "Ask my wife how beautiful she found my remarks."

Regina said, "I guess I know the answer."

"I embarrassed her in front of the entire community. I 'e-mo-ted.' I 'wore my heart on my sleeve.' Can you imagine criticizing someone for his heartfelt tribute to an employee? What kind of person says some-

thing like that after the fact? When the words have already been spoken? It's very cruel. Heartless, really."

Regina nodded sympathetically. "How was Sunny today?"

"Subdued. Heartbroken, of course. But still very hospitable." Dr.
Ouimet's chin began trembling.

"I should call her," Regina murmured.

"Who?" asked Randy as he came through the back door, a charred
hamburger on the end of a long-handled spatula.

"Sunny."

"I just saw her at the club. In fact, I was going to tell you that we may
have buried the hatchet today."

"What hatchet?" asked the doctor.

"The old one, from high school. Some pranks we pulled."

"Who's 'we'?"

"The guys on the golf team. We thought we were riotously funny."

"What happened at the club?" Regina asked.

"I gave my side of the story, which was that she could have been a
better sport, and I conceded that we guys could have been a little more
inclusive." He smiled. "Chet fine-tuned some of the sticking points, but
we ended up in what I judged to be a sincere handshake."

"Hard to believe," said Regina. "Unless she felt too worn down to
argue her case." She turned to the doctor. "Was her mother working for
you back when Sunny was being harassed?"

"What year?"

"It started her freshman year . . . fifteen, sixteen years ago?"

"Yes, she was. But it was so like Margaret to leave her problems at
home."

"She didn't know the whole story," said Regina. "Partly because
Sunny didn't want to upset her and partly because she knew Margaret
would go to the principal, who'd call in the coach, who'd squeal to the
boys."

"I think I can speak for the boys," said Randy. "She was an easy tar-
get, because she was so serious about everything and knew the rule
book, chapter and verse—"

"Then it's even a worse disgrace that she wasn't the captain," said Regina.

Dr. Ouimet was chewing slowly, as if it required thought. He swallowed, then said, "I do remember Margaret wearing a Lady Terrapins sweatshirt to work the day after Sunny got her letter of intent from Maryland, but otherwise she was very professional. Very discreet. *Always.*"

Randy glanced across the table at his wife.

Dr. Ouimet confided, "There's a chance—very slight, and I hate to take credit for today's summit—that Sunny was feeling a bit stronger after my visit."

"Because . . . ?" Regina prompted.

"I brought her a check, which represented Margaret's unused vacation pay, accumulated sick pay, and what would have been her Christmas bonus. A not-insubstantial amount." He turned to Regina. "This might ease your mind a bit."

"I wish you'd consulted me first," said Randy.

"About what?" asked Regina.

"Writing checks for not-insubstantial amounts."

"Why would you care if he paid Sunny what was due her mother?"

Randy looked to Dr. Ouimet, who blotted his mouth, then said, "I'd be comfortable taking Regina into my confidence. The whole town will know sooner or later."

"Know what?"

The doctor sat up a little straighter. "After twenty-eight years of marriage, I may have walked out on Mrs. Ouimet today."

" 'May have'? You don't know?"

"I did it in the heat of an argument. She is doubtless convinced that I am merely out on my walk, blowing off a little steam."

Regina reached over and picked flecks of corn from the baby's hair. "But you left. For good?"

"I didn't know it myself until I'd passed my half-mile mark—the hydrant in front of Wheeler's Garage—and then I said, Do you know what you just did, Emil? You left Christine. You said what you've wanted to say for a very long time—"

"Which was . . . ?" asked Regina.

When Dr. Ouimet hesitated, Randy said, "I'm sending him home, irrespective of his wishes to run in the opposite direction."

"You'd want to anyway, wouldn't you? You can't just leave and never go back for your stuff," offered Regina.

"I'm sending him to Marc Weiss in Keene," Randy told Regina.

"When you say 'go back,' you understand that I won't be sleeping in Mrs. Ouimet's room, correct? Or trying to patch things up. You're not suggesting that?"

"Are you?" Regina asked her husband.

"If Christine knew I was discussing such deeply personal matters with strangers . . . well, I can't even imagine the force of that blast."

"Except," said Regina, "the irony here is that Mrs. Ouimet knew a lot about us."

"She did?" asked the doctor.

"Sure. Personal medical stuff. She's the one who got all the test results back and called us. Or didn't call us."

"She's a registered nurse," said Dr. Ouimet. "In fact when I was doing my surgical rotation at the Brigham, she was head nurse on that service."

And an utterly unsympathetic one, thought Regina. Her mother had changed doctors and driven all the way to West Lebanon for her appointments because of Mrs. Ouimet's imperious gatekeeping. "Will she be devastated?" Regina asked.

"Of course," said the doctor. "As will our boys."

"Nothing has happened," said Randy. "This may still prove to be a spat. Doc may feel completely different in the morning."

"May I be frank? Now that my cards are on the table?"

"Absolutely," said Regina.

"Ordinarily I wouldn't discuss this in mixed company. But I feel as if there's been a sea change in me, that some vein has been tapped here and I can talk freely for the first time. Not that Margaret's death didn't break my heart, but another part of me has been resuscitated. And eventually I might have to testify to this in a court of law."

"Testify to what?" Regina asked.

Dr. Ouimet shielded his words from the baby and whispered, "Mrs. Ouimet and I haven't had marital relations since June of nineteen ninety-six."

Neither Regina nor Randy responded immediately. "Have you been keeping records?" Randy finally asked.

Dr. Ouimet tapped his temple. "Only up here. I remember the date because we went to Colonial Williamsburg that month, then toured Civil War battlegrounds. Our second honeymoon."

"Memorable," said Randy.

"Of course, Christine's view may well be that I haven't been keeping up my end of the marital bargain."

The baby dropped his chewed-up ear of corn over the side of his high-chair tray.

"Yuck," said his mother.

Robert bent over to study the corn cob on the floor, his arm hanging longingly over the side.

"No turning back now," said his father.

"All gone?" said the baby.

"Correct. On the floor."

"All gone," the baby wailed.

"Maybe he dropped it by accident," said Dr. Ouimet.

The baby straightened up and blinked at his new ally.

"Finish your hamburger," said his mother.

"Caw," he said mournfully.

"Cute as they come," said the doctor.

"We think so," said Randy.

"Where do the years go?" asked the doctor. He'd eaten his hamburger, bun and all, with a knife and fork, which were now crossed, tines down, on his plate.

"Another burger?" Randy offered.

"Absolutely not," said the doctor. He patted his still-convex abdomen. "You may have noticed a change for the better."

Regina felt an uncontrollable smile coming on, so she took the baby's hand and cooed some nonsense. *Not keeping up his end of the marital bargain. No sex since Gettysburg.*

I'm no lawyer, she thought, untying Robert's bib. I didn't promise confidentiality. Besides, Sunny won't tell a soul.

"Maybe I'll give Sunny a call after I put the baby down," Regina murmured.

"No bed!" pleaded Robert.

"Of course you'll send my warm regards," said Dr. Ouimet.

CHAPTER 23

Emily Ann Recants

Even though VACANCY flashed in halfhearted amber, the King's Nite office and all its units were dark, including number 1, where a blandly sleek and gleaming white rental car stood parked at an inexpert angle.

"How does this woman expect any drop-in business without even a porch light on?" Fletcher complained to Sunny, next to him in the Volkswagen.

"She doesn't want to be woken up. Besides, tourists don't come to King George. Not on purpose, anyway."

Fletcher ejected a tape from the player, read the label, and shook his head. "*Sinatra at the Sands.* Why am I not surprised? Miles had, like, three tapes in here. He who always claimed to be a big music lover."

Sunny didn't comment. She peered straight ahead at unit 1. "Isn't she expecting you?"

"She's doing wounded and withdrawn. C'mon. No way she's asleep."

"I'll wait here."

"You were the whole idea," said Fletcher. "That you'd be here to defuse things. She cannot possibly decide to sue me or seduce me in the face of our obvious and joint sorrow."

Suddenly, Fletcher was smiling and pronouncing words through clenched teeth in the manner of a bad ventriloquist. "Don't look now," he said. "Window."

A face was peeking out from the space where two halves of the beige drapes failed to meet.

"Is that Emily?"

"Emily *Ann*. You're not allowed to partition it."

"Or else?" said Sunny.

"She corrects you until you get it right. C'mon."

"Should we knock?" asked Sunny as they stood before the door.

"She's studying you intently," said Fletcher.

"How long do we wait?"

Fletcher landed two staccato knocks on the door.

"I'm thinking," said Sunny, "that if she ever opens the door, you should introduce me as your half-sister. Like immediately."

"Exactly what I had in mind." He wiggled his fingers in a coy wave, and the figure retreated. "Probably calling a consultant," he said.

"Or putting on lipstick," said Sunny.

Another half minute passed. Fletcher called her name. Emily Ann finally opened the door, wearing what appeared to be baby-doll pajamas in pale blue cotton. "Fletcher?" she asked, covering herself with dingy tan drapes.

"Didn't we just speak on the phone?" asked Fletcher.

"You said you were going to call first. Besides, I didn't recognize the car."

"Sunny Batten," said Sunny, extending her hand. "I think he did mention on the phone that he had a new apple-green vehicle."

"Meet my long-lost sister," said Fletcher. "If you turned on your porch light, you'd notice the uncanny resemblance."

Emily Ann shook Sunny's hand and said, from her funeral play-book, "Please accept my heartfelt condolences over the loss of your mother."

"Do you want to invite us in for a nightcap?" Fletcher asked.

"There's no room. There isn't even a chair, let alone a sitting area. I asked for an upgrade, but there's no such thing."

"Maybe this is a bad time," said Sunny.

Fletcher nudged her with his elbow.

"Or maybe just the opposite," she said brightly. "Maybe you're feeling claustrophobic and would like to get out."

"There must be a bar open somewhere," said Fletcher.

"There's an ice cream stand on Route 114 that used to stay open till midnight," said Sunny.

"I doubt very much whether Emily Ann eats ice cream, short of a political necessity," said Fletcher.

"Yes I do. Besides, I didn't have any dinner."

"Easily remedied," said Fletcher.

Sunny said, "Emily Ann? Did you catch what Fletcher said before? That I'm his half-sister?"

Emily Ann frowned. "Did I not react? Is that why you're asking?"

"Put some clothes on. We'll wait in the car."

Sunny climbed into the backseat. After a dry silence, Fletcher asked, "See what I was up against? That much charm and that degree of warmth in a political candidate?"

"So? No one's charming when she's angry and in pain. *And* feeling betrayed. Not to mention jobless and a stranger in a strange land."

"You are," he said. He examined the plastic bud vase mounted on the dashboard, then opened the glove compartment. He brought forth a leatherbound manual. "Now if you'll excuse me, I'm going to read about my new chick car."

"I think you should drop me at my house," said Sunny. "Sister or no sister, she was expecting you unchaperoned—if her outfit meant anything."

Fletcher tapped the manual triumphantly. "That sound I heard when I was on the highway? It must have been the retractable spoiler. Available only on a diesel."

"Don't look now," said Sunny.

Emily Ann was wearing a charcoal-gray suit with a short skirt and ankle-strap high heels.

"Ever seen such skinny legs?" Fletcher asked.

Emily Ann hesitated beside the car for a few seconds, as if not accustomed to opening doors herself.

"Entrez," Fletcher called, then exclaimed to Sunny, "As I was saying, I wanted to throw myself on top of it."

"On top of what?" asked Emily Ann, clicking her seat belt into place.

"My father's coffin. As it was being lowered into the Astroturf liner."

"I didn't mean to interrupt."

"Not at all," said Sunny. "Sometimes it's better to keep one's grief private."

"I was confessing a discovery, that I thought I disliked my father— *our* father, we now know—but death turns out to be a great psychoanalyst: i.e., feelings surfaced that I didn't know I'd ever entertained."

"Was it that way for you, too?" Emily Ann asked Sunny.

From the backseat, Sunny said, "Actually, I'd entertained these feelings when my mother was alive, so—"

"She was devastated from the first moment she heard," interrupted Fletcher, "whereas I was sucker-punched."

"Men are different from women," said Emily Ann. "It isn't just the way we're socialized, either. Our brains are different, which isn't something everyone likes to admit."

"I'm happy to admit it," said Fletcher. "It's why we're so much better at geography and math: spatial relations and mental rotation."

"You don't sound devastated to me," said Emily Ann.

"Because the Lord tooketh away, but in this case He also gaveth. I lost my father but I gained a half-sister, and don't we look like clones?"

"Is that what you're going on? Physical appearances?" asked Emily Ann.

"Turn on the dome light," he ordered.

"I have three brothers," Emily Ann said unenthusiastically.

"Older or younger?" asked Sunny.

"All older. I was a birth-control accident."

"I doubt that," said Sunny. "I bet your parents kept trying for a girl."

"Hah," said Emily Ann.

"Your old man worships you," said Fletcher. He turned the key in the ignition, put the car in reverse, and confided his disappointment over his father's choice of transmission.

"What makes you think my father worships me?" Emily Ann asked.

"Buying you a congressional seat? How many fathers do that? Finance their daughter's campaign and put their family name out there? And I noticed he didn't do it for any of his sons."

"It's free advertising. Besides, they're all happy where they are."

"Free advertising can backfire," said Fletcher.

"He means," said Emily Ann, her voice rising, "that my candidacy was such an embarrassment that any ballyhoo surrounding the Grandjean name would not sell one single stationary bicycle."

"Is that what your father does? Makes stationary bikes?" Sunny asked, trying to sound as if Fletcher had not enlightened her on the subjects of Emily Ann's trust fund, eating habits, and menstrual irregularities.

"My father owns Big John, Incorporated," she said flatly. "And every piece of Emily Ann Grandjean's campaign literature stated that fact. *Why?* Because my father thinks that when one goes into a voting booth, one votes with one's handlebars."

"I can't help noticing your referring to your candidacy in the past tense," said Sunny.

"It's over," Emily Ann snapped. She pulled down the visor, lifted the flap over the illuminated mirror. "How much do you know?" she asked, plucking angrily at her eyebrows.

"About what?"

"Did your brother tell you what happened on the way to your respective parents' funerals?"

Fletcher jumped in. "Sunny and I haven't even gone beyond dates of birth and names of family pets."

Sunny put her hand on Emily Ann's shoulder. "If you mean that unpleasantness on the airplane, I think he'd say he wishes he could take it back."

"He'd *say*? As if he isn't sitting a foot away from me? As if he's under a gag order?"

"Fletcher's not good at apologies," said Sunny.

Fletcher said, "Look, the God's honest truth about the incident on the plane is that I was just looking to do enough damage to get myself terminated. And now my fervent hope is that you don't go public. Or sue me."

Emily Ann swiveled as far as her seat belt allowed, in order to address Sunny directly. "See: Not 'I'm sorry.' Not 'I apologize.' Not 'I hope I didn't effectively destroy your future by disabling your campaign.'"

"What exactly have you told your father?" asked Fletcher.

"I lied! I didn't say I was touched inappropriately. I said, 'Fletcher quit,' and he said, 'He can't quit. It's a breach of contract.' And I said— you won't believe what I said. I actually said you were taking a moral stand. That it was just a trick to get me to resign and save me from further humiliation. *Me.* Like I needed intervention. Do you believe I'd protect him? Am I the most pathetic woman ever born?"

"I think you're being extremely honest," said Sunny. "And I think Fletcher is, too, in his own graceless fashion."

"Well, I'm furious," said Emily Ann.

"At yourself, or at me?" asked Fletcher.

"Both!"

"Do you want me to turn around and take you back to the motel?" he asked mildly.

"Fletcher!" said Sunny. "Emily Ann didn't come all the way back to King George to rant at the four walls of her motel room."

"He's not interested," said Emily Ann. "Why bother?"

"I *am* interested," he said unconvincingly.

"Have you officially withdrawn from the race?" asked Sunny.

"No! How could I?"

After a tactful pause, Sunny said, "You could have called a newspaper."

"Without a press officer?"

"One of my many hats," Fletcher murmured.

"*You* write the headline—EMILY ANN GRANDJEAN, VICTIM AND SEX OBJECT. And how do you like this irony: Now *I'm* the one my father's calling a quitter and a crybaby."

Fletcher was shaking his head emphatically. "Can I tell you why you characterized it as a simple, even noble resignation? Because you knew in your heart that it wasn't sexual harassment. You knew it was just me problem-solving."

Sunny said, "Up ahead, at the fork, you'll want to bear right."

"I swear, I never saw you as a sex object," said Fletcher.

Emily Ann turned around to face Sunny. "Tell your brother that he's only insulting me further and digging himself in deeper."

"I didn't mean you weren't attractive," said Fletcher. "And I now see clearly that in one moment of . . . temptation, I may have ruined my chances of ever being hired by a woman again."

"Temptation had nothing to do with it," Emily Ann barked. "I know where you stand, so let's not rewrite our emotional histories."

She turned to Sunny. "We spent hours and hours together—driving around, canvassing, leafleting, working late, drinking coffee from the same vessel—and there was nothing. Ever. Temptation was never on the table. In fact, I concluded what most women would have in this situation, which is to say zero interest. Way, *way* beyond no chemistry: dead nerve endings."

"Meaning?" asked Fletcher.

"That you're not attracted to women. Which I'm fine with. Completely. In fact, relieved by."

Fletcher said, less emphatically than Sunny expected and with a tinge of kindness, "Sorry, Em. I'm not gay."

"Not everyone knows when they are," said Emily Ann.

"As far as I know, I'm a heterosexual. But I can say with equal conviction that I don't let myself get involved with many women, because I do have principles. And the first of my ironclad rules is, Never ever sleep with a woman you work with or for."

"You just made that up," said Emily Ann.

Fletcher took his hands off the steering wheel to flail them in a surrender. "Hey! It's not my rule. It's the way all men should conduct themselves in the workplace."

"Are you following this?" Emily Ann asked Sunny. "He pinches my breast, then tells me what a right-thinking and noble professional he is."

"It's coming up on the left," said Sunny. "About three hundred, three-fifty yards ahead."

"How far to the green?" Fletcher asked, and laughed.

"What's so funny?" asked Emily Ann.

"It was a golf joke," said Fletcher.

"I don't get it," said Emily Ann.

"Her directions sounded like she was describing a fairway."

"You golf, too?" Emily Ann asked Sunny.

"When I can."

"She used to beat the boys," said Fletcher.

"They make the ice cream here," said Sunny. "There's an actual dairy farm behind the stand. When I was a little girl, my mother and I used to come out and stand by the fence and watch the cows."

"How little?" asked Fletcher.

"Three? Four? That age when you still find farm animals thrilling."

"I wouldn't know," said Fletcher.

"You grew up here?" Emily Ann asked Sunny.

"We moved here when I was two."

"My father impregnated her mother back in Philadelphia," Fletcher offered.

"How old are you?" Emily Ann asked.

"Same as me," said Fletcher. "Isn't that creepy? My old man impregnating two women at the same time?"

"They claim to have invented maple walnut here," said Sunny.

"Yet they found each other again? In their old age?" asked Emily Ann.

"We think they were an item the whole time," said Fletcher.

He parked directly in front of the slatted menu board. Behind the screened-in counter, two teenage girls in raspberry T-shirts stopped talking to stare at the Beetle. "I'm buying," Fletcher told his passengers. "Have whatever you want."

"I swear, nothing's changed since the last time I was here," said Sunny. "When was the last time you saw frozen pudding?"

"I don't see frozen yogurt," said Emily Ann.

"I'm going to have a banana split," announced Fletcher.

"If that's true, after a Deluxe Carnivore, I'm amazed," said Sunny.

Emily Ann said, "Appearances aside, you two seem like complete opposites."

"Too early to tell," said Fletcher.

"You should have a DNA test," said Emily Ann. "*I* would if I were in your situation. I mean, do you really want to declare yourself siblings without proof?"

Fletcher looked up into the rearview mirror and cocked his head. "*Do* we want that?" he asked Sunny.

"Neither one of us ever had a sister or a brother," she answered.

"Greatly overrated, believe me," said Emily Ann.

"Can I help you guys?" yelled one of the teenagers.

"We wouldn't even know where to go for a DNA test around here," said Sunny.

"I think, if this is the home of maple walnut, I'll scale back and have a cone," said Fletcher.

"Me too—a small," said Sunny.

"Tell her I want the lemon sorbet," said Emily Ann. "See if they let adults get the children's size."

"I'll ask no such thing," said Fletcher. "And if this is a working dairy, you might want to get a cream-based product. It's always best to go with the house specialty."

"Get a scoop of each," said Sunny. "He'll finish what you don't eat."

Fletcher restarted the car so he could lower the electric window. "Two maple walnut cones," he called out. "One *grande* and one *poquito*. And your smallest dish of lemon sorbet."

The older of the two girls, with a gold braid arranged over one shoulder, slid open her screen. "There's no curb service," she smirked. "And we call it *sherbet*."

Fletcher smiled and waved in friendly, obedient fashion as he said under his breath, "No tip tonight, little lady."

The girl held up a waffle cone and a sugar cone smartly for his vote.

"I guess I'll have to make an appearance at the window," said Fletcher.

"Be nice," said Sunny. "You live here now."

"Can't promise anything," said Fletcher.

"See if they sell water," said Emily Ann.

CHAPTER 24

9-1-1

When Emil didn't return from his evening constitutional exactly forty minutes after starting out, when she didn't see him stretching and cooling down in his usual unappetizing fashion between house and garage, Christine Ouimet locked every door. She was not going to forgive this outburst easily—not just the language and the loathing in his voice, but the public nervous breakdown over Margaret Batten's passing. Good riddance to secretaries worshiping their bosses, and vice versa. It was humiliating at best—this infidelity cloaked as employer lamentation.

She hoped he would appreciate the symbolism of being locked out, excluded, hungry, thirsty; without transportation or toilet and unwilling to relieve himself in the yard. What did that say about him? So fastidious that even on their one camping trip, when the boys were small, even in the middle of the night, he'd led them on a hike to the sanitation facility instead of twenty-five yards into the woods.

Maybe he wasn't coming back. More likely, he'd passed some patient along the way who had to describe her latest lump. He listened too readily; didn't like it when she reminded these encroachers that her husband practiced medicine Monday through Friday, at his office. Margaret, she surmised, was even better at the kind of armchair compassion patients equated with good medicine. Her own friends implied as much—never directly, but couched as praise for Emil's staffing talents. Some said "good listener"; some even used the word *nurse,* which Christine would correct. (Margaret had a certificate from a secretarial college she'd never heard of.) And while she may have been professionally gracious to Doctor's patients, she'd never been particularly warm to the doctor's wife. She'd heard it all—Margaret this and Margaret that, in life and in death: acts of mercy and clever bits of psychology she'd performed at the office; how a phlegmy, obviously contagious patient was led out of the waiting room, diplomatically shown to an examining cubicle, and compensated in the form of the latest issue of *People.*

Not that she had ever wished Margaret ill or dead. Certainly not dead. In fact Christine had been gripped in an unexpected way at the service, watching the daughter's face contorted with grief and seeing the tears of the better friends. The eulogies would have made her worst enemies cry—Doctor's performance at the top of everyone's list. She knew what people were reading into his waterworks: that he'd been transparently in love with the sweet, marvelous, albeit plain Margaret for years. And how shrewd of her to be buried next to that man, the intended—the out-of-towner Miles Finn—a beard if ever there was one.

It was ten minutes to eight, and she was *not* keeping his half of the Rock Cornish game hen warm. She'd followed her own example from when the boys were late, after promising to return from practice or a matinee by 6 P.M. sharp: She'd sit down and eat by herself. When they returned, she didn't jump up from the table the way some slavish mothers would. Her boys sliced their own meat, buttered their own rolls, poured their own milk. A small enough punishment to fit the crime of unreliability.

—

Dr. Ouimet walked home at less than his usual brisk pace, mindful that blood would be rushing to his stomach to aid digestion of his hamburger. Marvelous thing, the human body. He hadn't had red meat since last summer—another case of being a polite guest at a barbecue—but he always advised his dieting patients to be kind to themselves, to indulge their needs occasionally lest the deprivation result in something worse.

He'd gleaned from his new lawyer's instructions that he was not to abandon the house, the property, his belongings. Parallel lives, he chanted silently. *Parallel lives.* He already knew how to survive conjugal hypothermia, and certainly tonight's outburst was the declaration of independence he'd been unable to voice heretofore. This was a watershed night: One doesn't confess one's hatred, turn on one's heel, then reintegrate oneself into one's domestic routine after the customary four circuits around the neighborhood. He slowed down when he turned onto Puffton, and stopped altogether at his lamppost to pinch several dead petunias from their stems. His watch said 7:55. He noted with pleasure how light it still was on this twenty-third day of June.

No question, this would be unpleasant. He'd slip in the back door, ascend the back stairway, check with his service, change into proper clothes for his house calls even if none had been requested, and go out for a drive. There were always visits he could make voluntarily that would be no less appreciated than the solicited ones. The chronics, Christine called them in a less-than-charitable tone of voice. In fact, he was thinking fondly of the brave Albert Fournier, who had contracted polio a month before the Salk vaccine was distributed and now wrote poems on a computer with the aid of a mouth stick, when Emil Ouimet found the entry to his own home thwarted by a locked door. He tried the front door, then the cellar door, then the rusty nail underneath the back porch steps. It yielded nothing. He felt in the dirt where the spare key sometimes landed, then rinsed his hands in the sprinkler.

Annoyed, he pressed the back doorbell for longer than was necessary.

"Who is it?" Christine asked, visible at the table through the shirred curtain.

"Emil," he said, trying not to sound apologetic or at a disadvantage. He waited the few seconds it should have taken her to put down her teacup and her newspaper, and then waited longer before rattling the doorknob. "Open the door, Christine," he called.

She didn't. He moved along the porch to the picture window. She was reading. Above the headlines, he could see her eyebrows arched like those of an actress reading a newspaper too well, pointedly ignoring the man across the table.

MASS. MAN ARRESTED FOR COP SHOOTING, said the *Bulletin*. "TIP" HAS NEW MEANING AT DOT DINER, exclaimed its sidebar, under a photo of Winnie the waitress, mid-pontification. He rapped on the window.

Suddenly, Christine lowered the paper, folded it neatly, met his stare. Her lips formed, "How dare you?"

Which offense? he wondered. His declaration of hatred? The skipping of dinner? Or how dare he characterize her ass as fat, knowing about her concerns in that department and her thrice-weekly step classes.

"Let me in, Christine," he said sternly.

"Or what? You'll crawl in a window? I don't think so. Everything is locked. And I'd be very surprised if you had any kind of key." She moved the newspaper to display a collection: his key ring, *her* key ring, the discolored spare missing from its hiding place.

He returned to the door and pulled, causing no more than an unyielding click with each yank of the knob.

"Let. Me. In!" the doctor yelled, his syllables a crescendo.

"Go away," said his wife.

"Christine," he warned.

"I'm sitting here quite happily on my fat ass. And I'm not moving until hell freezes over," she answered.

He remembered his new counselor's advice. "I own this house and its contents!" he shouted. "And now I've returned. I want you to unlock this door immediately."

Christine jumped up from the chair and yanked the filmy curtain aside. "Well then," she said smartly, her nostrils flared, "you'll have to apologize, won't you?"

She had changed into a skirt and blouse and had swept her hair off her face with a zigzag tortoiseshell instrument he'd never seen before.

He forced what he hoped was an expression of reasonableness and possible rapprochement. "Open the door, Christine. We don't need to air our dirty laundry to all of Puffton Lane."

"I will if I have to," she yelled.

"I'm not apologizing through Thermopane," he answered. "And furthermore, it's not abundantly clear what I'm apologizing for, since you're the one who impugned the memory of Margaret and rubbed salt into my wound."

"Your wound!" she spat back. "Are you a man or a mouse? Not even a widower carries on the way you have in public. You're a married man, a professional, who buried his own mother without a whimper as I recall. And the first little word of criticism out of my mouth—"

"Shut up!" he yelled. "Shut up! Shut the *fuck* up!"

Never before had Emil failed to apologize on demand. And never had he used the "f" word. Christine's lips parted, then trembled. He might as well have slapped her, the way her hand flew to her face and the way she backed out of the room, unsteady and incredulous.

Even from the porch he could hear her sobbing, then the slam of the bedroom door.

Conciliatory words could have reached her ears if he'd wanted them to. Instead, he moved off the porch to the side yard and looked for something, anything, to get his wife's attention. A pebble thrown at the window, he decided, would be too soft, too apologetic. She'd think it was an invitation, Romeo paging Juliet. A pinecone hurled with all his might barely tickled the sill. He dislodged an ornamental rock from the perennial bed and launched it. It hit its mark, the screen, with a satisfying thump, and returned to earth.

"Open the door this minute," he tried one more time.

He waited on the front porch—a man without a key, without a change of clothes; without a secretary famous for her sympathies.

He looked around, wondered how loud their fight was and how much their neighbors had heard.

Too much, evidently. In an impressively short time, a siren wailed and grew closer.

Ambulance? Dr. Ouimet wondered. *Hope it's not for one of mine.*

Within seconds, King George's only emergency vehicle flew up Puffton Lane, lights flashing, radio squawking, and came to an abrupt stop in front of Dr. Ouimet's annuals.

Chief Loach stepped out of the cruiser, bullet-proof vest over an off-duty polo shirt, to mediate the least likely domestic dispute of his increasingly perilous career.

CHAPTER 25

A Place to Stay

All he's asking," Joey argued, stooping to enunciate into the mail slot, "is to change into clean clothes and pack an overnight bag."

"Where is he now?" Mrs. Ouimet demanded.

"He's sitting in my cruiser, ma'am."

"Is he under arrest?"

"He's cooperating fully."

"He's not who you think he is," said Christine. "But now the truth will come out." The door opened exactly the width of her red face. "And I suppose you think that a police officer's presence means I'm safe? Because I disagree. One can be surrounded by security and still be injured. Look at Ronald Reagan."

Joey read from his notes in order to stanch the flow of her lecture. "Dr. O alleged that the complainant—you—locked him out, at which time he tossed a rock at an upstairs screen to get complainant's attention."

"Our windows *happen* to have combination–storms and screens. The fact that glass didn't break is academic."

Joey said, "I understand. Right now, I'd like to sit down, take your statement. Maybe talk things over."

"I should have been the first one interviewed. *I* called you."

"It's all part of the record, ma'am. It doesn't matter who goes first. You were locked inside and he was outside—"

"What's preventing him from escaping and lurking in the bushes until you leave, then coming back here to storm the house, or worse?"

"Me." He motioned inside, as if the hospitality were his to dispense: *The couch would be fine. After you.*

Christine hesitated, then led Joey past the mauve sateen perfection of her living room toward the kitchen. She stopped abruptly at the threshold. "Is he handcuffed?"

"Yes," Joey lied. "I don't take any chances these days." He patted his vest.

Mrs. Ouimet asked, "Is it true you got knocked to the ground by the force of the bullets?"

"So I've been told. It's kind of a blur."

She frowned. "Are you on any pain medication right now?"

"Haven't needed it," he said, then added, "Your husband did such a good job on my injuries that I haven't taken anything since the hospital. And I certainly wouldn't be driving if—"

"Good job?" she repeated scornfully. "My understanding is that you were examined and kept overnight for observation."

"Still," said Joey. "Dr. Ouimet came right over, and he stayed for at least an hour, and he was very upset when he saw what a close call it was."

"Mr. Compassion," she huffed. "Except that charity is supposed to begin at home." She plucked the piece of paper he was carrying and studied it, front and back.

"Why don't we sit down," said Joey.

" 'Incident-slash-offense report'! That could be anything. Don't you have one specifically for spousal abuse?"

"We should," said Joey.

"I don't know if I can capture adequately the terror that seized me as he tugged on the doorknob like an insane intruder, shaking it until the whole house rattled. And then he was aiming projectiles at our bedroom window. I called you because I was terrified for my own safety." She sat down unhappily. "But I guess I have no choice."

Joey pulled out the chair opposite her. "May I?"

She paused. "Unless you want to wait in the car so you can guard Emil."

Joey pressed his lips together to suppress a smile, but Mrs. Ouimet noticed. "This isn't a joke! I knew this would happen—that I wouldn't be taken seriously. What does a man have to do these days before a wife is taken seriously? Kill her? Gun her down outside the courthouse after she's secured a restraining order?"

"I take your charges *very* seriously," said Joey. "I take every domestic disturbance seriously. I have to. If I didn't, I shouldn't be a police officer."

The front doorbell rang, several sharp peals.

"Don't answer that," said Mrs. Ouimet.

"It's probably my backup," Joey lied. "Please excuse me."

The unrelenting thumb on the bell belonged to Dr. Ouimet, who was near dancing in his discomfort. He strode past Joey, took the stairs two at a time, and was soon heard urinating forcefully and acoustically into a toilet.

Mrs. Ouimet rushed to Joey's side, frowning, one foot on the bottom step. "Emil!" she barked.

The toilet flushed.

Joey said, "Clearly it was an emergency."

"Well, that's just great. Now we have a situation: He's gained access, he's done his business, and he's ready to renew his hate campaign against me, police protection or no police protection."

Joey said, "I'm not playing judge and jury here, Mrs. O, but I don't think that lobbing a rock at a screen to get someone's attention is an arrestable offense, especially when it's the perpetrator's own house, he's in distress, and he's locked out. What would you have done?"

Mrs. Ouimet hissed, "He's dangerous. Something snapped—that's obvious. Either you take him away or I call whoever it is that you report to."

"He isn't under arrest—"

"So arrest him! You can release him tomorrow, can't you? On his own recognizance?"

They heard the sound of a toilet seat being slammed, water running in the sink, a face and neck being vigorously soaped.

"Emil!" his wife called sharply. She climbed up one step. "I'm not sleeping in the same house with you. Come down this instant."

When the rush of water stopped and Emil still didn't answer, Joey said, "I'll go up. You stay here."

He found the doctor in a pink bedroom, an unzipped garment bag already on the bed.

"You can tell my wife that she will not have to sleep in the same house with me. You can tell her that I'm packing and I'll be out of here as fast as I can." He opened the top bureau drawer and began inspecting identical pairs of dark socks.

Joey asked quietly, "Do you want me to tell her it was all a misunderstanding? That you had to take a leak badly, and that it won't happen again?"

"There's no talking to her," said the doctor. "And I have no desire to make things right. I returned because my lawyer said I shouldn't walk away from my house and its contents, but I think that's been taken out of my hands." He crossed to the closet and came back with a stiff, impeccably ironed white dress shirt.

"Do you have someplace to go?" asked Joey. "Friends? Your sons?"

"Both out of state," he said. "And my friends all happen to be married to friends of hers." He had been folding and refolding the white shirt defiantly, but stopped. "At least now, anyway."

"Now?"

"I had a confidante, but she died."

"I'm sorry," said Joey.

"So either I stand my legal ground, which I'm not inclined to do, or I go to that motel. If you'd be so kind as to drive me."

"You don't want to drive yourself?"

"My jailer has my keys and I doubt whether she'll give them up."

Joey said, "I think I can liberate your keys."

"And I'll need my wallet."

"She's got that, too?"

"It's not on the night table. I'm sure she appropriated it." He stopped, murmured, "Cuff links," and went back to the dresser.

Christine's voice rose from the first floor. "What's taking so long?"

"I'm packing the bare minimum of what I need until I can return to the house from which I'm being evicted involuntarily."

"Which suitcase are you taking? Not my leather carry-on?" she asked.

Emil looked more triumphant than aggrieved. "Did you hear that?" he asked Joey. "Which suitcase am I taking? This is my life. This is what I come home to every night."

"Emil?" she yelled. "I asked you a question."

"Go to hell!" he shouted back.

Joey walked to the top of the stairs. "Mrs. Ouimet? I need your husband's car keys. And do you happen to know where he put his wallet?"

She had ascended as far as the landing and was waving her report. "I'm finished. I assume it's confidential and that you won't be sharing this with my attacker."

"Actually," said Joey, "his lawyer will get a copy of it. Be sure it's signed and dated."

Emil appeared at his side, the garment bag in one hand, his dress shoes in the other. "Did she give you back my keys and wallet?" he asked Joey. They both looked down at Christine.

"Lawyer?" she repeated.

"What did you think happens when a wife calls 911 and the police takes the innocent party away in the paddy wagon?" asked her husband.

"Ma'am?" Joey prompted. "Dr. Ouimet's keys?"

"His car keys are on the same ring as the house key," she said. "So you can see the problem inherent in that."

"I don't know how you live with yourself," said Emil.

"If he needs to come back for more of his things, I'll accompany him," Joey promised. "Or one of my deputies will."

"You don't have any deputies," said Christine.

"Then hire a bodyguard," her husband yelled. "Jesus Christ! Give the man my billfold and let me out of here."

"Don't think I'm not calling your sons," she said. "Don't think they won't jump into their cars and race up here the minute they hear what you did."

"You do that," he said. "Then ask them which parent has always been the reasonable one, the loving one, the real mother in this family!"

"If I have one piece of advice—" Joey began. But Christine was storming back toward the kitchen. She returned in seconds and threw both keys and wallet up the stairs, hitting Joey in the chest.

"Assaulting a police officer!" barked Dr. Ouimet.

"I'm just here to keep the peace," said Joey. "Both of you. Let's go. Mrs. Ouimet—please get out of our way."

"Take my written statement," she said. "Here. Run it on the front page of the *Bulletin*. I don't care who sees it, because I meant every word."

"And so did I!" said her husband. "Shrew!"

To inconvenience him further, Christine had parked her car behind his and removed her keys from his ring.

Joey said, "I can go back inside and ask her to move it, or I can drop you off at the motel."

"Let's just go," he said.

The King's Nite office was dark, and there was only one car parked anywhere on the premises. "I'm losing my nerve," said the doctor.

"I can't let you go home. Even if I looked the other way, I doubt you're going to get your foot in the door."

"I meant about registering here. It's so . . . public."

"It's clean, if nothing else," said Joey.

"It isn't that. It's the harpy who owns this place. What do you think she'll make of a married man checking into one of her units on a Saturday night without his wife?"

"You mean she'll think you're fooling around?" Joey frowned. "Wouldn't she know that any guy cheating on his wife wouldn't check into the motel in his own backyard?"

"Not Florence Peacock! She always thinks the worst."

Joey reached under his vest and shirt to scratch the increasingly itchy edges of his bruises. "And do you care what she thinks? A mean old lady without the sense to illuminate her place of business on a Saturday?"

Dr. Ouimet didn't answer.

"Would you like to stay at my place?" Joey asked after a few moments.

"Do you mean your mother's house?"

"I meant at the station," said Joey. "I've got a setup in the back—a cot, a bureau, a sink, a toilet, cable TV, a microwave."

"Where would you stay?"

"At home. No problem. I go back and forth, depending on my schedule and whether I feel like company."

"And it wouldn't violate any police rule?"

"I make the rules," said Joey.

Dr. Ouimet turned to glance out the back window. "I could take my meals very conveniently at The Dot," he murmured.

"Well, it's not a long-term solution. I was thinking more of one night."

"What do I do if your phone rings?"

"Ignore it. Everything's being forwarded to Claremont until Monday morning."

"Then how did Christine reach you?"

"She called my house. My mother answered. And despite my having just said, 'I'm not here,' she handed me the phone."

"Sometimes there's just no hiding," said Dr. Ouimet. "Of course, Christine was always one step ahead of me. If the phone rang when I wasn't on call, I'd say, 'If it's so-and-so I'll take it.' But Christine always got there first. It made me cringe, actually: 'Doctor isn't home . . . no, I don't know what time he'll return. Dr. Lee is covering for him tonight.'" He shook his head sadly. "Heartless, really. Sometimes it was a simple matter of making one call to the pharmacy to renew a prescription." He signaled with a flutter of his hand that Joey had prevailed and should now proceed in the direction of the police accommodations.

Joey drove around the block to prolong the hundred-yard trip. "Ordinarily," he began, "it wouldn't be any of my business, but maybe it is now, since I've got you in my cruiser and your wife's incident report in my pocket. But you two might consider marriage counseling. I don't say that to the ones who are swinging baseball bats at each other, but it seems if you've been married this long, maybe you can get past this and remember what it was that got you this far."

"Cowardice," said Dr. Ouimet. He turned to face Joey. "Would you believe that a grown man could be afraid of his wife? Could feel no love for years and years, for as long as he remembers, yet feels powerless to change his situation?"

"I believe anything. The stuff I see . . ."

"And I wasn't just afraid of Christine. I worried about what my patients would say and how it would affect the boys—"

"In this day and age? You really worry that patients would care about a doctor's private life?"

"I'm not claiming to be logical or modern. I'm saying I was too worried about appearances to save my own life."

"Things could still work out, Doc. Tonight you'll have privacy and a chance to think. And—don't laugh—maybe a chance to miss your wife."

"Never. It's over. I said it to myself, and then I said it aloud. 'I hate you, Christine.' I used those very words. I don't *want* things to work out."

"I'm no authority on marriage—" Joey began.

"I'd like to rest now," said Dr. Ouimet. "Complete solitude and peace and no phone calls are things I rarely experience." His gaze left Joey's face and migrated to the sign above the doorway: POLICE.

"I'll come by in the morning," Joey said. "So why don't you stick around until I get there. We can go across the street for blueberry pancakes."

"Too high in carbs," said the doctor. "But I can choose something else." He smiled. "I love The Dot. So did Margaret. She usually ordered the LumberJill." His smile faded and he looked away.

Joey said, "It'll be okay. Someone's gonna get to the bottom of this."

"What do you mean?" he asked sharply.

"Psychologically speaking: why it took thirty-some-odd years to have a fight with your wife. Why, in the face of a lockout and a full bladder, you didn't piss on her doormat."

"Joey!" scolded Dr. Ouimet.

"What?"

After a long pause, he answered, "I'm the only doormat here."

CHAPTER 26

No Hard Feelings

After Fletcher dropped Sunny off at her mother's house, after he'd interpreted her pointed good-night stare to mean Be extra nice for the rest of the evening, he invited Emily Ann back for a drink. "I'm not looking forward to being there alone after last night," he added dolefully.

"Why? What happened last night?"

"I must've slept for a total of two hours. And no wonder: all the images of the funeral swirling around in my head. The dirt hitting the coffin. *Plop*. And sleeping in my father's bed, surrounded by his belongings. I could actually smell his aftershave on the pillow."

Emily Ann asked if he'd changed the sheets.

"Believe me, I will. First thing. I kept telling myself, Dad left here alive and well. He had no idea he wouldn't be coming back. There were clothes in the dryer and dirty dishes in his sink." Or Billy the juvenile delinquent's dirty dishes, he thought.

"I could change the linens for you if that would help," said Emily Ann.

One day earlier he would have retorted, When did *you* learn how to make a bed, Missy Em? But now he said, "Thank you. Thanks a lot."

"Is there a guest room?"

"Yes there is. A loft. Why do you ask?"

"You might sleep better if there's another person in the house."

"You'd do that?" He swallowed with the effort of his insincerity. "After all that's happened between us? After the way I treated you?" His right index finger was jabbing the radio's scan button. Emily Ann reached over and smoothed his knuckles. He knew then: The polite and politic thing to do was to act as if he liked her, to utter nothing that would stem this wave of sympathy. Sunny had been telegraphing this all evening, with every reprimanding glance, every time he sounded like the disdainful employee, the frustrated campaign manager. So as Emily Ann caressed his knuckles, he answered with a sickly smile meant to convey something approximating a sexual response.

If it had been the real thing and not a charity seduction, he'd have pulled the Beetle over to a dark spot and, at the very least, kissed her. Luckily, she didn't look too eager. He'd buy a little time—plead back roads and bucket seats; wait and see how things progressed back at his father's house. *His* house. Maybe he'd like it. Maybe she had hidden talents. She was a full-grown woman, at least on paper, who had hinted at past affairs and satisfied boyfriends. He could turn the lights off and pretend she was someone else.

They'd do it, and she'd return to New Jersey. He'd keep in touch, chipping away at the five hundred free minutes on his calling plan. Talking was good. Women loved that. With four states separating them, he could propose future weekends without delivering: ". . . as soon as my father's affairs are in order," or, ". . . as soon as I feel I can leave my sister alone." He sensed that Sunny was endorsing exactly this; that it was possible, with one act, to raise Emily Ann's spirits and save himself from a lawsuit. He guessed that her many allusions to the friendship they'd enjoy when the primary slithered to its unsuccessful end meant this: They'd fuck. The time had come. He'd send Emily Ann home happy. Well, "happy" was probably too optimistic; he'd send her away feeling something other than vengeful and litigious.

What he hadn't counted on was a disloyal penis that knew the difference between work and play.

———

Emily Ann didn't mind, except for what it said about her desirability and her failure to arouse Fletcher. He'd been polite enough to blame the deaths, his fatigue, and the psychologically unwise choice of employing his father's bedside condoms.

"I think you're being polite," she said. "I think it's me. You can't stand me, so not only am I fooling myself, but I'm breaking my campaign celibacy pledge."

"I *do* like you," said Fletcher.

"I can tell when someone's heart isn't in it," said Emily Ann.

"Maybe it's the employer-employee thing," he said. "Even if it doesn't apply anymore, it's still a powerful construct. Or it could be that all those months of restraint, and finally—"

"Is it my body?" she asked.

"No! I like skinny. Skinny's good. It's very . . . sinewy."

"I meant this." She managed to find some pinchable skin on her inner thigh.

"You're not saying that there's, like, an extra ounce of fat on your entire body? Tell me that's not what you're saying."

"Okay," she said obediently. "I'm not."

"It's not your fault," he tried again. And then cheerfully—the end in sight—"Maybe next time. On a return visit. I know you have to get home to withdraw formally from the race and close the office. Otherwise, if you didn't have to rush back, I'd take another whack at that celibacy pledge of yours." She was sitting at the edge of the bed, her back to him, affording him privacy to get something started by himself. "Especially," he chuckled, landing a dopey kiss on her neck, "if we were at a cheesy little motel instead of in bed with the ghost of my promiscuous father."

Emily Ann's spine and shoulder blades, just visible in the moonlight, produced an honest twinge of something in Fletcher—residual campaign camaraderie, he guessed. He pondered his options: Offer a drink. Offer a ride back to town. Point out the stairs to the guest loft.

Finally, Emily Ann murmured, "I never said I had to rush back."

———

It might have been minutes later, or hours, when Fletcher woke to hear, "I never really felt comfortable interrupting people's meals to shake their hands. I mean, I wouldn't want to shake hands with anyone while *I* was eating."

"Em?" he said thickly.

"I hated most of what I had to do, which is why I wasn't heartbroken to call it quits. And do you know the moment I knew I wasn't cut out for this? When we were at that drawbridge and the lights started flashing and you grabbed the campaign literature and said, 'Do you believe our luck? C'mon. Let's go. We're going to be stuck here at least fifteen minutes.' And while you were cheering for the bridge to go up, I was praying for the boat to make it through so I wouldn't have to jog through traffic and try to canvass people who didn't even want to roll their windows down."

"I hated it, too," said Fletcher.

"I didn't know I'd hate it this much. Or how bad our numbers could be. Or that it would be so humiliating," said Emily Ann.

Fletcher reached over and patted the closest bony rise. "Yeah. That part sucks. I'm not a gracious loser, either." He rolled over to his side and murmured—a childhood echo, unplanned and involuntary—"Get some sleep, hon."

———

He woke in his usual state of unaffiliated arousal, which dissipated as soon as he remembered his trouble of the night before. Emily Ann was not in his bed. He listened for sounds of human presence and heard a low murmur coming from the TV. "Em?" he called.

And then she was in the doorway, dressed in his white shirt, unbuttoned just so, legs bare, like a coy sleepover from central casting.

"Did you get any shut-eye?" he asked.

"I couldn't."

"Sorry about that. Was I tossing and turning?"

"No. You didn't move a muscle."

"Oh," said Fletcher. "And sorry about, you know—last night."

"It's not your fault. It was a terrible idea under these conditions." She gestured to take in the room, the house beyond, the ghost of Miles Finn. "Just let me say, I don't think any less of you. And I'm really sorry I said that thing last night when we were driving out to the ice cream stand."

"Which thing?"

"That I thought you'd never responded to me in any way because you were gay. I wish I'd never said that. Because now you'll think that *I* think—"

Fletcher sat up. "Jesus! I'm not gay. Is that what you thought the problem was?"

"No. It never occurred to me once things got started. I think last night was clearly my fault for having mentioned homosexuality at all, so I wanted to strike it from the record."

Fletcher remembered his long-term goal: to send her away entertaining affectionate thoughts about her champion and admirer, Fletcher Finn. He sighed and said, "Let's forget it, okay? I always have trouble on the first date, so how could it be your fault? Really. We should have left it at ice cream and conversation."

"What about the kissing on the deck when we first got back here? Are you sorry about that, too?"

"I had no problem with that," he said.

"I think what we're both feeling is that we should have waited, just like our mothers always told us to, instead of jumping into bed on what amounts to a first date." She lifted her arms and arranged them behind her head in a manner meant to be, Fletcher guessed, both balletic and crotch-exposing. "Although one could argue that we've spent hundreds of hours in each other's company, so this was, in fact, long overdue."

"One could argue," he said, his words ending in a yawn. When he didn't continue, Emily Ann ran her hands up and down her arms and shivered dramatically.

"Cold?" asked Fletcher.

"A little."

He might have offered her the warmth of his bed; he might have jumped out from under the covers and taken over the task of briskly massaging her arms. He might have said something flattering, romantic, or binding. He yawned again, then said, "That's the main difference between men and women: You're freezing, and I'm sweating under one flimsy blanket." He pointed behind her, toward the outer room. "There has to be a thermostat out there somewhere. You can turn it up if you want to."

Emily Ann said, "Here. You'll want your shirt back. Sorry to have borrowed it without your permission. And if you'll be so kind as to give me a ride, I'd like to go back to my motel now." She unbuttoned the shirt in a manner that was anything but flirtatious, balled it up, and threw it in the direction of the bed.

"Are you mad?" asked Fletcher.

"No, I am not mad."

"You're acting mad. You just finished saying it wasn't my fault."

She answered by striding over to her underwear and yanking it on as if weren't lacy, scanty, and virtually transparent. "For your information," she continued, "your problem was not last night. That only made you a touch human. Your problem is not knowing how to act the next morning. I should have expected as much, since I've spent hundreds of predawn hours in your presence. I'd forgotten that no conversation is possible until you've spoken into the microphone of a drive-through McDonald's."

Fletcher wondered why he hadn't noticed her underwear the night before. It suggested there were attractive parts beneath the lace of the bottom and the padding of the top. If she could dress and undress this easily—if she could argue and debate as she adjusted her various straps and checked her moles—then he could, too. It was now or never. He slipped out from under the covers, stretched slowly, frontally, before turning back to make the bed.

"Do you always do that the second you get up?" Emily Ann asked.

"Do what?" He smiled confidently.

"Make the bed."

"Oh. I guess so." He picked up last night's boxer shorts—patterned all over with license plates—from the floor. "How about breakfast?" he asked.

Emily Ann sat down on a plaid ottoman and shimmied her long, narrow shoes onto her feet. "I'm not stupid, Fletcher. I know you're working overtime to ingratiate yourself. But I'm not so needy that I have to spend time with a man who doesn't notice when I parade around his room stark naked."

"I noticed! I most certainly did notice. Why do you think I got out of bed? To level the playing field. Up till then I was respecting your wishes—to take the sex issue off the table. Temporarily, anyway."

"I see. Well, consider the issue off the table. Permanently."

"I didn't mean permanently. I meant until we get to know each other better."

She walked toward him, but only en route to the night table for her earrings.

"What if I could find some bagels?" he asked.

"You know I don't eat breakfast."

"Even on vacation?"

"Vacation! This is not my idea of vacation. I expected to find a grand white hotel with mountains above and a lake below. I didn't expect King George. And I certainly didn't expect the King's Nite Motel and an owner who acted as if she'd never seen an American Express card before."

What would Sunny do? he wondered. What words would work here, spoken in what tone?

"What about my guest room?" Fletcher asked.

She looked around, spotted her purse, opened it, and frowned at its contents. "What *about* your guest room?" she asked.

"It has a futon. There're probably sheets that fit. And it has a lake."

"And that is your way of saying what?"

"I wouldn't mind the company," he replied.

———

Joey's cot and bare-bones barracks reminded Dr. Ouimet of his on-call nights in Boston decades ago. He'd slept fitfully. Why had he thought that being away from home, in monklike quarters, would soothe his soul? And then he remembered: He couldn't have his own bed, his feather pillow, his white-noise machine, *and* his liberation. He'd chosen, and this was marital separation in the light of day. This was what he'd wanted. He'd get up early and read, then meet his host for breakfast at 9. He'd wished he'd said 8 A.M., but young fellows enjoy their sleep.

Joey had turned out well. He'd had a wild streak in high school. Or was he thinking of another boy on Mattatuck, the third Lussier boy? No, it was Joey whose hand he'd sewn up after some incident, some senior-class prank involving the maneuver of a car into the gym. He smiled. Boys could be rascals and still turn out all right. He thought of his own sons and his smile faded. They would have to take Christine's side. They might call his office and privately express their neutrality, but lip service would have to be paid to the sanctity of their parents' marriage, and to Mother.

He tried to concentrate on what was merely the turmoil of separation and divorce rather than that other, more acute pain and the inexpressible horror of losing Margaret.

He could have saved her. He could have banged on the door, or at least pressed the doorbell as if he were there on an urgent professional matter; interrupted their lovemaking and demanded an explanation, a resignation. He shouldn't have looked. There was the shame of that memory. And the shame of knowing that she'd glanced up and seen his face in the window, as if he were a common Peeping Tom. She had to know it was he, although the look on her face was alarm rather than recognition. And that man had jumped off of her, that lean, tall man with the body of a forty-year old, that runner, that dieter, that consumer of vitamins, his genitalia unbound and flapping with indignation.

Ironically, tragically, he'd walked away feeling that he'd done the right thing, shown restraint, hadn't demanded that Miles Finn . . . *what*? That had been the problem. He had no rights, only romantic wistfulness. Margaret had been so kind to him; had listened to his declarations; had, in a loveless period before Miles established year-round residency, allowed him to swing by after his house calls. He had said he'd accept the one-sidedness of their friendship, and her notion that hugs were chaste but that kisses meant adultery. He'd take whatever it was she could give him. He knew how she felt, though; he knew too well that his marital status was a social convenience and an excuse. Margaret did not find him attractive. Margaret did not want to have sex with Emil Ouimet, M.D., despite his willingness to cross all lines moral, religious, and EEOC. He offered to divorce Christine first. Would Margaret reconsider if he was free? If a whole year passed before they were ever seen in public? If they married first? Moved away? If he were a widower? *Anything?*

He had to tell someone soon, and Joey might be the one, although The Dot would hardly be the place for a confession. But who would be any more professional, any more convenient? And who in this town, be they counselor or clergy, wasn't a patient?

———

Dr. Ouimet accepted a small chrome teapot from Winnie but refused a menu. He waited, checked to make sure she was out of range, then said to Joey, "I must talk to you. There are things I should have told you that are tormenting me."

"Here? Or did you mean later?"

The doctor checked the booths on either side of them, then whispered, "I went to Margaret's house the night she died. I was on a house call—well, a trumped-up one. Fred Sturgess had a kidney stone, and truthfully, the renal colic was over when it passed into his bladder. But it was an excuse to get away." He winced. "I never betray doctor-patient confidentiality, but I thought you'd want to know every detail."

"Or maybe not," said Joey.

"I drove to the golf course and turned off the road. And when I got to Margaret's house, I saw his car—"

"Whose car?"

"That goddamn Bug! Finn's."

"Which night was this?"

"The night she died!"

"Okay, look. I'm going to suggest that we move this conversation across the street—"

"I saw them!"

"Mrs. Batten, you mean? Did you enter the house?"

"No. The front door was open. I heard . . . noises." He swallowed several rapid breaths.

"What kind of noises?"

"Giggles, moans. Noises one would emit during intimate relations, especially pleasurable ones. I don't think I have to paint you a picture."

"No," said Joey.

"I should have walked back to my car and driven away, but I didn't."

"You stayed?"

"I stayed. I very quietly withdrew from the porch. I went around to the side of the house." He met Joey's gaze directly. "To another window. Behind them."

"Doc!"

"I did. Just what you're recoiling from. I acted as if I were a common Peeping Tom."

"Doc, if you're going to tell me something that could link you in any way to their deaths, criminally—"

"I'm a sick man! That's what I'm telling you. I worshiped Margaret. All of that made me desperate and curious, and it made me do something I never thought I was capable of."

Joey leaned closer. "Emil, this is serious. This isn't something you confess at the local diner."

"I have to! I have to tell you everything I did so you can tell me if I could have saved her."

"Shh. Calm down. If you don't want Winnie dialing 911, then just take a sip of your tea and tell me calmly and quietly what you want me to know."

"I saw them!" He closed his eyes.

"Alive?" Joey whispered.

The doctor opened his eyes. "Of course alive. Very much alive!"

Joey did a quick check behind him for eavesdroppers. "And can you tell me what this is leading to?"

"I watched."

"You mean, through the window? You just watched? That's what you had to confess?"

"I didn't interrupt them. I didn't kick him out. I watched as if I were paralyzed. I stood outside the window prowling, lurking, skulking . . ."

"But you walked away. You had nothing whatsoever to do with their deaths, right? They were alive, breathing, having sex? You left, and next thing you know, you got a phone call saying they had died, right?"

"Worse! I heard it at the breakfast table. From my wife, without a shred of compassion in her voice!"

"Doc, you drove to her house because you've been carrying a torch for Margaret for years, correct? You saw her fiancé's car—"

"Alleged! That was never formally announced!"

"Okay, alleged fiancé. You went to the door—at what time?"

"Eight-thirty; nine at the latest."

"Okay: a very decent hour, on your way home from a house call. You don't want to be seen, so you move around to a side window. You watch them having sex, and you don't interrupt. Neither party calls me to report anything amiss. You leave, no doubt devastated, and you go home. Correct?"

Dr. Ouimet blotted his eyes with a paper napkin, then blew his nose. "Except for one thing, which I'd like to confide to you off the record, something I did that links me to the site. I wanted to come to you before your investigation brought you to me."

Joey said, "Emil. There *is* no investigation. The autopsies were conclusive. The deaths were ruled accidental: carbon monoxide poisoning. There was a crack in the heat exchanger. The air conditioner tripped the thermostat. Case closed. So if you're going to confess what I think you're telling me, some private act that had nothing to do with their deaths, then I wish you wouldn't."

"I should have stopped them," he whimpered. "If I hadn't been so timid. If I hadn't been so . . . fascinated. Or so weak . . ."

"Doc, what difference would it have made? You'd have taken a swing at Miles Finn and at best sent him packing. So what? Margaret would have gone to bed alone and still would have died in her sleep. I think I know what you're getting at—you watched, you got a little excited, you left some evidence, right? But what you did behind Margaret's house is not illegal. Believe me. Every teenage boy in America would be in jail."

"But I thought—we both watch the news—what if someone found my DNA at the scene and I had never mentioned being there that night? Or my shoe prints were found leading around to the bedroom window, or my tire tracks in the driveway?"

How much longer can I listen to this without cracking a smile? Joey wondered. Before choking on my coffee?

Dr. Ouimet continued, "I know I can trust you, and I know as a doctor and a man of science that what I did was not an aberration. I always tell my patients who are feeling me out on the subject—"

Joey covered his face with his hands.

"If you'll permit me to continue, Joseph," the doctor chided.

Joey managed, "Go ahead, but I gotta tell you, I don't really need to hear it."

"It didn't happen at the window, as you may be imagining, which to my mind would have been the moral equivalent of renting an X-rated video. It was a very private act, away from the house, in a very dense thicket of bushes . . . into my own handkerchief."

Joey by now was patting the doctor's forearm, hoping to thwart the unbosoming. "That's enough," he said. "I'm not a priest. I know you've suffered a terrible shock and you need to tell someone everything, and I don't want to hurt your feelings. But this isn't in my job description. If you need to talk about it, you should talk to a professional."

"There's nothing left to tell," said Dr. Ouimet. "That's all there is. I'm a man like any other. I wish I had interrupted them." His voice changed to a gravelly whisper. "Because maybe he would have left, and I would have comforted Margaret and confessed my feelings, and might have been invited to stay—even in a chair in the parlor. And I would be out of my misery now."

"You don't mean that," said Joey. "C'mon. You're upset—"

"What do I have now? You tell me one thing I have to live for."

"Your kids," said Joey. "And your patients. What would this town do without you? And even though you just had a terrible fight with Mrs. Ouimet, you have her. She'd come running if she knew what you were saying."

"I'm talking about having someone to love."

Joey said, "I don't want to be cruel, Doc. But I think you might not have a good grip on where Margaret stood in all of this. I know you loved her—you've told me ten times in the past twenty-four hours. But she was engaged to another man. Maybe, because she died, you've talked yourself into another scenario."

"He wasn't right for her. I'd have been there when that crumbled. I was willing to wait. Even though she didn't reciprocate my feelings, she never gave her notice. She was by my side every day. Whatever you want to call that—friendship, companionship, administrative assisting—it was what I lived for."

Joey said quietly, "Doc, c'mon. Let's you and I go for a ride somewhere, find some nice soothing place where we can talk and review your options."

"The cemetery," he said.

"I was thinking maybe I could drive you to one of your sons' houses. Does either one have an extra bedroom?"

"Peter does."

"And where does Peter live?"

"Too far. Providence. I have rounds tomorrow morning. And a full office schedule. At least a dozen camp physicals."

"Mrs. Ouimet can cancel anything that needs canceling. I bet she'd love to jump back into that saddle."

"Or Sunny could," said the doctor weakly. "I offered her Margaret's old job. She could start tomorrow, even if I'm not there. All she'd have to do is come in early and call the patients—"

"No," said Joey, more sharply than he'd intended. "You're going to stop making Sunny offers, and you're going to stay away from that house."

"Joey!" said Dr. Ouimet. "I'm deeply hurt. I don't think I deserve that."

"Deserve what?" asked Winnie, suddenly at their elbows with a coffeepot.

"We're having a private conversation here," said Joey.

She cocked her head toward him. "The chief used to think I should mind my own business, but he's come around since I fingered his perp." She stared at Dr. Ouimet for a long, diagnostic moment, then asked Joey, "He okay?"

"He's a little blue. Understandably. I'm going to drive him home."

"Or maybe to a place where they have . . ." She mouthed, *antidepressants.*

"I'd appreciate it if you didn't feel the need to share this with your public," Joey said quietly.

Winnie leaned in and said, louder than necessary, "Doc? Anything else? More hot water?"

His lips trembled. "I hope not," he said.

Winnie patted his shoulder. "I'll get your check, hon," she said.

CHAPTER 27

Things Are Looking Up

Mrs. Loach ironed Joey's shirt and was pleased to be enlisted. It was new, short-sleeved, of muted grays and blues, a print too splashy and a size too big, she thought, but handsome. Soft but breathable; that must be the rayon. Rayon amazed her these days. She did her best job, even with Joey butting in to snap, "Gotta go, Ma. That's good enough."

She suspected, from his choice of shirts and the gift-soap smell about him, that he was meeting a woman. "I'm assuming you won't be eating at home tonight," she said as nonchalantly as she could.

"I'll pick something up," he said.

"Are you going out with a friend?"

"Kind of."

"Someone new?"

"Yes and no."

She sat the iron upright on its heel. "Do I keep guessing or do you tell me?"

"Oh. No big deal. Didn't I say? It's Sunny Batten."

Mrs. Loach understood it was best to disguise the fact that she was tickled. "How is that poor girl getting along?" she asked.

"It's hard," said Joey.

"Does she have family up here? Grandparents? Aunts or uncles?"

"Not that I know of."

"Did you see any out-of-state license plates at the cemetery?"

"A few." He helped himself to the shirt before she had turned the dial to OFF.

Mrs. Loach mused, "Margaret could easily have parents who outlived her. If she was fifty-seven, they could be in their late seventies."

"I've never heard any mention of grandparents."

"From Sunny, you mean? In recent conversations?"

"Correct," said Joey.

"I know you've been helping her out," prompted Mrs. Loach.

"People usually need help after their mothers die in freak accidents." He smiled. "I know *I* would."

She tapped his shoulder, meaning: Turn around; inspection.

Joey said, "What? Something's wrong. Why are you looking at me funny?"

"Are you going like that?"

He plucked his shirt away from his chest. "How shocked can you be if you just ironed it?"

"I meant your dungarees.... Don't you think a nice pair of chinos would be more suitable for dinner?"

"No, I do *not*," he said.

She followed him downstairs, through the kitchen, across to the screen door. "If anyone calls?" she prompted. "I'll tell them you'll be back ... at what time?"

"No one will call. Everything's being forwarded to Claremont."

"Joey?"

"What?"

"Her house. Is it safe? I mean, is there any chance there's still poison in the air?"

"No chance. Besides, we're going out."

"Where?"

"Haven't decided yet."

From the porch, she tried, "You wouldn't wear your vest, would you? No one would see it under that roomy shirt. And I'd feel so much better."

He scratched his chest. "Itchy. Besides, once a week I'm supposed to air it out."

"Oh, you," she said.

———

Sunny's dress was silky, navy blue; it showed her arms, showcased her legs. Almost lost in her hair, silver earrings like little wind chimes dangled. "You look nice," he said.

She looked down. "Same dress I wore to the wake. I think Mrs. Dickie Saint-Onge was horrified by it."

"Why?"

"Sleeveless. Not black. Probably too short."

"I disagree," said Joey. "I go to funerals and wakes all the time, and I see people in the funeral party wearing purple sweatpants and Hooters T-shirts. You look very proper."

Sunny murmured, "Then maybe I should change."

He smiled neutrally, waited for clarification. Had he heard her correctly? Was she saying, Last thing I want on a date with you, Joe Loach, is to appear proper? Or was she alluding to his open collar, his dungarees? "Don't change," he said. "You look great."

"So do you," said Sunny. "I knew sooner or later I'd catch you out of uniform."

Best behavior, Joey scolded himself. Accidental double meaning. No jokes. "Would you believe that my mother wanted me to wear my bullet-proof vest?" he asked.

"Where did she think you were going?"

"Into harm's way. *Always* into harm's way."

"Where *are* we going?" she asked.

"A new place. Well, new since you've been gone."

"Named?"

"La Quiche. It's French. It's usually pretty quiet."

Sunny gestured in spokes-model fashion to the china cupboard that had become her mother's unprepossessing bar. There were shiny chrome utensils on a dish towel next to a pair of martini glasses and a half-empty, clouded jar of olives that must have garnished the drinks of Margaret's gentlemen callers. "I've never made a martini, but there was a recipe booklet in the set. They were something of a rage at Harding faculty parties. Do we have time?"

"Sure," he said. "No hurry."

"No reservation, right?"

"None," said Joey. "In fact, I never get behind the wheel until I metabolize the alcohol."

"You're an exemplary citizen," said Sunny.

"I have to be," he said.

She gave the martini shaker a few gentle tilts, smiling self-consciously. She attached a strainer, filled two glasses, fished out four olives with a two-pronged fork.

"A toast," she said.

He waited; watched her face sink into melancholy, then struggle back to a shaky, hospitable smile.

"C'mon," he said. "We're going to have a nice evening. We're going to make an optimistic toast and try to forget the last couple of days, which I mean as no disrespect to your mother." He raised his glass. "To a long life. And to things looking up."

"To things looking up," echoed Sunny.

They clinked their glasses. Sunny stared at him intently, appraisingly, until he asked, "What?"

"Nothing."

"Then don't be rude. Drink up."

"Your eyes are actually hazel," she said. "I was under the impression they were brown."

Joey grinned. "Are you leading up to a compliment?"

She took a sip and said, "Whoa. Strong."

Joey said, "Perfect. You're a natural."

Sunny turned the gin bottle to inspect its label. "My former boss, two jobs ago, used to tell the waiter, 'Very, very, very dry. That's three verys.' He also specified the brand of gin, and once canceled the order because they didn't have Bombay Sapphire."

"Was this something you observed over dinner with this ex-boss?" Joey asked.

"Twice: my welcome-aboard dinner and my farewell/no-hard-feelings dinner."

"Nice guy?"

"Not bad. Very boring. All he could talk about was Harvard. He went there, and his wife, naturally, went to Radcliffe, and his kids, thank goodness, all got in. It came up six times in every conversation."

"I never do that," said Joey.

Sunny smiled and handed him a cocktail napkin. It was printed with a bowling ball and three white pins dancing in mid-air. "Shall we sit?" she asked.

There was only one choice, the black velvet love seat. Joey gestured: *You first.* When Sunny took one extreme end, he anchored the other.

"Mrs. Angelo sent a cheese tray," she said, and popped back up.

"Later," said Joey. "Sit."

She did, a body's width closer. "I think Dot and Gus assumed I'd be having people back after the service. I told them I wasn't, but then I found this giant tray—three or four kinds of cheeses, crackers, red and green grapes—on the porch."

"They feel terrible," said Joey. "Everyone does. People even call me to see what they can do."

"And what do you tell them?"

"I tell them to make a donation to the memorial scholarship. Or send a card. Or give you a little time, then call."

Sunny looked toward the kitchen. "The answering machine still has my mother's message on it. I don't necessarily want to pick up, but her voice startles me no matter how many times I hear it."

"We can fix that right now," said Joey.

Sunny shook her head.

He stirred his drink with his skewered olives, and tried to think of a topic that didn't lead to Margaret. He glanced over and she smiled.

Embarrassed, both looked away. Joey, after another silence, asked if she liked to fish.

"Fish?" asked Sunny.

"The water temperature's just right now. There's some great trout fishing up here."

She touched one of her earrings, freeing its silver drops from a tangle of hair. "I like to *eat* trout," she said. "If that's a prerequisite."

Joey said, "Not necessarily. But that's good to know."

"Blackened," said Sunny. "Or amandine."

"Or smoked," said Joey. "But that requires a smoker."

They sipped their drinks in silence until Joey asked, "Has Finn turned up again?"

"Fletcher? Not since he dropped me off last night."

"How was that?"

"He's trying. I mean, in his own fashion, which is to say, studying the brother handbook. He treated. And he was intent on loaning me the Beetle tonight."

"Why?"

"An unmarked car to go out to dinner in, maybe? He said we could drive over to the lake and get his Bug."

"Would Fletcher be part of the deal?"

"No. Not invited."

"Does *he* know that?"

Sunny said, "He's busy."

"I'd just as soon take the Tahoe," Joey said. "If that's okay with you. I mean, it's fifteen minutes to the lake, which would add a half hour on to dinner."

Something in her face changed. He reached over and touched her wrist. "That wasn't what I meant. It came out sounding as if I wanted to rush home."

"It's fine. Really. It was a stupid plan." She stood up and walked to the bar. On shelves beneath it were a turntable and a stack of albums. Sunny said, "I thought I'd put something on, if you don't mind Broadway musicals in a time warp."

Sunny sat on the floor and read, her head tilted sideways, *"Annie Get*

Your Gun. Brigadoon. West Side Story. South Pacific. Camelot. My Fair Lady—original cast recording or movie soundtrack. *Oklahoma! The Sound of Music. Half a Sixpence. Bye Bye Birdie. Funny Girl. Funny Face. A Funny Thing Happened on the Way to the Forum.*"

"You pick," said Joey.

He couldn't tell what her choice was until she placed the needle on the record's surface and one inadequate speaker spit forth the overture to *My Fair Lady.*

"They gave the movie role to Audrey Hepburn," said Sunny. "Supposedly it broke Julie Andrews's heart."

"Come sit," said Joey.

They listened politely, Sunny once again at the far end of the love seat.

Between overture and first cut Joey said, "I'm lucky they let me use the cruiser for personal time at all. Some municipalities restrict their fleet purely to police work. And, of course, for commuting."

"Shocking," said Sunny.

"Which means if I worked in Nashua, let's say, or Concord—and, I think, Manchester, Merrimack, and Portsmouth might be in that category—I'd need a second car."

"Although tonight would probably qualify as duty, don't you think?" Sunny asked. "A follow-up home visit to the daughter of the deceased, collecting evidence, checking the furnace and the air quality?"

"I think I know what you're asking," he said.

Sunny added, "You'd probably earn overtime now that you have to stick around until your alcohol metabolizes."

Joey rubbed his face and smiled. "Are you asking if this is a date?"

She put her glass down, crossed her legs, uncrossed them, stared at the expanse of limb, slipped off her navy-blue flats, bent over to touch her toenails, and came up frowning. "I don't think the polish was totally dry when I put my shoes on," she explained.

Joey wanted to laugh. He also wanted to run his palm down one smooth leg and up the other.

"I don't suppose you want a refill," she said, "which would make you a virtual prisoner of your blood-alcohol content."

"Is it all mixed?"

Sunny said, "I doubled the recipe."

"No hurry. When I finish this one. Which is to say, I'm in no hurry. I'm here as a matter of personal preference and free will."

"I caught that," said Sunny.

"Nobody has to put a label on it, though, right? We're listening to music in your melon-colored living room and talking."

"It's caviar," said Sunny.

Joey pointed to her feet. "I must say, though, I took it as an excellent sign that you painted your toenails caviar for the occasion."

Sunny reached down and put her flats back on.

"On the other hand, I know the timing is lousy," Joey offered. "You're probably still in shock—all this talk of dates and such coming from the guy who delivered the worst news you ever heard."

Sunny said quietly, "I'd feel better if I *were* in shock."

"Better about what?"

"Me. My character. My reaction."

"To your mother's death? You're saying that you want to feel worse than you do?"

Sunny closed her eyes. "Would a truly grief-stricken daughter go directly from the cemetery to the golf course? Or, between the wake and the funeral, give herself a pedicure? Or put an egg-white mask on her face this afternoon? From her late mother's eggs?"

Joey said, "Come here."

Sunny slid to his side. He put his arm around her shoulders. "I deliver a lot of bad news—too much. And everyone's different. The ones who scream and beat their breasts aren't necessarily the most loyal spouses or the most devoted kids. Believe me, I see all kinds of stuff. I think people need to do normal things, like hit a bucket of balls or mow the lawn, after they get terrible news. It gives them a routine, and reminds them of how life might be again someday."

"Or maybe I'm an incredibly shallow person who, in the face of tragedy, thinks only about herself."

"Keep going," said Joey. "Hit me with your best argument. Because so far I'm winning this debate."

"I meant this," said Sunny, moving her index finger back and forth between them. "Tonight. Is this the dictionary definition of mourning? Did I invite my mother's friends back after the funeral for cheese or crackers or a candlelight vigil? Or did I invite one very attractive man over for cocktails?"

"Me?"

"Of course you!"

Joey sat up straighter. "How does that make you shallow? I started it. I don't offer my services to every person who comes to town for her mother's funeral. I thought it was obvious—the police escort every time you left the house, the station flag at half-mast. And who asked who out for tonight?"

"First of all, Fletcher arranged it by saying, 'Have pizza with me tonight and Joey tomorrow.' I couldn't read anything personal into *that* invitation, could I? Second of all, this isn't an ordinary death. Of course you'd have to get involved and investigate and put up police tape and squire around the loved ones."

Joey smiled. "How old are we?"

"Thirty-one?"

"So let's be direct. Is there a boyfriend back at home?"

Sunny said, "Hundreds."

"That was a joke, right? The coast is clear?"

"Embarrassingly clear."

"I figured that much. I figured that a boyfriend would have jumped on the first plane and would be here for the wake and the funeral, and would be keeping you company during your travails. And would be here now. Where a boyfriend would be: here." He pointed to his own lap.

"And have we established whether or not *your* coast is clear?"

"We never discussed this? How my wild oats were behind me since I became a pillar of the community and chief law enforcement officer, especially since there's only one, closely watched motel in town?"

"Which doesn't mean you haven't settled down with a female pillar of the community."

"I haven't."

"Hard to believe," she murmured.

"And why is that?"

Sunny tilted her head, narrowed her eyes. "A nice-looking, hazel-eyed boy like you? With flattering shirts, civic pride, a company car—"

"Who lives with his mother and works seven days a week; who doesn't even come across a single woman in the course of the day unless she's driving drunk?"

"Please. Those days are behind you—the woman shortage. You're a celebrity now. Superman. You can bet I wasn't the only one who noticed you naked from the waist up on television."

Joey threw his head back and laughed. "I've been busy. I haven't had time to read my fan mail, let alone answer it."

When Sunny didn't smile, he said, "I was kidding! I didn't get any fan mail. Everyone but you shut off the TV when Channel 9 showed me naked."

"Hardly what I'd call naked," she murmured.

"I meant, you know—my hematomas."

Sunny asked, "How *is* that badly bruised famous torso of yours?"

Do I show her? he wondered. Do I undo a button? Two? He sneaked a glance. She looked concerned. Better than concerned. Interested. Inclined.

These are my options, he thought: Kiss her; or don't. Wait. How long has it been since her mother died? Five days? Don't blow it. Assume nothing. Assume no interest except that of a grateful taxpayer for her chief of police. Expect the next sentence out of her mouth to be: I'm flattered but not interested. I'm seeing someone. I'm getting married next month. I'm gay. I'm moving to Seattle. I'm suffering from a terminal illness that I forgot to mention in all the commotion.

"What are you thinking about?" Sunny asked.

Joey removed his arm from her shoulders. "Truthfully? I'm trying to figure out what to do next. I don't want to get us into an awkward situation where you have to explain how I misread the cues, and you're vulnerable, and even though you like me very much as a friend, it's getting late."

Sunny began shaking her head halfway through his speech. "This is *exactly* what I was saying: People don't know how to treat me, because of the mixed messages I send. One minute I'm weeping and the next minute I'm shaking martinis. Do I stay home? Go out? What do other people do? What would a grief counselor tell me to do?"

Joey said, "You know what I think a grief counselor would say? That if something makes you happy, you should do it, regardless of the timing, because nothing is going to bring your mother back."

"That's the modern argument. But in some cultures, there's a week of mourning and prayer, or maybe it's a month. I forget. And some people don't date for a whole year."

"I think that's for widows," said Joey. "I think daughters can date as soon as a nice bachelor comes along."

Sunny smiled. "I think I read that in the Old Testament."

"And this might be self-serving," he continued, "but your mother liked me. I think she would have approved. We know she had a pretty healthy social life of her own—ahem—and she would *not* want you to follow any religion that prohibited making out on her couch just because she died there."

She tucked her hair behind her ears, then leaned back against his arm.

Still, he waited. He remembered this was the Sunny from study hall, straight of spine and A in conduct. He leaned in with every intention of dispensing the respectful, consoling kiss that her orphan state required. But that was seconds before their lips actually touched; before she kissed him back; before they shut the door and closed the blinds; before Rex Harrison finished singing or dinner was forgotten or La Quiche was closed. Hours before Mrs. Loach, across town, checked her bedside clock and fell reluctantly to sleep.

CHAPTER 28

No Secret in King George

Emily Ann had hoped for press coverage, but her dropping out of the race was greeted with more equanimity and fewer column inches than she would have dreamed possible. When Representative d'Apuzzo issued a statement praising her quixotic public spirit and her plucky idealism, one lone reporter bothered to track her down in King George, and then only for comment on her opponent's choice of adjectives.

Had anyone bothered to ask, she would have labeled her stay a retreat, which she hoped would be understood in the meditative rather than the military sense. No one, she reasoned, would believe that Emily Ann Grandjean, Nantucket summerer and St. Bart's winterer, would choose King George, New Hampshire—no spa, no beach, no craft galleries, no darling cafés offering gourmet take-out, no concierge—as a vacation destination.

Fletcher, on the other hand, seemed to her annoyingly content. If anyone asked what drew him to this speck on the map, he could answer without spinning: a father to mourn, a history to reconstruct, a grave to visit, a house to inherit, a car to wax, a sister to adopt, a book to write.

After several breakfasts alone—Fletcher slept till all hours—Emily Ann met a potential friend at The Dot, an older woman, who noticed her tennis racket and her *Wall Street Journal*. Fran Pope, dressed in tennis whites, made the overture, asking Emily Ann to join her in her booth and finding a way to slip her Republican State Committee credentials into the conversation. Even before Winnie had warmed up their coffee, Mrs. Pope asked, "Are you by any chance interested in theater?"

"Of course," said Emily Ann.

"Have you ever acted?"

"Not on a stage," said Emily Ann.

"And aren't you, coincidentally, a lawyer?"

"Why 'coincidentally'?"

"Our local group is doing *Inherit the Wind*," said Mrs. Pope, "and we need women. The courtroom is jammed with spectators."

"I'm no actress," said Emily Ann. "I learned that on the campaign trail. Besides, I don't know how long I'll be in town."

Mrs. Pope appeared stumped, but only momentarily. After a sip of black coffee, her recruiter's smile returned. "You know what would be an enormous contribution yet wouldn't take any time at all?"

"What?"

"A consultant." She patted Emily Ann's hand. "Of course you know it's the Monkey Trial, with Clarence Darrow and William Jennings Bryan, and with men wearing straw boaters? Well, just the way soap operas have a doctor on the set to make sure no X ray is read upside down, we'd be looking for the judicial equivalent."

"You're not rewriting any dialogue, are you?"

"No! Heavens no. I was thinking of gestures, objections, when to sit, when to jump to one's feet. Body English. Those little moments that make an attorney come to life on the stage."

"No thank you," said Emily Ann.

Mrs. Pope tried again a few days later, on their first official outing.

The two women were waiting on a bench on a knoll above the one municipal tennis court that had a net. "Have you given any more thought to joining our group?" she ventured.

"No," said Emily Ann.

"I talked to some Players—we're the King George Community Players—and they agreed it would make such a difference if we had something like a verisimilitude coach."

Emily Ann asked, "Isn't your son an attorney?"

"My son," said Mrs. Pope proudly, "is a combination workaholic, public servant, and golf addict. Which doesn't leave any time for the performing arts. Or for his mother."

"Is he married?"

"Yes," said Mrs. Pope.

"Do you like her?"

"She's a sweet girl." She paused. "Italian. Former schoolteacher."

"Are they happy?"

"They seem to be. Randy's doing very well. He has a partner, a receptionist, and a secretary who's studying to be a paralegal."

"Can't one of them help you with *Twelve Angry Men*?"

"Twelve angry men?" Mrs. Pope repeated.

"Isn't that what you told me? Your play?"

"No, but how funny that you would mention that. We considered staging it, but we don't have twelve men—angry or otherwise. In any event, my point is we'd very much like you to join us. We think you'd fit in very nicely, and we're prepared to offer you the title assistant director."

Emily Ann nodded toward the teenagers on the tennis court. "Do they know we're waiting? They could be fooling around here for another hour."

"I know the girl. She'll lose interest in five minutes." Mrs. Pope reached into her canvas bag for a bottle of water, the slightly obscure brand that Emily Ann favored.

"You can get that here?" Emily Ann asked.

"Easily. At Foodland, our supermarket." She handed the bottle to Emily Ann. "Please. I have a spare."

After a passionate swig, Emily Ann asked, "So what would legal consulting involve? Watching one rehearsal?"

"Or two. Whatever time you could donate."

"Couldn't you just rent the movie? Or tune in to Court TV?"

"We could, I suppose . . ."

"Besides, I wasn't a prosecutor or a litigator. Except for moot court, I've never been before a judge. I've never practiced law outside my father's company."

Fran Pope's smile revealed that she had done her research and treasured the knowledge that Emily Ann's father was the Grandjean of Big John, Inc. "That must be very interesting—corporate law? Exercise law?"

"My official title was consultant, but my hours were pretty flexible. I had a lot of demands outside of work."

"Political, I'm sure."

"*All* political. Until last week."

"Of course. When the tragedy occurred."

"Tragedy?"

"Miles Finn! I understand his son was your campaign manager."

Emily Ann liked this interpretation; liked the image of her campaign derailed by an act of God. She nodded sadly. "I couldn't ask him to go on. It was like the air going out of a balloon, and it all seemed so pointless after the phone call came. How do any of us know how much time we have left and how we should spend it? I mean, look what it's done to Fletcher: He's virtually dropped out of society and taken up residence in an unventilated cabin on an obscure lake."

"Like the Unabomber," said Mrs. Pope.

"Except," said Emily Ann—and with this she couldn't help but flash a superior smile—"other than quitting his job and leaving my campaign in ruins, he's displaying no antisocial behavior. He's more of a person now, no question. I had a terrible time during the months we were on the road together establishing any kind of intimacy. And you know I don't mean in the physical or sexual sense."

Mrs. Pope waited. It was a delicate matter that she and Christine Ouimet had already spent a good deal of time speculating over. They both had grown children, living in cities, sleeping in queen-size beds. Among young people, cohabitation could mean splitting the rent and nothing more. "It makes perfect sense, even to an old fuddy-duddy like me: You and Mr. Finn are colleagues, presumably friends, and what would be the alternative if you wanted to visit? The King's Nite Motel? It's the last place any of us would stay. It's always a dilemma—where to put our out-of-town relatives." From her canvas bag Mrs. Pope brought forth a cellophane package. "Flatbread?"

"Maybe a half," said Emily Ann, reaching over and breaking a corner off one seeded cracker.

"He's a very attractive young man," said Mrs. Pope. "There's something intense about him that I think a young woman would find compelling."

"I'm sleeping in the guest room," said Emily Ann. "In case that was what you were asking."

"No! Of course I'm not. But I will confess something naughty on my part, and that's my ulterior motive: There are several single professional males in the Players who would be delighted to meet you. As for your sleeping arrangements, it never crossed my mind, nor would I ever ask anyone a direct question about her romantic attachments."

"I'm much too busy for romantic attachments," said Emily Ann. "And that applies to Fletcher. Luckily, we're in the same place right now."

"I understand completely: same place, separate bedrooms."

"I meant figuratively, emotionally."

Mrs. Pope nodded and chewed her flatbread, waiting for amplification.

"I don't want to jinx it," said Emily Ann. "But Fletcher and I are working through some problems."

Mrs. Pope smiled and nudged Emily Ann with an elbow. "In the old days, when I was single, it served the cause to introduce a little competition."

"In what sense?"

"Men. *Other* men. Actors, for example. We choose our members carefully, by invitation only—"

"You're kidding! By invitation and not auditions?"

"Certainly auditions. But that's within our circle, after they've been invited to join. We tried open casting calls, of course, but we weren't happy with the results. A number of people tried to sign up because they thought it would launch them into King George society. And once in a while we'd get someone insufferable who'd ushered in summer stock and thought he could show the locals how it's done. And there's the occasional man who thinks it's a socially acceptable way to kiss and nuzzle a woman who isn't his wife."

"Really? You think some get into it just for the sex?"

Mrs. Pope leaned in to confide, "Not sex per se. But we've had situations where two characters are in bed together."

"Nude?"

Mrs. Pope closed her eyes.

"I take that as a yes?"

"It started with a male director, who's since moved back to Long Island, who felt that the woman's bra straps undermined the whole scene."

"Did it cause a big stir?"

Mrs. Pope said, "For better or for worse, it was our best box office ever."

"What was the play?"

"*Same Time Next Year*. Do you know the premise? Two characters, married to other people, have an annual liaison—much of it under the sheets. Accordingly, we closed our rehearsals, which of course was all the publicity we needed for many years. We'd be in the black if we continued in that PG-13 vein, but it wasn't to be."

"Why not?"

Mrs. Pope crushed a piece of cracker and threw the crumbs at a brood of pigeons. After a beat, she said, "Because our trailblazer died."

"Sunny's mother? She was the one under the sheets?"

"Pulled up to *here*." She traced a line from her left armpit to her right. "What was underneath the sheets . . . well, no one really knew except her co-star."

"Which was who?"

"Bill Sandvik for a few weeks. Then, after Petra Sandvik put her foot down, Bill Kaufman."

"Really? His wife made him quit the play? In this day and age?"

"It was almost too perfect a casting job," explained Mrs. Pope. "Bill, the first Bill—well, the chemistry between him and Margaret may have been a bit too evident. They wanted to rehearse *au naturel,* ostensibly to get comfortable with each other's bodies. Luckily, by opening night, Bill Kaufman was able to rekindle the sparks." She sighed. "It was a turning point for us. There had never been any scandal associated with the Players, and suddenly we were the subject of rumors."

"And it was Mrs. Batten's fault? Is that what I'm hearing in your voice?"

"Margaret was very talented. No question. And willing to take that particular artistic risk."

"More than once?"

"When she first came on board, she was a shy widow, unworldly. Not liberated in any sense. And certainly not enjoying any kind of social life."

"So then what happened? She came out of her shell? I've heard of that—people who can turn into someone else onstage. Shy people who come to life and stutterers who can speak fluently."

"I was—and I mean this sincerely—very fond of Margaret. I honestly believe she was a sweet woman, and very kind. People responded to her. Men were drawn to her initially because of that." Mrs. Pope pressed her lips together and turned back to the pigeons.

"Initially drawn to her?" repeated Emily Ann. "And then what?"

Mrs. Pope said, "You're a modern woman. I think you can fill in the blank."

"This was before she was engaged to Fletcher's father, though, right?"

"I'd rather not get into it. Margaret considered me her friend, and friends don't say unkind things about each other, especially after one has passed away."

Emily Ann asked, "Are you saying she slept around?"

"How did we even get on this subject? All I wanted to do was invite you to join the Players. Now I feel like a gossip. And, worse, a prig. What you may be hearing in my voice is my conviction that people should respect their marriage vows."

"But she wasn't married."

"I meant the men."

"She fooled around with married men?"

Mrs. Pope began studying the tennis game in front of her. "Neither goes to the net," she said.

"Wasn't she a little old to be running around?"

"Fifty-seven. I'd prefer to drop the subject."

"Did Fletcher's father know any of this?"

"Miles Finn—" Mrs. Pope stopped herself.

"Say what you were going to say. I won't tell Fletcher. Or anyone."

"Miles Finn and Margaret Batten had a bond. Whatever forays they made into the dating scene, they eventually returned to some kind of understanding: They were each other's backup or, if you'll forgive me, they met each other's physical needs during the dry spells. Which is to say, it was like an open marriage without benefit of clergy."

"Did Sunny know about her mother's sex life?"

"We don't think so. After all, they shared a bedroom until Sunny went away to college."

"Fletcher thinks Sunny is his half-sister," said Emily Ann. "He's getting their DNA tested if he can talk Sunny into it."

"We're all wondering how we missed the obvious. Well, yes we do know: Sunny went away blond and came back looking like Miles Finn reincarnated. And then the son walked onto the scene! Most of us almost fainted at the graveside. And suddenly the double funeral made sense. We knew they were a couple of some sort and that there was a very long history. Margaret once confided to me that Miles didn't take her seriously until other men entered the picture."

"And was that what she wanted? To marry Miles?"

"We thought so. We were all a little surprised when she continued to see other men, to *entertain* other men at her house after she and Miles went relatively public."

"How did you know she was entertaining other men?"

"Because." She stopped. "No one was spying. It was unavoidable. We all play golf—"

"Who's 'we'?"

"The women in the Players. Margaret's house is just on the other side of the rough, through the bushes on seventeen. It did not require snooping to notice a car parked in her driveway, and who drives what vehicle is no secret in King George."

Mrs. Pope stood and called sharply to the teenage girl, who was seconds away from kissing her boyfriend over the sagging net. "Alison! Don't you think you've had enough of a workout for one day?"

Alison peered nervously into the sun. "Mrs. Pope?"

"I happen to know she's not supposed to be seeing this boy," Mrs. Pope said to Emily Ann.

"Okay. It's all yours," said Alison. "Jason has to get back to work anyway."

"He dropped out of school," Mrs. Pope murmured. "He was suspended for smoking in class; worse—in a chemistry lab. And he didn't bother to finish the year."

"How do you know all these details?" asked Emily Ann.

Mrs. Pope looked perplexed. "*Do* I? It's just common knowledge that Jason Bonner was suspended for smoking and didn't go back. I think anyone in King George would be aware of the bare facts."

"I see," said Emily Ann.

"The *Bulletin* has to be very thorough. There's so few of us to cover and so much space to fill."

"I understand," said Emily Ann. "I've been on the receiving end of reporters' insatiable appetites for stories."

"Is that a problem? Because if you were our legal consultant for *Inherit the Wind,* it would be news."

"Really? On the front page?"

"I can see it now: CONGRESSIONAL CANDIDATE DIPS HER TOE IN THEATRICAL WATERS."

"*Ex*–congressional candidate."

"Still, you'd be very big news. Candidates pass through all the time, but no one in recent memory has stayed the night. And certainly there's never been an overlap with the Players."

Emily Ann stood up, bent one leg back and held it firm by the ankle.

"What if it we did it all in one evening?" Mrs. Pope asked. "Two or three hours at the most? Followed by a small dinner party?"

Emily Ann stopped mid-stretch. "I haven't been to a social gathering other than a fund-raiser for practically a year. I hope I could circulate without shaking hands and asking for votes."

"You'll be the guest of honor. I'll do the introductions, and I'll be sure that there's an eligible bachelor on either side of you. Which means I've just decided: cocktails first, followed by a sit-down dinner with place cards."

"I don't eat meat," Emily Ann said.

"Nor do I," said Mrs. Pope. "At least hardly ever."

"Do I bring Fletcher?"

"That's up to you. I'd love to meet your parents if they're visiting."

"They're angry with me right now, my father especially. He didn't want me to run in the first place. He thinks I'm a quitter, and an expensive one."

"But it wasn't your fault! It's like saying you're responsible for the death of your campaign manager's father. How could you have seen that coming?"

"You're absolutely right," said Emily Ann. "I only wish Daddy saw it that way."

Mrs. Pope patted the empty bench beside her. "Parents are supposed to love their children unconditionally, don't you think? Anytime you feel like talking, you call me. I have three children, and I have wonderful relationships with all of them. I also have very good instincts about what makes people tick, men especially." She smiled. "After thirty-six years, Ansel still rushes me home from the club on Saturday night."

Emily Ann sat down again, shuffled the contents of her big green bag, and brought forth an indigo-blue Palm Pilot. She touched her stylus to the screen and poised it over the results. "I'll pencil your dinner in for what night?" she asked.

CHAPTER 29

The Member-Guest

They walked, carried their own bags, replaced their own divots. Fletcher had intended to work his way up to the subject, perhaps after Sunny had sunk a dramatic putt or posted a few birdies, but he was too distracted and only mildly envious watching her. Her swing was all at once beautiful, classic, easy. Too bad, he thought: In the right hands, the right family, the right clothes, she could be the star of a Titleist commercial.

Finally, as they walked up the fairway on five, side by side, bags bobbing and clubs clanking, he brought it up: a lab on the Internet—great ad by the way: a pregnant Mona Lisa above a headline reading, WHO'S THE FATHER? A kit, a mailer, a swab, no doctor . . . results in three weeks. Still better, the coroner had all the DNA samples they'd ever need from Miles—blood, tissues, the works. Factor in the father, according to the lab guy at the toll-free number, and you get 100 percent certainty. His treat. How about it?

"Okay," said Sunny.

He stopped for a few seconds, then caught up with her.

"Just like that? No argument? No stalling?"

"It's all you've talked about since the minute we met."

He repeated, "It's painless. No doctors. A do-it-yourself kit. And we'll know in three weeks."

"I said okay, Fletch."

"What happened to 'I don't know where I'll be in three weeks. How long can I impose on the good people of King George for charity housing and free refills at The Dot?'"

"You're putting words in my mouth. Besides, where would I go?"

Fletcher was tending the flagstick. He lifted it as she made the long putt, swiftly and into the center of the cup. "Nice one," he said.

"What about you?" Sunny asked. "How long do you expect to stay?"

"I'm in no hurry. Why would I rush off and start paying rent somewhere?"

"Where did you live before?"

"Oh that," said Fletcher. "Let's just say I lost it with my job."

"Like me," said Sunny. "Only something tells me you weren't a dorm parent."

"I had a condo—get this—which Grandjean père had bought solely for his dog."

"No!"

"I'm not kidding. He had this old geezer of a dog, some hulking French breed, and Mrs. Grandjean couldn't stand the smell of him even when he was fresh from his bubble bath. So Rex and his wholesale bales of dog chow lodged in the family's pied-à-terre near the main plant, where various Grandjeans and dog walkers visited him daily."

"That was your roommate? A dog?"

"Who understood only French."

"Still, a free apartment, and one without horrible fifteen-year-old boarders to police and tutor."

"That's what I thought at first—free. But within a week I discovered that a half a dozen people had keys, and no one felt the need to ring the doorbell before entering. It's why I get down on my knees every night—well, figuratively—and thank my father for the renovated roof over my head and the solitude."

"Solitude?" she repeated. "What about Emily Ann?"

Fletcher sped up, but she stayed with him. "You know that she likes you," said Sunny. "We've established that. But I would have thought by now familiarity would have bred a little contempt."

"Don't get cute," said Fletcher. "It's me playing host. Me sleeping in a bed and her on a futon, a floor above. Me convincing her that if my hand brushed against her breast in mid-air, it was turbulence."

"Poor Em," said Sunny. "You should take the futon and give her the bed."

One hole later, a second away from making her putt, Fletcher asked, "Do I editorialize on the subject of your personal life?"

"Constantly."

"Let me see your stroke," he said.

She backed off and demonstrated.

"A little wristy," said Fletcher. "Did anyone ever tell you that?"

Sunny smiled without looking up.

"Ever try something a little more from the shoulders?"

Her putt traced an impossible arc toward the cup, hit the lip, circled 180 degrees, and dropped in. "Me and Arnie," she said. "Too much wrist. But I'll keep it in mind."

"I thought you couldn't play. I thought you'd lost the magic in Maryland."

"This is different," she said. "This doesn't count. I try not to analyze what I'm doing. I need to let it happen, without me. No brain. Just the club and the nerve endings." She fished her ball out of the cup. "Watch me on the next hole. The mere fact that we discussed it will ensure that I slice it into kingdom come."

He did watch her closely on seven. Her backswing, when her hands were neck-high, could be frozen and photographed, he thought. Or cast in bronze. She smashed the ball. It flew forever and landed on the fairway, midway between two long, shallow bunkers.

"Not bad," said Fletcher. He looked up from his own practice swing to find Sunny studying him. "What?" he asked.

"Do that again."

"Why?"

"I was thinking that you could keep your lower body a little quieter."

"Don't be fresh," said Fletcher. He addressed the ball, then took his most ferocious and unlovely swing. The ball hit a huge sycamore and ricocheted back onto the short grass. Sunny laughed.

"We're good, aren't we?" said Fletcher. "I think our grandma would be happy to see us out here, reunited at last, killing the ball, making par."

Sunny said, "Par, par, birdie, bogey, par, par, likely birdie."

"Not my point. My point was the genetics of things, not the play-by-play."

"Your Victorian grandmother? She'd be horrified by my very existence, low handicap or not."

"It was probably all her own damn fault—off playing the circuit and leaving Miles at home to find affection in the arms of other women." He grinned broadly. "We'll know soon, won't we?"

"The test, you mean?"

"It's in my glove compartment. It comes with a mailer."

"It's here? You already ordered it?"

"They overnighted it."

"And this is what you want? To know for sure?"

Fletcher asked, "Are you serious? We've taken this brother-and-sister thing as far as we can on the anecdotal evidence, so let's get validated. That's who I am: A sister isn't some feel-good palsy-walsy thing I can adopt without documentation."

Sunny took an angry practice swing with her pitching wedge. And another. "Fine. I wouldn't want that, either—a brother without proper papers."

"I mean, we'd still be friends. And I'd still want to play golf with you."

"Thanks."

"I think I'm a good influence, don't you? Judging by the first seven holes, you're in that zone you talked about—all nerve endings and no analysis."

"I wouldn't go that far."

"We could be a team. Seriously. Do they have a member-guest tournament?"

"Not interested," said Sunny.

"It would have to be coed, of course."

Sunny pointed at his ball. "Hit. People are waiting. You're talking too much."

He chipped nicely onto the green, then studied his scorecard. "Coming up: shortest hole on the course—a hundred forty-four yards."

"I aced it once," Sunny said. "But I was playing alone. No witnesses. I jumped up and down and made a lot of noise, but it was too early in the morning for anyone to hear. I've mentioned that before, haven't I? That I used to sneak on at sunup or sundown, before or after the members?"

Fletcher shook his head. "You really depress me," he said.

"Why?"

"Your Little Orphan Annie past. And now it's the real deal: zero parents. No job. No car. All I can say is it's a good thing I came from a broken home, too, or I'd feel even worse."

"I didn't tell you any of that so you'd feel sorry for me. I was bragging about sneaking on. I thought it made me sound brave and adventurous. I've had a perfectly good life. We had a roof over our head, food on the table, clothes on our back. And an eighteen-hole golf course for a backyard."

"I still don't like it," said Fletcher.

"What?"

"This loner thing. You think that's the way things are supposed to be—with you on the outside, your nose pressed against the glass."

"That's not true—"

"From what you've told me, it's always been true: the town, the golf team, the country club, the faculty of that school you left, your mother's social circles. Your mother's—shall we say—dance card?"

Sunny dropped her golf bag with a jangle of clubs and strode over to him. "I thought we settled this. I thought you understood that your father was committed to my mother, that he was not in the wrong place at the wrong time in a stroke of horrible one-night-stand bad luck. They were getting married. Why are you still talking about my mother's dance card?"

"For no reason at all. Just forget it. I'm sorry. I must've meant . . . nothing."

"Did Dr. Ouimet come crying to you about how he was in love with my mother?"

"No. Absolutely not. I've never talked to any Dr. Ouimet."

"You're lying. You heard something, and I want to know what."

"Shh. There's a ball in play. Please move back so I don't brain you." He shimmied into position, then looked back over his shoulder to see if she was out of range.

"Did you overhear something at The Dot?" she persisted.

"C'mon. What are you getting so riled up about? Emily Ann met some dame and they started talking and your mother's name came up. It was chitchat—mindless chitchat between two ladies of leisure."

"I don't care what you call it. And if people are insulting your late father's late fiancée, you should be riled up, too."

Fletcher looked back at the tee, at four retirees watching and waiting. "We're holding up play. Do you want to finish or pick up?"

"I want to pick up," she said.

———

They sat on the first bench they came to, next to a footbridge that spanned the brook. "Even if it's pure rumor," said Sunny, "even if it's untrue, I want to know who's spreading lies about my mother."

After a long pause, Fletcher said, "Fran? Is there a Fran?"

"Fran Pope."

"She's befriended Emily Ann. They're cooking up something with the local theater group."

"Go on."

"She was telling her about plays they've staged, and one thing led to another."

"Such as?"

"Your mother starring in one where she took her clothes off."

"So?"

"Well—and don't take this the wrong way—the word *chemistry* came up. Which led to a discussion of the group's social dynamic, which apparently led to a little reminiscing about who your mother went out with."

" 'Went out with'? Is that a euphemism?"

"Sort of."

"For what?"

" 'Fooled around with'?"

"Kissed? Slept with? What?"

"According to Emily Ann, all of the above. Apparently, in a town this size, when a woman is naked onstage, even if she's under a sheet, it's seen as very . . . out there. Liberated. Hence her popularity."

Sunny asked, "Was it *Same Time Next Year*?"

"I don't know. Does it matter?"

"That was ages ago. Right after I left home."

"So?"

"So if that's what made her popular, she's been popular for a long time."

"Popular's good," said Fletcher.

"Was Mrs. Pope implying that my mother was promiscuous?"

"I only got it secondhand. I don't know exactly what she said or what words she used. Besides, who knows what the Pope's criterion is for fast and loose? It could be dancing too close at the thespians' Christmas party."

"She must have been implying plenty or you wouldn't be working so hard to spare my feelings."

"I'm trying to spare your feelings because your fears are groundless. Emily Ann doesn't know another soul in town. Even if she wanted to spread a rumor, she couldn't. Besides, she'll be gone soon."

"You don't know when she's leaving! And if Mrs. Pope blabbed to Emily Ann, a perfect stranger, you can bet everyone else in town has gotten an earful."

"I'm sure that's not true."

"Yes it is! I can see it in your face. Everyone in King George, with the possible exception of me and Dr. Ouimet, knows. Even the tourists are getting briefed."

"Emily Ann only knew because she's been recruited for the play, and she only told me because my father was a casualty. Which I use in the forensic rather than figurative sense."

"Well, she's an idiot! Didn't she think it would kill you to know that your father was the unlucky loser in my mother's boyfriend roulette, delivering take-out the night her furnace kicked on?"

"Not that I'm defending Emily Ann, but she wasn't gossiping per se. She thought she'd found the missing piece of the puzzle—that my father didn't tell me about his engagement ... because he wasn't engaged."

"That's great! So you and I were not out of the loop after all. We weren't the last to know. We weren't the total strangers to our parents that we thought we were."

"Something like that," said Fletcher.

Sunny got to her feet.

"Where are you going?" he asked.

"Home."

"To do what?"

"I don't know—look around, pull out some drawers, look for signs."

"Of what?"

"True love. Monogamy. Matrimony."

"I think ... wouldn't you have found that by now? Wouldn't there be some engraved invitations or caterers' menus or, at the very least, a list of deejays lying around?"

"Not if they were going to slip away and have a quiet ceremony before a justice of the peace. Just the two of them."

"But wasn't your mother very social? Wouldn't she have wanted a big wedding, with all her friends and a party at the country club?"

Sunny returned to the green bench and sat down heavily. "That would be a little awkward, wouldn't it? Especially if she'd slept with every man on the guest list."

"Whoa, Sun. C'mon. Don't believe everything you hear. Consider the source: Emily Ann Grandjean. Via me. *Me!* Deaf to nuance. I could have it all wrong. And Emily Ann is extremely literal. Probably this dame said something like, 'Margaret was perfect for the lead in *Same Time Next Year*,' and Emily Ann took that to mean, Margaret herself was no stranger to adultery."

"That's not being literal. That's the opposite of being literal. That's making a giant deductive, presumptuous, small-minded, puritanical, Republican leap."

"Okay, bad example. I'm trying to unring the bell, as we spin doctors say."

"Well, you're doing a shitty job of it. Emily Ann told you my mother was the town strumpet and you believed her, hook, line, and sinker."

"Look, maybe I bought into Emily Ann's report, but that's because of her rhetorical skills. She's amazing at framing an issue and presenting the salient—"

"No she's not! All you ever complain about is what a dud she was on the stump."

Fletcher sighed. He tried to put an arm around Sunny, but she moved away. "C'mon," he said, "I thought we were a team. I thought we were in this together."

Sunny turned squarely, unhappily, toward him. "Explain to me, please, how we're in this together."

"Your mother. My father. They're buried in the same plot, for God's sake. Isn't that enough of a statement to the outside world? Isn't that the ultimate wedding ceremony?"

"That's what I don't understand. Even if my mother played the field—even if she slept with a couple of guys over the years—so what? Can't she have a past? She made a public commitment to Miles. Why didn't that put the rumors to rest?"

Fletcher rubbed his nose with his fist, repeatedly. Finally, he said, "Emily Ann's impression—and I'm paraphrasing here—was that Miles and Margaret ... had sex with each other in a nonexclusive, recreational mode."

"Which means what?"

"On and off. When they weren't getting it from other people."

"I don't believe it," said Sunny. "Not my mother. She was a little mouse. At best, a late bloomer. You heard the eulogies: Every single speaker raved about her generous heart and her open door. To know her was to love her."

"Apparently so," said Fletcher.

Sunny pulled her visor down over her eyes, slumped, and crossed her arms over her chest.

"You okay?" He jiggled her knee. "Sunny?"

"I give up. No wonder everyone's been so nice to me. The charity lives on. Poor Sunny. It's hard enough losing a mother in a freak accident, let alone one who was the town pump."

Fletcher said, "Why did I open my big mouth? Now you'll think even less of me than you already did."

"I'm going home," she said. "By myself. Back the way I came."

"Are you sure? Do you want me to take your clubs and drive them over?"

"I've got them," said Sunny. She stopped after a few yards. "The DNA test. You wanted to get that over with."

"Another time," he said. "No hurry."

"Since when?"

"Since I'm working overtime to dig myself out of the hole I've just dug."

"Give me a day or two," she said.

"Or longer. Whenever." Doesn't matter, he thought, then repeated aloud, "Are we sure it matters?"

She didn't respond, except to walk away. He watched her cross the footbridge, trudging like a disgraced caddie in retreat, across one fairway, then another.

He cupped his hands around his mouth. "Call me," he shouted, but she didn't stop. On a distant green, men nodded solemnly as she passed. It must have been the seventeenth hole and the shortcut home, because seconds later she was gone.

CHAPTER 30

The Moms

She hadn't yet opened the sealed manila envelope bearing the medical examiner's return address and containing the deceased's personal effects. Randy Pope had tracked it down, in person, and found it misfiled in Concord. Regina brought the envelope to Margaret's house, along with a carload of empty cartons. "I have two hours of child care," she announced. "Where do I start?"

"It *would* be nice if I didn't have to face a full closet every morning," said Sunny.

"Done. You tackle something easier," said Regina. "How about her books?"

"Better still, her record collection," said Sunny.

"Anything I think you'd use goes on the bed. But I'm ruthless. Especially clothes, which I'll have to approve of."

"I know," said Sunny. "That's why I hired you."

"The wigs—all that First Lady stuff: Out, correct? To the dump?"

"Agreed," said Sunny. "And anything too scandalous and skanky for the poor box."

Regina walked out to the first step of the porch and addressed the clouds. "Mrs. Batten? It's okay. Sunny's a little upset because she was the last to know. But she'll come around. Some of us are happy you had a fruitful sex life."

She turned back to the house, gave Sunny a playful swat, and said, "Leave everything to me."

Sunny remained on the glider, the State of New Hampshire's official envelope on her knees. After a minute, she emptied the contents onto her lap. Out slid only the ancient, small-faced Speidel with its gold-filled bracelet, its chipped crystal, its safety chain. And the ring—misinterpreted by Joey as a token of Miles's intentions—was the same one her mother had worn all of Sunny's life, the forlorn engagement symbol that John Batten didn't want back.

Regina called her name, then appeared in the open front door holding a bulky white garment bag. "First thing I tackled," she said. "Faye's Bridal Finery. Wherever that may be."

"Under the circumstances," said Sunny, "maybe Faye will take it back."

"Not these," said Regina. She unzipped the bag. Inside were five child-size dresses—some cross-stitched, some smocked, some trimmed with lace or edged with braid—the most labor-intensive of Margaret's projects. There was a taffeta plaid, an organdy pinafore over black velvet, a pinwale red corduroy, an organza party dress of lavender sprigs on pale gray, its starched sash still holding a majestic bow.

"What she *used* to do with her evenings," said Sunny.

"Take that back," said Regina. She touched the white plastic buttons decorating a pink gingham shirtwaist. "Look at these."

Sunny smiled. "Golf balls. She thought they would make me wear it; thought they might do the trick." She turned up its hem. "Six inches wide. Ever hopeful, she'd make them extra deep so she could let them down as I got taller. I have this mental picture of her sitting in front of the TV, wearing her thimble, biting off threads." Sunny slipped the organza party dress off its hanger and held it to her. "I think I was in third grade for this one—eight or nine, and still cooperative."

"You wore all of these," said Regina. "I remember you at birthday parties. So don't you worry about how cooperative you were. You never gave her a moment's grief."

Sunny put the flowered dress back on its hanger and zipped up the bag. "If Robert were a girl, I'd give them to you," she said.

"I wouldn't take them," said Regina. "These were saved. These are for *your* girl, Sun."

———

Joey was on the phone and smiled when he looked up, mistaking her grim expression for a reluctance to interrupt. He scrawled on his memo pad, *A.G.'s office—the kid who shot me has chix pox!!*

She took his pen and wrote underneath it, *How long have you known about my mother?*

Joey's reaction—apparent incomprehension—gave Sunny hope that the grapevine hadn't reached every resident of King George. He held up one finger, then snapped into the phone, "Send me the papers. I'll look them over. It'll depend on what my town counsel advises and what kind of mood I'm in."

He smiled at her then—her ancient blue jeans were rolled up at her ankles, and her faded gray PROPERTY OF KGRHS ATHLETIC DEPT. T-shirt might have fit her at fifteen—but she didn't smile back. When she continued to pace in front of his desk, he leaned over and caught her by the wrist.

What's wrong? he mouthed, then said gruffly to the party on the phone, "I wouldn't give much of a flying fuck about that, would I? Let him rub on calamine lotion. Or give him some oatmeal. My mother used to give us oatmeal baths when we itched."

She saw, just above his Adam's apple, a spot of tissue dried to a shaving nick. She could also see that it was her behavior and not the State of New Hampshire that had put this puzzled and anxious look on his face.

"What happened?" he asked her before the receiver was even in its cradle. "What *about* your mother?"

She stared at the poster behind his head—NEW HAMPSHIRE'S TOP 20 CHILD SUPPORT SCOFFLAWS—as she recited in an overly modulated voice, "Fran Pope told Emily Ann Grandjean, who told Fletcher, who told me, that my mother was, essentially, the King George Jezebel. From which I—not to mention Fletcher—have deduced that their double funeral was a sham."

"How so?"

"Their alleged engagement."

"And you're asking me what?"

"For some goddamn confirmation."

The phone rang but he didn't answer it. His prerecorded voice advised the caller to try Chief Loach at home. At the same time, a man in a business suit stuck his head in the door and asked if this was where one obtained building permits.

"Upstairs," said Joey. He waited until the man was gone and the woman on the phone finished describing the irregularities of her powder-room walls and inquiring as to whether or not Joey did marbling or other *faux* techniques.

"*Do* you?" asked Sunny.

He closed his eyes; opened them as if it took energy he didn't have. "Where are you going with this funeral-as-sham nonsense? And what ever happened to *rest in peace*?"

"In other words, I'm right," she said. "You're confirming that Miles Finn, entombed at my mother's side for all eternity, was nothing more than a foot soldier in her sexual army."

"Who said that?"

"I told you: Mrs. Pope told Emily Ann, who went running to the ever frank Fletcher—"

"So Fletcher's the one who got you worked up about this? The guy who brags about having no knowledge of his father's private life? And he's certainly no authority on King George mating habits."

Sunny put one foot up on the visitor's bench and retied the laces of a threadbare sneaker. "That may be true," she said over her shoulder, "but he was happy enough to pass on Mrs. Pope's hearsay. And Fran Pope certainly has no trouble posthumously besmirching my mother as the loosest woman in the Players."

Joey grimaced and pressed his lips together.

"This isn't funny! I'm pretty sure everyone at the funeral was thinking, Poor Miles. Terrible timing. Lousy luck. And poor Sunny. Too bad she doesn't have a clue."

" 'The loosest woman in the Players'? Everything is relative. They're all old bags. Your mother was single. She went on dates. Maybe she played the field."

"What about Miles?"

"Miles got around."

"But with my mother?"

"Sure. Definitely."

"I can't seem to find any hard evidence that they were getting married."

"I'm sure they were," said Joey. "I used to see them at The Dot, and sometimes at the movies. And they always had their heads together. They looked like they were having fun."

"Fun enough to have set a date? Fun enough for a double funeral?"

"Have you been hanging around with my mother? Do you need an announcement in the society pages before you believe it was official?"

"Apparently I do," said Sunny.

"They were definitely an item. Ask anyone. Maybe your mother didn't need a wedding to feel married to Miles—"

"Oh please. My mother was not some nonconformist who didn't need a wedding ring on her finger to feel committed. She didn't even like the way *single mother* sounded, so she made up a story about her widowhood."

"People can change," said Joey. "If I didn't believe that, I wouldn't be signing off on William Thomas Dube, would I? Your mother stopped worrying about King George Ladies' Auxiliary code of conduct and started having a little fun. She worked hard and she memorized her lines and when she got up there in her fancy costumes, she looked great and people noticed."

"Do you mean men?"

"Sure I mean men."

"Like, dozens?"

"Over the years, maybe. But when it comes down to the math—what's that? One a season? Big deal. Don't be an old lady."

"More than that! There was a line out the door, if you listen to Fran Pope."

"I used to have about four dates a year myself, and no one put *me* in the stockade."

Sunny finally offered a pallid smile. "*Used* to have four dates a year? What happened?"

"I thought you knew." He came out from behind his desk, sat down on the visitors' bench, and pulled her onto his lap. She resisted, then sat stiffly, spine tilted away from him. "A girl came back," he began. "Someone I used to moon over in study hall. Seventh period, I think, during which she actually studied, unlike me, and therefore went off to college. I grew up, found out I had half a brain, found gainful employment. I didn't see her for years and years, though occasionally there would be an article about her in the local paper. Which I clipped. I went to some of her mother's plays, because what else was there to do and because they never filled the house. And because maybe, if I was very nice to the mother, she'd write to the daughter and say, 'You know who didn't turn out so bad? Joe Loach. That dumb guy. His acne cleared up and his manners improved. Children look up to him.' Then tragedy struck her, and almost struck me, but it turned out for the best. I mean, not to take anything away from her mother's death, but it did bring the girl back to King George."

Sunny said, "You clipped stories about me from the *Bulletin*?"

"Only the ones with pictures."

"Go on," she said.

He smoothed her hair back from her face and hooked it behind her ears. "And since I was in charge of the investigation, I had to walk her through a few things and explain the way the world works. Nothing big. Just life and death. And her mother's popularity."

In their silence, the noise of station business grew louder—the clock, the faxes, the callers talking to the answering machine. "How well did you know my mother?" Sunny finally asked.

"Pretty well. Occasionally we shared a booth at The Dot during peak hours."

"Really? Did you tell me this before?"

"I probably didn't because it didn't add up to much over the years. But enough, I think, for her to like me and vice versa."

"Did you ever talk about me?"

"Sure we did."

"What did she say?"

"Well, it wasn't so much what she said but how she looked. Like it was her favorite topic, and she was glad to be having breakfast with someone who knew you from high school and was rooting for you and didn't hold a grudge for that old stuff—making the boys' squad and getting the scholarship."

"Besides that—besides looking pleased to be talking about me—did she seem happy?"

"Always," said Joey. "That's why I never paid attention to any rumors. Not that I heard any—and I'm in an excellent position to have fielded whatever passed through town. But in retrospect, I know what really mattered was that she was always a good person and—I don't know— peaceful."

"Peaceful?" said Sunny. "Really?"

"Sure. Like, whatever she was doing, it felt right."

Sunny said, "I think you're making this up. I think you would have told me ages ago if you'd been having breakfast with my mother at The Dot and could report firsthand that she was so happy and proud and filled with alleged peace."

"I didn't know you ages ago. And I couldn't confide any of this at the wake or at the funeral because I was out of range, directing traffic."

"You might have told me Sunday night."

Joey said, "Sunday night . . . I was a little distracted Sunday night."

His hands were on her shoulders, but he slid them down her arms. "I'm still distracted. In fact, five minutes ago I told an assistant attorney general to send my attempted murderer home to his mother."

Sunny leaned back against him. "Maybe that's good. Maybe he'll turn his life around and won't ever do another felonious thing as long as he lives."

"What's this?" he asked. "A new, sunnier, optimistic Sunny?"

"I'm just thinking of his poor mother. First he gets arrested and now he gets the chicken pox."

"First he stole a truck and shot a police officer. Second he gets arrested."

"How old is he?"

"Sixteen."

"And his mother's willing to take him back?"

"Yeah. With a juvenile service officer and the state of New Hampshire paying for his therapy."

"What about a father?"

"Not in the picture."

"Brothers and sisters?"

"Grown. Gone."

"Then definitely do it. His mother's all alone. And this way she won't have to hang her head in the local diner when people say, 'How's your baby? How's Junior? What's he up to?' "

"Maybe," he said. "We'll see."

"I bet in ten years you'll get a thank-you note from him saying he found religion and he's a Big Brother, and has a degree in social work."

"Ha," said Joey.

"Will you keep me posted?" Sunny asked. "Will you forward his testimonials?"

His hands left her arms and he didn't answer.

She sat up. "Joey?"

"What?"

"Did I say something wrong?"

"Nope. Not at all. I understand. You'll give me your forwarding address. I'll drop you a line and let you know the disposition of the case.

Or Randy can tell Regina, and Regina can put it in her Christmas letter."

"Back up a minute," said Sunny. She found his right hand, which was gripping the bench. "Your synopsis? Of the girl who moved away and came back when tragedy befell her mother? I cut you off. You didn't finish."

"You finish," he said. "I lost my place."

"Okay. Give me a sec." She closed her eyes and settled back against him. "The girl came back. She met the aforementioned boy, now a full-grown man, who was indeed helpful. Very. She had to get to know him herself, because her mother had been too busy to fill her in, too busy to write her to say he wasn't the same Joey Loach from tenth grade. That children looked up to him now. That his manners *had* improved—not only did he no longer get detention, but he was the chief of police. And the girl took one look at him, and, embarrassingly enough—I say 'embarrassingly' because she'd been summoned home for a very tragic reason—more or less fell at his feet. Amazingly enough—'amazing' because he'd grown up to be extremely handsome—he wasn't married, engaged, gay, or on anyone's dance card. Also amazingly, the feeling appeared to be mutual—as much as one can assess these things across police tape and from riding in the front seat of a cruiser. A few days after her mother was laid to rest, they had their first date. After an awkward start, it took a turn for the truly great. At least *she* thought so. Before long, Fran Pope would spread rumors that the girl was lap-dancing with said officer while visiting him at the police station, or so it appeared when viewed through her pocket binoculars from the diner across the street. But the girl ignored Fran Pope, because—not to take anything away from her mother's death—she was happy for the first time since she could remember. And the part about forwarding the kid's letters in ten years? That's called fishing. That's a line that a calculating woman throws out in hopes that the man says, 'I want you to stay.' "

"I want you to stay," said Joey.

"Even if I hate it here?"

"I hate it here too," said Joey.

"Good," said Sunny. "That'll be our bond when the sexual flame burns out."

He laughed. She could feel it next to her ear, buried in her hair.

"When's our date?" he murmured.

"Tomorrow."

"Can we move it up, like, twenty-four hours?"

Sunny looked at the wall clock. "How's seven?"

"How's the minute I get off work?"

"My place?" she asked.

He laughed again. "It's either there, or here, or the King's Nite."

"Should we go out to eat first and pretend it's a real date?"

Joey said, "If you want to dine first, in public, and keep your hands to yourself, we can do that. Sure."

Sunny slipped off his lap, took a step toward the door. He pulled her back. "Maybe I'll cut out early."

"Like, what time?"

"Like—don't you need a ride home now?"

She looked down at her threadbare sneakers, at the woeful tread on their soles. "You're right. But I'm buying a car as soon as I get a job. Your gallantry is costing the taxpayers too much money."

"It's their pleasure," said Joey. "They almost lost me. I know they'd insist I drive you home and secure the perimeters and make love to you in the afternoon to the original cast album of *I Can Get It for You Wholesale,* because they want what I want."

"What a generous town," said Sunny. "To think that I blamed them for all of my grief." She leaned over to kiss him—a kiss unsuited to a public space or a man hampered by a bullet-proof vest.

The footsteps on the stairs announced an intruder. Joey jumped to his feet. Mrs. Loach came through the door, slightly out of breath, rubber gloves in one hand and a bottle of bleach in the other.

"Hi, Ma," he said.

She stopped, appraised the scene, tried not to look too pleased.

"Oh, go ahead," she said.

CHAPTER 31

Deal

It was Fletcher knocking at her front door, in what had to be Miles's seersucker shirt, speaking from behind a full-grown azalea.

"You didn't have to," said Sunny. She stepped out onto the porch, wearing her mother's red satin kimono over its matching slip.

"I thought I did," he said.

There was a clanging of pipes from inside the house, then the sound of a shower sputtering and a muffled male voice singing.

"I take it that a police car in your driveway first thing in the morning is no longer a cause for concern," said Fletcher.

"That's right," said Sunny. "I'm entertaining the troops. Like mother, like daughter."

"Very amusing. Now read the card," he said, transferring the plant to her.

It was not a card but a check, creased and canceled, drawn on the

First National Bank of Philadelphia, signed carelessly by Miles H. Finn, paid to the order of Margaret Batten. Dated February 1, 1982. Stapled to a budding branch.

"What's this?" she asked.

He sat down, smiling smugly, arm flung across the back of the glider. "Oh, nothing much. A canceled check made out to your mother."

"I can see that."

"One of many such canceled checks. Always paid on the first of the month. Always for the same amount."

She pried it off the branch for a closer inspection. It looked like checks of old, blue tweed waves, watermark, good paper. Margaret had endorsed it in her modest, pre-autograph hand.

"Well?" he demanded.

"It's certainly made out to my mother."

"And?"

"It's almost twenty years old."

"It's a child-support payment! Isn't that obvious?"

"Not really," she said. "There's no notation on the memo line. Maybe he was paying for sexual favors."

"Sunny! You're ruining my moment here. This was not me hiring a detective. This was not me putting a stethoscope to a wall safe. This wasn't even me going through Miles's papers. This was me looking for nutcrackers, and unable to open a desk drawer because it was jammed with canceled checks."

"Why were you looking for nutcrackers in your father's desk drawers?"

"Because I bought lobsters, two-pounders—live and kicking from a tank at Foodland. His desk happens to be in the kitchen. Adjacent and contiguous to the utensil and junk drawers. Voilà. I never found the nutcrackers, but we spread some newspapers on the deck and used a mallet. Would you believe Emily Ann ate a whole lobster? Even one or two bites dipped in drawn butter?"

"No, I would not," said Sunny. Her mother's name and the date were typewritten. Miles's signature was an *M*, an impatient dash, a nod to an *F*, a squiggle. She could picture him, fountain pen uncapped, checks placed on his executive blotter by a secretary—for electric, gas, telephone, mortgage, Diners Club, love child.

"Aren't you even mildly dumbfounded?" Fletcher asked.

"How many of these did you find?"

"Enough! One in every statement."

Sunny murmured, "Two hundred dollars and no cents. Fifty dollars a week. I wonder what judge awarded that amount?"

"Not my point," said Fletcher. "And frankly, I was expecting a little more enthusiasm."

"You're convinced this tells the story?"

"I know the story! I knew the minute I saw you at the cemetery. Suddenly my father's mysterious black hole of a life made sense. Why he'd drop everything and run to New Hampshire, waxing ecstatic about his idyllic sanctuary on his breathtaking lake, when in fact it was a pit and when in fact he was coming up to see his daughter."

"But he wasn't," said Sunny. "He had nothing to do with me. You seem to have forgotten I didn't know him."

"This isn't wishful thinking on my part. This isn't me saving five hundred bucks for the DNA-by-mail test. These are, no question, payments to Margaret Batten from Miles Finn for the support of his child. Besides, if he wasn't coming up here to live his double life and play father, then what—no offense—would be the draw?"

"A very nice, very sympathetic, adoring woman," said Sunny. "And I don't mean the popular and allegedly promiscuous Margaret. I mean the Margaret of old, the one I knew."

"That goes without saying," said Fletcher. "No Finn has to travel six hours for sex."

Sunny, after a few moments, said, "Okay then. Let's call it official. You're my brother and I'm your sister."

"That's it? In that tone of voice? *Thanks, Fletcher. If I need an organ donor, I'll try you first?*"

"It's not as if we didn't already suspect," said Sunny.

"Now I'm *really* depressed. I thought this was going to be huge. I thought you were going to throw your arms around my neck and sob into my collar."

Sunny touched his arm. "I did like the canceled check on the azalea bush. That was a nice touch."

"You can thank Emily Ann for that."

"Where *is* Emily Ann?"

Fletcher checked his watch. "Ten A.M. Either exercising or purging. Or both."

"No, c'mon. You wouldn't be having lobster dinners lakeside if you couldn't stand her as much as you say you do."

"I'm counting the days until the play ends, and then it's good-bye: Good-bye, Em. Good-bye, house guest. Good-bye, Celine Dion. Good-bye, dainty hand washables drying on my towel bar. Good-bye, makeup bag on my sink. Good-bye, contact lens paraphernalia. Good-bye, Tampax."

"Where is she going?"

"Home. You will not be surprised to hear that Daddy stumbled upon an opening in Big John's legal division."

"I bet you'll miss her."

"I will *not* miss her."

"Trust me. Everyone thinks solitude is so great until they get it."

"The reason I won't miss her," said Fletcher, "is because I'm going back, too."

"To New Jersey?"

"To my new job." He held up his hand. "Don't ask. It's too embarrassing. I won't be able to face myself in the mirror every morning."

Sunny laughed. "Then it has to be either working for the opponent—what's his name, the incumbent . . . ?"

"Tommy d'Apuzzo. Wrong. Not that I didn't send him a résumé . . ."

"Or for Big John, Incorporated, Emily Ann Grandjean, vice president."

"Bingo."

"In what capacity?"

"Paying down my debt. I may or may not have told you that I was compensated up front for my campaign work."

"And what's the job?"

"Don't tell anyone this, either: an executive training program. A month in this department, a month in that, learning the business from the ground up." He mouthed the words *assembly line* and shuddered. "After a year, they decide if they like you."

Sunny smiled. "It's not out of the question. Try to ingratiate yourself with the rest of the Grandjeans. If my experience means anything, they'll come around."

He nudged her with his elbow. "Was that the tiniest, subatomic quiver in your voice? Like, you'll miss me? Like, this wasn't the worst news you ever heard?"

"Which?"

"The siblinghood!"

Sunny said, "Maybe. I'm probably still digesting it."

"Because you're stunned! You finally got what you've always wanted, a birth half-brother. Then, in the same breath, he drops the bomb that he's abandoning you." He put his arm around her shoulders for a squeeze. "I'll be up. Often. I mean, I have a car, I have a country house at my disposal. Presumably, I'll get weekends off after the factory whistle blows."

"Seriously? You're going to travel five or six hours for a night away?"

"I'll get the occasional Monday holiday. And summer vacation."

"How many weeks?"

"Two to start. Pathetic, isn't it? He wouldn't budge on it."

"What about the rest of the year?"

"In what respect?"

"The house," she said. "Our father's house. I mean, would he want history repeating itself? Would he want me defrosting your refrigerator and dropping off a casserole in anticipation of your quarterly visits? Or would he want his only daughter to enjoy more gracious living than his two hundred dollars a month provided?"

Fletcher asked, "What's wrong with this place?"

Sunny reached behind them and peeled a splinter of paint from the clapboard. "Would *you* want to live here?"

"On the golf course? Absolutely."

"That served its purpose. The thrill is long gone."

"What about when I need the house and possibly some privacy?"

"You'll call ahead. I'll find a warm bed elsewhere for a few days."

Fletcher said, "Don't think this very idea didn't cross my mind when I was buying the azalea and the woman said, 'It needs at least partial shade,' and I wondered, Where is she going to plant this against that little shitbox baking in the sun?"

"That was sweet," said Sunny.

He closed his eyes. "Give me a minute to weigh the pros and cons."

"Pipes freeze up here. Desperadoes squat in vacant cottages. If I were you, I'd want a caretaker."

He narrowed his eyes. "Who pays the utilities?"

"I do."

"What about upkeep?"

"For instance?"

"If the walls needs refreshing? Or if the ceilings peel?"

"That's too easy," said Sunny. "You've forgotten Joey's sideline."

"Am I being stupid here? Are you going to change the locks and get a restraining order?"

"Nope. Just the opposite. I'm going to make it a shrine to you. I'll keep an overnight bag packed for a quick getaway. As you come in the front door, I'll slip out the back."

Fletcher grumbled, "I suppose it wouldn't kill me to sleep on the futon for a weekend."

"Then we have a deal?"

"Deal," said Fletcher.

"Can I tell people?"

"Do you mean your boyfriend?"

"I mean, can I officially notify the town fathers that they can rent the Abel Cotton House to the next indigent family?"

"As long as they don't evict you before I leave town."

"Which is when again?"

"In ten days. After the play."

"You're staying just for that?"

"Have to," he mumbled.

"What are they doing?"

"*Inherit the Wind.* Emily Ann is Scopes's girlfriend."

"We'll get tickets," said Sunny. "You can sit with us."

"Can't," said Fletcher.

"Why not?"

His cheeks colored slightly. "Because William Jennings Bryan can't sit in the audience."

"No! You didn't."

"Don't laugh. I'm good. I have presence. I auditioned for both leading roles and got my choice."

"You picked Bryan over Clarence Darrow?"

"Bryan won," he said.

From upstairs, the shower stopped with a clang of pipes. "Sunny?" Joey called.

Fletcher said, "I think the sheriff needs a towel." He jabbed the burlap-covered roots of the azalea bush. "Should I leave the peace offering here or take it back to its future home?"

"That depends. Will you plant it or just leave it propped against the house?"

"Prop it," he said. "And probably kill it."

"Leave it," said Sunny. "I'll do it when I get there. Which is—remind me—what date?"

"We leave on the seventeenth."

"A month in King George," said Sunny. "That sounds about right."

"Yes and no," said Fletcher. He backed away. "This isn't good-bye, in case you were thinking of making a scene. I'll see you plenty before I leave."

"I know."

"We'll get out there and play a couple of rounds before then."

"Absolutely," said Sunny.

He nudged the plant again. "They said you could exchange it if you wanted something else. It was between this, a rhododendron, and a mountain laurel."

"No, this is perfect," said Sunny. "The blue of the check against the pink of the blossoms. You did a good job."

He walked down the three steps to the path. "I left something at the cemetery, too. Nothing fancy. White. Some kind of bulbs. In a pot."

He turned away quickly so he wouldn't have to see how little she expected, how amazed she looked. "Gotta run," he said.

At the end of the driveway, he stopped the car and lowered his window. "Tulips," he yelled.

Sunny cupped her hand behind one ear, took a few steps closer.

"The flowers," he said. "They were tulips. As in, from Holland."

"Foodland?" she called back.

He shook his head: *Forget it; no matter.*

Sunny shrugged. They both smiled. She waved, and he waved back.

Acknowledgments

How lucky I am that James E. Mulligan, a childhood friend, grew up to be deputy chief of police in Nashua, New Hampshire, and an ever-obliging source of things procedural and constabular. Special thanks to Lee Boudreaux, divine editor, for her enthusiasm and attention to all of my words—written, spoken, unspoken; Luke Ryan for his willingness to talk about his golf demons; Bonnie Covey, the first person to suggest I put a club into a character's hand; and the golf resource under my own roof, Bob Austin.

I cherish my association with the good people of Random House and Vintage and the boffo team of Ginger Barber and Jennifer Rudolph Walsh.

I'd still be turning sentences around if it weren't for Mameve Medwed and Stacy Schiff, who drop everything (no small matter) to read my chapters as I write them and egg me on sternly, drolly, lovingly. Thank you both.

About the Type

This book was set in FF Celeste, a digital font that its designer, Chris Burke, classifies as a modern humanistic typeface. Celeste was influenced by Bodoni and Waldman, but the strokeweight contrast is less pronounced, making it more suitable for current digital typesetting and offset-printing techniques. The serifs tend to the triangular, and the italics harmonize well with the roman in tone and width. It is a robust and readable text face that is less stark and modular than many of the modern fonts and has many of the friendlier old-face features.

ALSO BY ELINOR LIPMAN

Elinor Lipman

The Ladies' Man

'Hilarious. Superb entertainment.'

Time Out

The Dobbin sisters, attractive red-headed spinsters Adele, Lois and Kathleen, live together in relative harmony. Until Adele's ex-fiancé Nash Harvey makes a sudden reappearance on their doorstep.

Nash is incorrigible, debonair and pathologically unreliable. His arrival causes havoc, but he soon finds out that scorned women do not make gracious hostesses.

'A charming and funny writer who is also very wise. Your spouse will hate you for reading this book; you'll stay up late nights, shaking the bed with laughter.'

Arthur Golden, author of *Memoirs of a Geisha*

'Full of charm, verbal sparkle, and funny genial sex. I adored it. Every page. Definitely her best.'

Anita Shreve, author of *The Weight of Water*

'Delicious and hilarious – the ladies' man and all his ladies are sublime.'
Jane Hamilton, author of *A Map of the World*

4th

Elinor Lipman

The Inn at Lake Devine

'I loved this book . . . Utterly addictive.'   *Independent on Sunday*

'The Inn at Lake Devine is a family-owned resort, which has been in continuous operation since 1922. Our guests who feel most comfortable here, and return year after year, are Gentiles.'

It's 1962 and all across America barriers are collapsing. Except in Vermont, where Natalie Marx's mother's enquiry about summer accommodation elicits an extraordinary reply. For twelve-year-old Natalie, who has a stubborn sense of justice, the words are not a rebuff but an infuriating, irresistible challenge.

'Imagine, if you can, a cross between Philip Roth and Melissa Bank: it has a water-tight, self deprecating humour that will make you laugh out loud.'   *Independent on Sunday*

'A delightful novel: funny, sad, romantic and with an author who was born with an auto-immune system already primed against clichés and an ear for dialogue sharper than an electronic listening system. Her situations and her characters sparkle with life.'
                                                                            The Times

'A taut, witty novel that tackles love, death and intermarriage against a backdrop of small-town anti-Semitism.'   *She*

'There is a sharp, provocative edge to her comedy.' *Sunday Times*

All Fourth Estate books are available from your local bookshop.

For a monthly update on Fourth Estate's latest releases, with interviews, extracts, competitions and special offers visit
www.4thestate.com

Or visit
www.4thestate.com/readingroom
for the very latest reading guides on our bestselling authors, including Michael Chabon, Annie Proulx, Lorna Sage, Carol Shields.

London · New York